The
LIONS
Share

DONNA J. BROWN

ISBN 978-1-0980-4504-3 (paperback)
ISBN 978-1-0980-4505-0 (digital)

Christian Faith Publishing, Inc.
832 Park Avenue
Meadville, PA 16335
www.christianfaithpublishing.com

Printed in the United States of America

God is not mocked
The Bible declares.
Man reaps what he sows
With his evil dares.

Lions share equally
Their ill-gotten gain.
God watches their lair
With utter disdain.

Daniel they've taken
For their evil plot.
They test him severely,
This wicked lot.

But Daniel stands strong,
And Daniel rings true.
With God-given courage
He sees the test through.

1

September 2, 1985

Hands clasped behind his back, "Adolf" paced his room at the Bergerstein Lodge located in the San Bernardino Mountains of Southern California. He strolled to the window and stared through the rain-splattered glass, not seeing the forest but visualizing his plan. This place suited him, somewhat far from Orange County, but otherwise perfect. He'd get back at the Bergersteins, and at the same time carry out his revenge against Captain Baker, the police officer responsible for his imprisonment. *Captain Baker, you will rue the day you testified. You tore me from my son for fifteen years. I will tear yours from you forever.*

Adolf did an about-face and took quick strides to the bathroom. In the mirror, he saw an ordinary short man with black hair and mustache. He picked up the comb, styled his hair like his hero, and imagined how he would look with his mustache cropped—from ordinary to extraordinary. He saluted Adolf Hitler. *Like you, men will fear me. The mind wields power, not the body.* Adolf combed his dark hair back in place and strode to his room.

He thought about Mr. and Mrs. Bergerstein. Never again would they cheat him or anyone else. Every year they closed the lodge after Labor Day and reopened December 1. This year while they were in Germany for three months enjoying their undeserved winnings, he would use their "establishment."

Modeled after a lodge in Germany, the rough-hewn log structure was too cold, too dark, too austere for American taste. The

Bergersteins had built the place in 1955. They never advertised, never catered to tourists or sportsmen. Their European clientele came to enjoy the camaraderie and special amenities the place afforded—high-stakes poker being one of the word-of-mouth attractions.

Adolf, as well as others, had lost thousands to the Bergersteins. He couldn't prove they cheated. No one could. Like him, everyone returned several times each year to even the score. Futile, Adolf thought, futile. When he finished using their lodge, he planned to burn the place to the ground. That would even the score. The owners would only have left the valuables they put in storage so they could leave the place unattended.

It had been easy to get a copy of the keys. Adolf's mouth curved into a sinister smile. *Really, Herr Bergerstein, you are a most careless man, losing your keys. You should learn to be more careful in the future.* He laughed. *Of course, in the future you won't need your keys.*

Close to one o'clock on Saturday, October 26, 1985, Adolf's Jeep Wrangler ascended the road into the San Bernardino Mountains. He'd made good time from Brea. "Needles," his thirty-year-old son, had slept the whole way. "Doc" had said he would sleep most of today and tomorrow. By Monday, he would be fine. *Doc better be right,* Adolf thought. *Needles must carry out his part. This operation depends on all of us.*

Adolf surveyed the whitening landscape. "Of all the blasted luck," he muttered, "Snow." He couldn't remember it ever falling in October. For three weeks, rain had pounded the lower elevations. Adolf didn't mind rain, but snow didn't bode well. Was it a bad omen? He pushed the windshield wipers to the max. They fought to remove the large flakes fast enough, and Adolf almost missed the unmarked side road. Would the others miss it? His Jeep ascended a steeper gravel road that wound through pines and firs. A clearing revealed the Bergerstein Lodge standing like a fortress against the elements. A row of garages had been built under the south wing. Adolf stopped near the garages, unlocked four doors, and raised them. He heard vehicles rumbling up the hill—one would be the van belonging to "Cookie" and "Doc." It would be parked in the enclosed carport near the kitchen door. He, "Lefty," "Muscles," and "Einstein" would keep their cars in the garages.

Adolf drove up the steep driveway to park in front of the lodge. He'd have one of his men stow his Jeep undercover later. "We're here," he told his son who only opened one eye in acknowledgment. Adolf had never taken his son to the lodge—too many people—too many germs for his weakened immune system. Yesterday, Doc had given him another injection of a drug he'd developed to combat and knock out the HIV virus. Hatred for Captain Baker roiled within Adolf every time he looked at his son's emaciated body and sunken blue eyes.

"I feel sick," Needles said in a voice so low, Adolf barely heard him.

"I know you do, but we'll be inside the lodge soon."

Adolf helped his son out of the Jeep and assisted him to the front porch. He kept an arm around Needles's waist, even though his son held onto the wooden railing while they climbed the slippery snow-covered steps.

Inside the lodge, Needles shivered as his father led him to the east wing living area. "I know you're cold," Adolf said. "Lie down on the couch. I'll get some blankets." Before he could head down the long hallway, the front door banged open. Five men entered, stomping snow off their boots. Their loud boisterous voices shattered the silence. "Doc," Adolf ordered, "get Needles's bed ready. He'll be using the front bedroom in the north wing. There's no sense his lying on the couch when he'd be more comfortable in bed. Grab sheets and blankets from that closet."

Bedrooms lay to the north and south of the two entertainment-living areas. Two massive side by side fireplaces separated the rooms. Doc hurried down the corridor as Adolf continued speaking, "The rest of us will sleep in the south wing. Einstein, our bedroom is the one with the bathroom."

"Good," Einstein said.

"I want you to get one of the heaters and take it to Doc before you help Lefty and Muscles bring in wood."

The three did an about-face and tramped back outside. Cookie walked straight past Adolf to the kitchen and unlocked the side door. Adolf wondered what Doc's young brother planned for dinner. He took the logs stacked next to the rock fireplace and placed them in the massive hearth facing this room. Before the men hauled in a week's worth of wood, he had a fire roaring.

Adolf, Einstein, Muscles, and Lefty started moving furniture. From the west wing, they moved couches and chairs to the larger living area that also had a twelve-foot dining table with black leather-upholstered chairs.

"Lefty," Adolf ordered, "you and Muscles haul in the plywood from your truck to block the window where we'll put Baker's son. Use long nails. I don't want him prying it loose. Muscles, pound the bolt into the floor where I marked."

Adolf checked the front room's heavy drapes to make sure no light could be seen from outside. The back room faced a steep hill. He didn't worry about its huge windows or the sliding glass doors. Everything arranged to his satisfaction, he took quick strides to the kitchen. From the doorway, he observed Cookie preparing dinner. Probably close to Needles's age, the chef stood robust and two inches taller than Needles's five-foot-eight. Cookie's deep brown eyes held a sorrowful look as if he considered being deaf a raw deal. *Better than being a druggie with AIDS.* Adolf's eyes narrowed. *That's not Needles's fault. Because Captain Baker testified, I was sent to prison and couldn't watch over him.* He tapped Cookie on the shoulder. When the man turned to face him, Adolf said, "What time do we eat?"

"Five."

"That soon…nothing gourmet tonight?"

"No."

Adolf strolled to the coffee maker and poured himself a cup of fresh brew—strong and black—just the way he liked it. Cookie had gone back to tearing lettuce into bite-size pieces. One thing about Cookie, Adolf thought, he never talks too much. Was he really deaf? He sure didn't have trouble reading lips. It didn't matter. Doc's brother was a fantastic chef, and Adolf enjoyed gourmet food.

Close to five, Cookie set carafes on the table. Everyone except Doc and Needles grabbed a seat before he could bring in the food— two casseroles of lasagna and a huge bowl of salad. The chef pulled out a chair and joined them. Each man heaped his plate and dug in without a word. Doc hurried into the room a few minutes later.

"How's Needles?" Adolf asked.

Doc sat across from him. "He's fine. You should know by now the medication always upsets his system for a few days. Tomorrow he'll be stronger."

"Can I assume his condition isn't worse?"

"Would I be here if he were getting worse?" Without flinching, Doc's gaze met Adolf's. Of the five men, only Doc would have dared to do this. Not even Needles challenged his father.

Adolf's mouth curved into a thin smile. "Cure him, Doc, and you'll make more than your million. You'll make history with your new cure for AIDS. If my son dies, I may not let you live to spend your million. Do you read me?"

"Loud and clear." Doc's confident smile indicated he didn't fear Adolf's threat.

Adolf passed Doc the salad, holding onto the bowl as their eyes met. "Just remember, we have a lot at stake. I don't want to worry about the kid."

"Acknowledged." Doc filled his plates—one heaped with salad, the other with lasagna.

The meal finished, Cookie cleared the table before Adolf stood. "Let's go over the plans. First, Einstein, get the map and spread it on the table. Show us where you intend to plant the bombs."

Einstein spread a detailed map of Orange County on the table and handed folded ones to each man. "Yours are marked."

Adolf noted the dead serious expression on Einstein's face and the emphasis he'd placed on his last words. For the first time, his men appeared to realize this was no fun-and-games caper. "I do believe you have their rapt attention now. Please continue."

"I've marked our routes to and from the lodge in yellow. The blue dots show the stores we intend to hit."

While they nodded, Adolf smiled as if listening to a prize pupil giving a lecture. He gestured Einstein to continue.

"To keep law enforcement too busy to tail us and to show the corporations we mean business, I'll have bombs planted I can detonate by remote control. These are the green dots on the map. Each red dot represents the store to be destroyed should their corporation refuse to comply with our demands. Any questions?"

A dozen bombs could be set off during their crime spree. Adolf licked his lips in anticipation. "Good job, Einstein. Now, concerning our mole in the police department, is she trustworthy?"

"She's eager to do her Judas-part. Not only does she love me and wants her million, I think she'd do this for free just for the chance to get back at Captain Baker's son. She loved Daniel Baker long before he married, and he wouldn't so much as buy her a cup of coffee. Now she hates his guts."

*****

Sunday, October 27

In a small rural town not far from Fullerton, youth pastor, Daniel Baker, found his Sundays falling into a pattern. He would leave for church an hour earlier than his wife, Cindy, and their three sons. Dan liked walking to the church. Cindy and the boys would ride in their four-door Ford station wagon. Rarely could he leave right after the service and ride home with his family. By the time he walked the mile to their country home, Cindy had their main meal ready. After eating, he'd hurry out the door to visit shut-ins and hospital patients. He had to be back at the church by four-thirty to counsel teenagers and lead the five o'clock youth meeting held before the evening service.

Today would be different, and Dan relished the unexpected break from routine. There would be no evening service. Most of the adults, including Pastor Richards, didn't want to miss the conclusion of the evangelistic meetings they'd been attending all week at a large church in Fullerton. Since few teenagers had gone, Dan decided not to attend the last service so he wouldn't have to cancel the youth meeting. Blessed as he'd been by the stirring messages, he'd felt a twinge of guilt. Cindy had been too tired to go, and his attending meant she didn't get a moment's break from taking care of their three sons. Tonight, he'd be home early. Tonight, he'd be there for her.

Since they only had sandwiches for lunch, Dan anticipated a special dinner. Cindy knew he loved fried chicken. Would she fix that or would she continue to make him eat crow? "I will be home by six-thirty," he had promised her. "By hook or by crook," he added to himself.

Black ominous clouds replaced white puffy ones by the time Dan finished his visitation rounds and headed for the church to lead the youth group. When the meeting ended and no one hung around, he breathed a sigh of relief. He'd be home on time. Rain pelted his VW as Dan drove home wondering how he could get Cindy to forgive him. How could he make the evening special? Surprise registered on her face when he dashed into the house before six-thirty. "I told you I'd be here," he said, reading her thoughts.

"Dinner's ready."

Her flat tone told him crow was still on the menu. Cindy hadn't even given him a peck on the cheek. All day she'd given him a cold shoulder. Dan drew in a breath and slowly exhaled. *It's up to me to make amends.* He wouldn't be able to do so until the boys were in bed. Curbing his impatience, he tried to make the evening appear normal. Like him, Cindy kept up a cheerful countenance at the dinner table. He complimented her on the spaghetti despite the fact he knew she'd chosen to cook the boys' favorite meal, not his.

"When can you teach me to ride my new bike?" five-year-old Danny asked, his eyes shining with expectation.

"Probably tomorrow."

"Teach me too," three-year-old Timmy said.

"The bike's too big for you, but I'll bet you can keep up with us on your tricycle."

After dinner while Cindy nursed six-month-old Jonathan and put him to bed, Dan roughhoused with his two toe-headed sons who'd inherited their curly locks from him. When Cindy returned to the living room, Dan said, "Okay, boys, time for p-jays and prayers." He took each by the hand and led them to their room. He helped Timmy and sat on the lower bunk while the boys brushed their teeth. They dawdled, spending twice the time than normal.

When they finally came out of the bathroom, he dropped to his knees in front of the bed. His sons took their places on either side of him. Timmy prayed his usual prayer, asking Jesus to take care of everyone in the family. Danny's long-winded prayer included some missionaries who had recently talked at church and prayed for all of his sick friends. He thanked Jesus for his new bicycle and the chance to learn to ride it tomorrow. Dan fought to curb his impatience. He'd given up trying to retain a prayerful attitude. When Danny finally said "Amen," Dan scrambled to his feet, kissed each boy good-night, and tucked them in bed. Outside their closed door, he prayed, "Please, Lord, let Cindy forgive me before we go to bed. And please forgive my impatience tonight."

Dan found Cindy in the kitchen putting dishes away. He slid his arms around her slim waist and nuzzled her cheek. "They're down for the night."

She closed the cupboard door and turned within the confines of his arms to face him. "So?"

He grinned, trying to counteract the anger her flat-toned reply conveyed. "The night is young, and you're so beautiful." This cliché usually brought a smile or a chuckle. Her lips drew tight. No twinkles sparkled in her brown eyes. "Cindy," he implored, "don't look at me like Danny looks at pea soup." No smile. "Hon, I don't like being called away almost every night, but someone has to counsel distraught parents and teenagers. Someone has to do hospital visitation when others can't."

"Can't? You're the one who immediately says yes. You don't even try to find someone else."

"Cindy, be reasonable."

"Reasonable? I didn't mind you being gone for the meetings during the week. In fact, I encouraged you to go. But, Daniel, there were no meetings yesterday, and your not being here for Danny's birthday is inexcusable. Turning five was a big deal to him, and I counted on your helping me. You didn't get home until his bedtime!"

Dan closed his eyes as he tried to control his temper. She hadn't accepted his apology Saturday night, and today she'd been in a huff. Ever since Jonathan's birth, they argued over finances and his working so much. Under control, he said in a quiet voice, "I'm sorry I couldn't be here."

"And you were gone when we had the earthquake two weeks ago. I needed you here to help me calm the boys."

"You did a better job than I could have. I never would have thought of crawling under the table and pretending to sit in a boat, rocking on waves."

"What if the next quake is a jolting one, not a rolling one?"

"Aren't you blowing things out of proportion? I can promise to be home more often. But for earthquakes?" He rolled his eyes before giving her his best contrite look. "I don't want to fight. Can we call a truce?"

Her frown melted into an I-can't-stay-mad-at-you-forever smile as she nodded. Dan realized with relief she'd finally forgiven him. "If it weren't raining outside, we could make up under our avocado tree." He brushed his lips teasingly across hers, hoping her desire would mount as fast as his. Sunday night was to him what Friday night was to a lay person, a chance to relax. Tonight was his chance to make love to Cindy.

The phone jangled, parting them before the second ring. Dan lunged for the receiver, thinking unfitting thoughts. He took a slow deep breath to regain his composure and mask his irritation. "Hello." He cast Cindy a wistful glance but froze at the caller's words.

"Pastor Baker, this is St. Jude ER. We've got an injured boy here calling for you."

"What's his name?"

"Don't know. No ID. Someone found him lying on the sidewalk...pretty incoherent." The man talked loud enough for Cindy to overhear. Her hand flew to her mouth; her worried eyes met Dan's.

"I'll be right down." He hung up and raised his hands in helplessness. "Hon, I've got to go."

Her lips were pursed, but she nodded. "Do you want me to come with you? I can get Mrs. Andrews next door to stay with the boys." She followed him to the hall closet.

"If I need you, I'll call." Dan yanked his navy jacket off a hanger, slipped into it, grabbed his Angels baseball cap, and crammed it on, covering most of his brown curly hair.

"Take the umbrella," Cindy urged.

"Too cumbersome."

When he kissed her, she clung to him as if she'd never see him again. Her eyes met his. "Be careful."

"Hon, what's wrong?"

Cindy trembled. "I…I'm afraid. Please, watch yourself."

Dan brushed his lips over the freckles on her nose before giving her a gentle reassuring kiss. The lines in her forehead deepened. "I'll be careful," he promised. He liked driving his VW, but he added, "I'll even take the station wagon. The brakes are better."

Cindy's police training had left her with the uncanny ability to sense danger. Her extra precautions and warnings had prevented near accidents.

Remembering her words, Dan drove the speed limit, his mind alert as he entered the freeway and headed for Fullerton. He turned the wipers full blast to push away the sheets of rain. For weeks, torrents had fallen. If this kept up much longer, there would probably be mudslides. He exited the freeway. From the corner of his eye, he saw a car run the red. Dan swerved in time to avoid a collision then thanked God for His protection and Cindy's premonition which had made him more alert. He relaxed. He thought about Cindy. He had never dated anyone so close to his height. He stood six feet, and Cindy, five-ten. When they first met, it struck him funny that such a tall stately woman would have freckles. Cap, his adoptive father, who was a peace officer, had introduced him to Cindy at the police family Christmas dinner. Cap had insisted he attend with him, Amanda, and their two girls. "I've invited Cindy Matthews to sit with us. She's only been on the force three months and doesn't have an escort." When Dan tried to refuse, Cap said, "You're twenty-two, no longer a kid. You can't avoid holiday fun forever." Dan got the message—get a life.

To say they didn't get off to a good start would be an understatement. She acted like a threatened she-bear, and he like a rejected male. During the predinner mingle, Dan asked if he could bring her some punch. She said, "I can get my own."

Cindy declined his arm when dinner was announced and seated herself before he could pull back her chair. Irked, Dan decided to chuck her attitude and enjoy the food. When she didn't notice her napkin had fallen off her lap, he retrieved the linen and waved it. "Yours?" he teased, hoping she'd lighten up.

She glared at him and yanked it from his grasp.

Okay, he thought, two can play this game. After they'd finished dessert, Cap and Amanda's oldest daughter, Susan, asked Cindy to tell everyone about her most exciting police experience. Dan couldn't resist saying, "Please, Cynthia, tell us the story of how you slew the dragon single-handed."

Cindy tossed her napkin on the table. "Excuse me, I need to leave."

Dan stood before she could. "No, you stay. I'm the odd man out."

At home, Cap said, "You bullheaded fool. Whatever possessed you to be so...so..."

"Crude? Crass? Chauvinistic? I got tired of being a gentleman and her refusing to be a lady."

"So what if she bruised your ego? Do you realize what a woman goes through when she becomes a police officer? She not only has to prove her worth to every man. She has to prove it to herself."

Dan had sent Cindy a dozen long-stem red roses and a card that said: I apologize, not for trying to be a gentleman but for when I stopped being one.

The next time he saw her was six months later at the police family picnic. He walked toward her, saying, "Remember me?"

"Ah, yes, the gentleman who wanted a bedtime story." She grinned. "I was hoping you'd be here."

Dan inhaled, trying to recapture the fragrance she'd worn that day and was probably wearing right now, waiting for him to come home. He pictured Cindy in her blue satin nightgown, clinging to every curve. His mind's eye saw her seated in front of the vanity mirror brushing her long honey-brown hair until it gleamed as it cascaded over her creamy white shoulders. If Dan was impatient and needed her to come to bed quicker, he'd grab the brush, pull it gently through the strands, then kiss her neck and shoulders. A few moments of this made her moan with pleasure, and soon she'd be in his arms. Dan fought the urge to turn around, forget the world, and spend the night making love.

The lights of St. Jude Hospital summoned. Dan's thoughts returned to the situation at hand. His mind sounded a warning when a red Mustang pulled into the parking lot after he did. Hadn't that car been behind him quite a while, getting off the freeway when he had? So what? He shrugged, drawing into a vacant parking spot. He locked his car and thought about the injured boy. "Please, Lord, don't let it be serious." Before he entered the hospital, he shook the rain from his cap. Sunday night in the emergency room rarely looked different from any other night. Tonight was no exception, with no empty seats. "I'm Pastor Baker," he told the receptionist. When her inquisitive expression didn't change, he added, "Someone phoned that an injured boy was brought in who keeps calling for me."

"Let me check." Her face remained perplexed. She disappeared behind closed doors and returned, looking doubly puzzled. "Are you sure the caller said St. Jude?"

"Yes."

She shook her head. "Strange as it may seem, no young people have been brought in tonight. Perhaps you should check the other hospitals. I'd do it for you but…" She waved her hand, indicating the crowded room. Dan thanked her as she swiveled her chair to face the desk. Since no phone book existed in the room, he went to the lobby and called the other area hospitals. None had record of the situation he described. He ran his fingers through his wavy brown hair. *What's going on?* Disgruntled, he jammed on his cap and trudged toward the door.

"Daniel?" A familiar feminine voice called.

Dan cringed inwardly before turning. He smiled despite the feeling he was ready to be pounced upon by a wily mature feline. Chance run-ins with Leslie Adams had been all too common, even after he had married Cindy. Leslie worked in dispatch at his father's precinct, and every time Dan happened to be in the building, he ran into her. Cap and Cindy had been amused when he mentioned he thought she had designs on him, but they wouldn't have smiled if they'd seen her face the day he told Leslie he was marrying Cindy.

Anger had flashed in her green eyes as her lips had mouthed, "That's wonderful." At least, this meeting was pure chance.

"It is you," Leslie said. "I hope nothing's wrong with the kids."

"No, Cindy and the boys are fine."

"I just finished sitting with my aunt in ICU." Leslie sighed as her countenance fell. "Very depressing. She may not last through the night, but at least she recognized me and knew someone cared enough to come." Leslie blinked back tears.

Despite wanting to put distance between them, Dan put a comforting arm around her. "Would you like to go to the hospital cafeteria and talk over a cup of coffee?"

"How sweet of you to ask, but I need to rush home. Missy's due to have her pups tonight, and she needs me. Maybe another time?"

"Sure," he said, praying another time would be decades away. "I'll walk you to your car."

"That's gallant of you, but I'll make a mad dash to mine while you run to yours."

They walked out together and stood under the overhang. "Sure you don't want me to walk you to your car?"

"I'm parked close." She pointed. "The red Mustang. But I will take a rain check on the coffee. For old times' sake?" She flashed a smile, revealing her nicotine-stained teeth as she drew a scarf around her cat-black dyed hair and gave him one last glance before she ran.

Dan waited until she had her keys in the door. He lowered his head to the blinding rain and dashed across the parking lot before she could pull out and possibly stop and offer him a ride. Harmless as this meeting may have been, he felt like an escaping mouse and saw his car as a safe haven. Something didn't add up. If her red Mustang had been the one following him, she sure hadn't spent much time with her aunt.

He fingered the keys in his pocket, wishing he could chew out the person who'd put him in this spot.

"Pastor Baker," a deep voice called, similar to the one on the phone.

Dan pivoted.

"I'm glad I caught you. About that boy…"

A sudden wind gust must have drowned out the rest of the words. Dan started toward the man cloaked in a hooded poncho. He took two steps and froze at the sound of sloshed footsteps behind him. A blinding pain slammed the base of his skull.

The mugger flipped his blackjack twice before jamming it into his pants' pocket under the floppy poncho. His partner retrieved Dan's keys and unlocked the Ford station wagon. Together they managed to cram Dan's dead weight onto the back seat before anyone entered the parking lot. Both removed their ponchos and placed them over Dan. The mugger climbed into the passenger seat. "Sure easy, Riles," he said.

The other man slid into the driver's seat. "You meathead! Don't call me Riles. A slip like that could foul up this operation. I'm Lefty. Get that through your thick skull. You're Muscles." He started the car and shoved it in reverse.

"Hey, Geek," Muscles shot back, "this name game is dumb city. That Bible thumper ain't gonna see daylight after this caper, no how."

Lefty drove slowly through the parking lot and gave a thumbs-up to a man parked near the exit. "Muscles, what if because of your slip of tongue, he somehow manages to tip the police to our real names?"

"We'll waste the lot of them."

Lefty snorted, "And where will we be then? You'll wind up in concrete, and we'll all be back to square one." He checked the rear-view mirror to make sure Einstein was following. "Mr. Adolf doesn't put up with dumb jerks."

"Why does he keep Needles around?"

Lefty's lip twisted as he shrugged. "Family's family."

They arrived at the secluded rendezvous spot five miles away, turned off the lights, and waited for Einstein who pulled alongside a few minutes later. Lefty and Einstein rolled down their windows.

"Any trouble?" Einstein asked.

"Never knew what hit him," Lefty said.

Muscles retrieved his blackjack and stroked it fondly. "Want I should slug him again? Make sure he stays out?"

"Put that thing away. I just hope you didn't hit him too hard. Lefty, tie and gag him before you transfer him to my station wagon. You'll ride back with me. Muscles, ditch Baker's car where I showed you. Wipe it clean. Doc will pick you up." Einstein raised the rear door of the station wagon, moved his toolbox to the side, and waited for Lefty to carry Dan over. "Muscles didn't hit the preacher too hard, did he?"

Lefty shrugged. "No harder than I've seen him slug others." He laid Dan down on his back and tried to shove him in. "Better get on the seat and lean over and grab him. We should have put a blanket on that rubber mat so he'd slide easier." Together they managed to push and pull Dan's lanky frame in far enough so they could close the door. After they covered him, Lefty said, "I need a smoke."

"You'd better make it quick," Einstein said, getting in the car. After Lefty snuffed out the butt, Einstein started the engine and pulled out as soon as Lefty closed the door.

"Kidnapping that guy was sure easy," Lefty said after they were on the freeway.

"Mr. Adolf plans down to the last detail. He leaves nothing to chance."

"What about tomorrow night?"

"That may be trickier. You and I may have to bide our time, wait for the right moment, and act quickly."

They discussed possible situations that could arise and how to handle each.

When Einstein pulled up in front of the lodge, he asked, "Do you need help getting Baker?"

"No sweat," Lefty bragged. "He may be a tall lug, but I've lugged bigger."

Einstein watched him grab Dan's ankles, haul him out, put his arms around Dan's waist, and hoist him over his right shoulder. Einstein marveled at the guy's strength but instead of parking the car in the garage, he decided to follow Lefty in case he needed help. Sure-footed as a mountain goat, Lefty trudged to the porch as if he were hauling nothing more than a twenty-pound sack of potatoes. However, when he came to the steps, he planted each foot and gripped the railing as he ascended.

The door opened the moment Lefty's feet touched the porch. Adolf stepped back to give him room. "Take Baker to his bedroom and lay him on the bed. Untie him and remove the gag while I pad-lock the chain around his ankle. Doc will inject a sedative to make sure he stays out for the next eight hours."

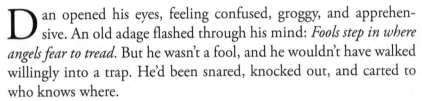

Dan opened his eyes, feeling confused, groggy, and apprehensive. An old adage flashed through his mind: *Fools step in where angels fear to tread.* But he wasn't a fool, and he wouldn't have walked willingly into a trap. He'd been snared, knocked out, and carted to who knows where.

Why?

Whoever had done this must know he wasn't wealthy, only a youth pastor who didn't know from one year to the next if the small community church would be able to support him. Dan lifted his head, winced, and sank back on the bare mattress where they'd left him. *Man, they slugged me hard. Cindy, your premonition was right on target. I'm definitely in a hard spot.* "Lord, let her and the boys be okay."

Why wasn't he bound and gagged? Why wasn't someone guarding him? Did they expect him to stay unconscious longer? The door stood open, letting light shine in from the hallway, but not enough for him to read his watch. Dan listened intently. He heard only the wind howling through the rafters and what sounded like ice pellets scratching at the window. Despite the blanket tossed over him, Dan shivered in the freezing room. Had they taken him to the mountains? He glanced around. The walls and ceiling were of rustic-hewn lumber such as one might find in a cabin. It didn't matter where he was. He had to escape while he had the chance. Despite the throbbing at the base of his skull, he sat up. *What?* He threw off the blanket, drew his right leg toward him, and fingered a padlock securing a heavy chain around his ankle. He followed the links lying on the mattress to where they were bolted to the wooden floor. *I'm chained! Like an animal!*

Dan clenched his hands in silent rage before he managed to take a deep breath and calm down. He opened his hands and rubbed nail-indented palms. How secure was the bolt? Trying not to jar his head or make noise, he eased off the bed, holding the chain so it wouldn't clank. The penetrating cold and the frigid floor against his bare feet made him shiver. The thought of escaping without shoes irked him, but he couldn't waste time searching for them.

He stared at the chain. If he freed it, lugging the heavy links would be cumbersome but would make a handy weapon if someone tried to stop him. First, he had to pull out the bolt. Dan inched forward, drawing up the chain link by link—no noise. *So far, so good.* He knelt to examine the metal bolt that looked strong enough to hold a bull elephant. Was it embedded only in the floor planking, or had it entered a joist? With great care, he laid the chain on the floor and grasped the bolt, pushing and pulling until his head throbbed. No go. He sat back on his haunches and glanced around the room for something to give him leverage. A card table and three chairs filled the corner left of the door, but their flimsy legs would never stand the pressure. What he needed was a tire iron or crow bar. *Fat chance.*

Dan studied the old, wooden-style bed frame. Could it possibly have metal slats? Carrying the chain, he retraced his steps, laid the links on the bed, and looked underneath. He gritted his teeth as stabs of pain knifed the back of his head. He saw nothing useful. Dan sat on the mattress and waited for the throbbing and a sudden attack of queasiness to subside. There had to be a way to free the bolt. "Lord, please show me," he pleaded. *The closet?*

Dan rose. Dizziness assailed him. Frustrated and angry, he waited now for the buzzing in his head to pass. When he felt steady, he walked to the closet, quietly stretching the chain links behind him. "Lord, please don't let the door creak." He sighed with relief when it didn't. The clothes bar caught his eye—four feet of two-inch-diameter steel, one end set in a hole, the other lowered in place by way of a slanted groove. Dan removed the empty coat hangers and set them on the shelf before he gripped the metal and lifted. It was wedged tight. He twisted. The rod moved a fraction.

Despite the pain and awkwardness, he backed into the closet and under the bar, his head touching the shelf, his shoulders striving to dislodge the bar. He shoved harder and felt the rod move, but the shelf tipped, sending the hangers crashing to the floor. Enough noise to—Running feet pounded the floor, the light flipped on, and a man in a sweat suit rushed through the doorway before Dan had a chance to move. He stood trapped, staring into the barrel of a gun.

The man, holding the .45 in his left hand, stood close to Dan's height—six feet. He had black hair and a swarthy complexion. With dark eyes riveted on Dan, he said, "Remove the bar, set it down, and roll it to me." Dan toyed with the idea of hurling it. "Now!" He lowered his aim to four inches below Dan's belt.

Bluff or not, the hair rose at the nape of Dan's neck. Heroics would be foolish at the moment. He eased the rod out of the groove, set it on the floor, gave it a shove, and fought back another wave of dizziness when he straightened.

"Now, back to bed."

Dan met him eye to eye. "I was set up, wasn't I?"

"Bright boy." He gestured the gun toward the bed. "Move."

Dan plotted as he took slow deliberate steps. Whatever this southpaw and his partner had in mind, it didn't seem to involve a tight timetable. He sat on the edge of the bed. "Where am I?" he asked, not really expecting an answer. "Why was I kidnapped?"

The man picked up the clothes rod and left.

Racking his brain about his situation exasperated Dan. He turned his thoughts to Cindy. Mentally he talked to her. "I'm okay, Hon, but your premonition sure was right. I wish I knew what's going on then again, maybe it's better if I don't." He stretched out on the hard bed. *They didn't even give me a pillow. I guess I should be thankful for the blanket.* He remembered telling others no matter what happened, God was in control; no matter how bad the situation, God could turn it around for good. The truth of that had come home after Cap and Amanda adopted him.

Dan thought about the past. What if his father hadn't been an alcoholic? Would things have turned out differently? He recalled the joy on his mother's face the night his father had accepted Jesus as his Savior. *What caused him to start drinking I'll never know, but the alcohol changed him from stern to abusive.* Dan shuddered, vividly remembering his last beating, but at least he'd deserved that one. *Boy, was I stupid. How many kids today succumb to peer pressure just like I did?* He'd been dared to take a drink and ended up driving home drunk. His father was livid, especially after Dan had said, "I thought you'd be proud of me. Like father, like son. But I managed to drive up the driveway without mowing down the bushes." After that beating, Dan vowed never to take another drink. If only his father had taken the same vow.

Depressed, he tried to push the past out of his mind. The present presented enough problems. He tried to think of every conceivable reason why someone would want to kidnap him. Exhausted, he fell into a troubled sleep. In a nightmare, he saw his father killing his mother. He relived his struggle to save her, gasped for breath as his father choked him, felt his own fingers wrap around the paperweight he grabbed to strike his father. "Mom," he began calling in despair.

*****

Monday morning while Dan slept, everyone except Needles gathered around the table for breakfast. Lefty relayed how Baker had tried to escape. "Good thing I heard him," he said, his chest puffed with pride. "I stopped him. And I stayed awake until I was sure he was asleep."

"Did you look in on him again?" Adolf asked.

Lefty hee-hawed. "Yeah, after I heard him yelling for his mommy. He must have been dreaming the bogeyman was after him."

All five had a good laugh while Cookie served breakfast. When Adolf finished eating, he wiped his mouth, folded the linen napkin and laid it on the table. He caught Cookie's eye. "That was terrific, the best omelet I've had in years. When you open your restaurant, I'll be the first one in line."

Praise seldom came from Adolf, and Cookie's crestfallen face brightened.

Adolf turned his attention to the others. "Einstein, while we're in San Bernardino getting last-minute supplies, I want you to check on Needles if he isn't awake by noon. When he does get up, make sure he eats something. Cookie's leaving sandwiches in the refrigerator for all of you."

"Anything else?" Einstein asked.

"Take no chances with Baker…you either, Lefty. He may be a little testy today. Tomorrow, I promise he'll be gentle as a lamb." He laughed. "Won't he, boys?"

"Yeah," Muscles blurted. "He'll be surprised."

All laughed in agreement except Doc and Cookie who only nodded.

Adolf studied them. "Do you two have a problem with this part of my plan?" He saw a spark of anger in Cookie's eyes. "Are you two going to go soft on me?"

"Soft?" Doc said. "No. However, I do have a problem with your assuming Baker will be subdued. His father is a police chief. Mark my words…you'll only be able to push his son so far." He glanced at Cookie before he continued. "We share one concern about Needles. He's the one person who can foul up this whole operation. If you don't keep him under control, he'll turn Baker into a raging lion."

"And if I choose to let my son have a little fun?"

"Don't even think about it," Doc challenged. "You'll wind up only getting your revenge against Captain Baker. I won't stand being deprived of my chance to grab one million dollars."

His men's narrowed eyes told Adolf they agreed with Doc. "All right, it's understood. Doc's room is off-limits to my son. It will be up to each of you to keep an eye on Needles." He realized he'd made a pun, but none of them cracked a smile, so he continued, "Will that suffice? Doc? Cookie?" Both nodded. "Now, concerning all your rooms, did you do as I ordered?"

"Sure thing," Lefty said. "Baker won't find anything useful in our room."

Einstein grinned. "Since you and I bunk together, you know our room is clean, except for the key and gun you put on the chest of drawers."

"Boss," Muscles said, "why'd you do that? Why let Baker roam?"

"The key is useless and the gun empty should he happen to find something to reach them."

"But why are you toying with him?" Einstein asked.

"Why does a cat play with a captured mouse?"

"You really like tormenting people, don't you?" Doc said.

Adolf eyed him with amusement. *Doc is so straight, so unimaginative.* "Torment? I see it as a controlled sporting chance. Tomorrow, we'll all go back to locking our rooms. Today let Baker have some fun."

Doc shrugged.

"You and Cookie did secure your room, didn't you?"

"Of course, Baker can search all he wants. He'll come up empty-handed."

"Good. Now, that takes care of business. Einstein and Lefty, we should all be back around two."

*****

Dan awakened with a start—bereft and angry. His father had torn him from his mother, and now his kidnappers had taken him away from Cindy and the boys.

From light filtering into the room, Dan read his watch: eleven-thirty. Cindy would soon be fixing lunch for the boys. How was she handling his disappearance? When he didn't return, he knew she'd probably called the hospital before Cap and Amanda. Had anyone found his car, or was it here? "O Lord, please watch over my family. I know Cindy is worried sick. Let her police training stand her in good stead. She needs stamina and courage as well as her faith in You."

Dan sat up and groaned. The dull ache at the base of his skull became an explosion of pain. He laid his head in his hands and waited for the banging to subside. *Why am I being left alone—to wear me down—for what? Why was I kidnapped?* Realizing he needed to walk around before his nerves got the better of him, he swung his feet to the ice-cold floor. The frigidness raced up his spine. He yanked the blanket off the bed and draped it around his shoulders. It did little to stop his shivering. Trying to ignore the thirty-some feet of chain wriggling behind him, he walked around the foot of the bed to check the large window. Strips of plywood covered it on the inside as if someone had rushed to hammer them on so he wouldn't be able to break the glass. Sunlight slithering through the cracks offered him a glimmer of hope. Could he pull the wood off? Dan tried to slip his fingers between the widest cracks but couldn't. He examined the large nail heads and groaned in frustration.

The light flipped on. "Looking for a way to escape?" a cold voice asked.

Dan turned. A short bony man with sparse brown hair stood in the doorway holding a revolver. His black-rimmed glasses sliding down his nose gave him a comical appearance, but the eyes behind the rims showed neither warmth nor humor. They looked deadly alert as if expecting Dan to try something, but he shifted his feet nervously. *A timid soul—one more easily caught off guard? Does he have the key for the padlock?* Dan decided to play a friendly nonthreatening role. He smiled. "Where's Lefty?"

Wide-eyed, he asked, "You know him?"

Dan masked his surprise. "No. I just noticed he was left-handed. Is that his name?"

"As far as you're concerned, yes."

How incongruous, Dan thought, that Lefty and this mouse of a man were partners. Where was Lefty now? "What's your name?"

"Einstein."

"Fictitious?"

A proud grin spread across his face. "I'm the genius around here…the electronic whiz…the bomb expert."

The bold-faced revelation sent icy jabs through Dan. He tried to keep his tone casual. "For what?"

"Not for me to say." His voice and manner turned business-like, as if he realized he'd already said too much. "Are you hungry?"

"A condemned man's last meal?"

"Not yet. We didn't go to all this trouble just to knock you off. No, you're going to be quite busy."

Not yet, Dan repeated to himself, but he knew he'd be killed when his usefulness was over. He masked his fear. "What am I going to be doing?"

"That's Mr. Adolf's department."

Another partner? "Who's he?"

"There's a bathroom across the hall if you care to wash. The chain will take you as far as the dining area archway."

Dan realized the man could keep mum when he wanted to. "Could I have my shoes?"

Einstein's sinister smile said "no." He did an about-face and hurried out.

Dan decided to explore. He couldn't help but wonder why his chain was so long. Why let him roam? After glancing in the bathroom, he walked the hallway to his right, turned the corner, and went as far as the chain allowed. Through a doorway at the end, he could see a refrigerator, and the smell of coffee drifting his way told him that was the kitchen. When Dan started back, he opened a door and flipped on the light. The small room had twin beds with rumpled covers. He saw nothing useful to help him escape. The huge bedroom across from it had two carefully made beds with suitcases underneath. Dan spied a key and a gun on top of the dresser in front of the window. Try as he might, he couldn't reach them, and there was nothing around or in the suitcases to help him. Frustrated, he turned off the light but didn't bother closing the door. He entered the room next to his and saw three quilt-covered beds, two dressers, and a card table with four chairs. Dan searched everywhere. Three suitcases and men's clothing hanging in the closet indicated three more criminals. A shiver zigzagged Dan's spine.

Seven people? Daniel, you've landed in the lions' den.

How was he involved in their scheme? He dragged back to the bathroom. A cold dampness and the foul odor of past use clung to the room. Four damp towels hung on wall hooks. To his surprise, a clean bath towel lay folded on top of the counter with a scrawled note: Just for you. The bathroom mirror appeared ancient. Its clouded surface distorted his image, but not enough to hide the puzzled brown eyes staring back at him or the brown hair flying every which way but down. He wet his hair and tried to smooth the waves but winced when he touched the tender spot. Dan looked sideways into the mirror, trying to see the lump at the base of his skull, but couldn't. He parted his hair and ran his fingers over the area. Whoever had slugged him had done it hard enough to keep him out for hours but not enough to break the skin. *A professional? Adolf? Lefty? No way could it have been the mouse.*

The chain grated on the floor as Dan's bare feet carefully walked over the worn wooden planking to the end of the hallway. On his left was a large, dimly lit empty room about twenty by twenty. The sturdy wooden door had a hammered-metal speak-easy—like ones Dan had seen in gangster films. Heavy drapes covered the walls. He could make out a hallway on the far side. Were there more bedrooms around the corridor? No way could he find out if they were occupied, but at least he knew now the place must be a lodge. Two side by side fireplaces and bookcases separated the rooms. The hearth facing this room was cold. The other, which faced the larger room, radiated warmth.

Dan walked to the archway Einstein had mentioned, but the chain stopped him from entering. In contrast to the dark room behind him, light flooded this area. The heavy drapes, pulled back from the huge picture windows and sliding glass doors, gave him a picturesque view of a steep snowy hill rising behind the lodge. Dan couldn't see the top even when he stooped to get a better view. He studied this living area. It looked as if the furniture from the front room had been crammed into this one—three couches, four recliners plus an extended dining room table with black leather chairs.

Dan stood in the archway, trying to absorb the warmth from the blazing fire as Einstein watched him from the kitchen. "Are you, Lefty, and Adolf the only ones involved in my abduction?" Dan asked.

"No, there's Doc, and he is a bona fide doctor. You'll have close contact with him."

Dan shuddered.

"You're afraid of doctors," Einstein bellowed.

"I'm cold! I'd like to sit by the fire."

Einstein gave a smug smile. "Does your chain go that far? Sorry, Baker, you'll just have to get used to the cold. Did exploring satisfy your curiosity? Adolf thought you should be allowed to roam so you'd know we don't intend to leave anything useful lying around within your reach. Did you find the key and gun? I thought that was a nice touch."

Dan clamped his lips. *So it was all a game, and Adolf seems to be the ring leader.*

Einstein sauntered out of the kitchen balancing a tray with one hand, the gun held in the other. "Your face tells me you found them. It must have been frustrating not being able to reach them. Now, back to your room." He gestured and stayed well behind until Dan entered the bedroom. He waved the gun toward the bed. "Stand over there while I put the tray on the table."

Dan walked backward and stood against the bed. This man might be a mouse but a nervous, cautious one. Fear could make for an itchy trigger finger.

Einstein set the food down, scurried back to the doorway, and waved his hand toward the table. "Have a seat. How do you like your private accommodations? Large room. Soft bed."

Dan rolled his eyes. "Large and soft, my foot." He slid onto a folding chair. "If this is my private room, why are there three chairs?"

"Maybe we'll find you some company?"

Dan's hands balled into fists. "Why was I kidnapped?"

"You can give us leverage."

"How?"

"Your old man's a police chief."

Breathing hard, Dan fought back his anger. "It won't work," was all he could say.

Einstein gave another conceited smile. "It'll work." When Dan glowered, he said, "Better cool it. Be smart. Eat and rest. While you can," he added, laughing before he hurried out.

Too angry to eat, Dan stood. Heedless of the noise the chain made, he paced from one corner of the room to the other. *It won't work. No matter what they have in mind, Cap won't allow himself to be manipulated, and I won't cooperate!* He gasped as he remembered Einstein's words. "I'm the electronic whiz, the bomb expert," he had bragged openly as if assured their scheme was foolproof. *What if innocent lives are at stake?*

*****

Einstein left Dan's room wondering what kind of a man they had kidnapped. This guy had guts, and from what Lefty said earlier, Einstein realized Baker wasn't stupid, and he would undoubtedly be bull-red angry tomorrow morning. Could they keep him under control? He was glad Doc had voiced his concern. None of them liked Needles. The last thing Einstein wanted to do right now was check on him, but orders were orders.

He hurried down the hallway to the front living area but took his time as he approached the hallway leading to the bedrooms on the north side of the lodge. *Instead of bunking with me, Mr. Adolf could have had his own room next to his son. Evidently, he doesn't want to chance sharing a bathroom with Needles either.* Einstein had no desire to share anything with Needles. When he peeked in on the sleeping addict, a chill ran down his spine. Death warmed over seemed an apt description. He hoped the guy wouldn't awaken until Mr. Adolf returned. *Let him touch him to see if he's alive.*

Einstein backed out of Needles's room and sprinted to the living area. He crossed under the archway and stopped at the end table next to the couch where Lefty lay sprawled. He flipped on the radio.

Lefty sat up. There's nothing good on. "The World Series is over."

"I want to catch the weather report."

Lefty snorted. "Look out the window. It quit snowing."

"And for how long?" He refrained from adding *Dummy.*

Lefty shrugged. "Is Needles awake?"

"No, thank goodness."

Lefty scrambled to his feet. "Then let's eat before he gets up." He headed for the kitchen.

Einstein caught up with him. "You fill the carafe and grab the mugs. I'll carry the plates and sandwiches." Einstein listened to the radio while he ate his ham-and-cheese sandwich. *I wonder if everything will go smoothly tonight.* When the newscaster mentioned the disappearance of youth pastor, Daniel Baker, Einstein smiled. "My, my, what could have ever happened to him?"

Lefty hee-hawed. "That reporter sounded bored. We'd better rustle up some action. A few of your bombs should do the trick."

"Quiet. I want to hear what the weather predictions are." After the forecast, Einstein said, "Clear skies for the rest of the week means it will probably be colder up here, but…"

"We won't have to fight snow or rain on these winding roads," Lefty interjected.

"My thoughts exactly, but tonight we may have to watch for black ice."

"That's your problem. You're driving." Lefty grabbed two sandwiches.

Einstein took the last one, leaving none for Needles. He could have canned soup. That's better for a sick person anyway, he reasoned.

"I sure don't like having to drive to Orange County every day," Lefty said. "If Mr. Adolf wanted to use this place, why didn't he plan this for summer?"

"The lodge isn't empty then."

"Why even use it?"

"He has his reasons, and we'll live longer if we don't question his motives."

Lefty shrugged. "Are you and your girl going to buy a mansion after you're married?"

"We could with the two million we'll have between us, but I think I'd rather travel around the world in style…live like a king."

The two played a friendly game of cards until Adolf returned about two-twenty.

"How's Needles?" he asked Einstein.

"He just got up. I heard the shower going."

"Did you check in on him earlier?"

"Of course, I did," Einstein said. He'd been given an order, and no matter how distasteful, he would obey the man his million rode on.

"I'd better go check on him."

Einstein watched him hurry toward his son's room. He'd finished his sandwich and taken the last swig of his coffee when he heard the van pull up next to the kitchen door. He gestured his head toward Lefty. "You coming? They could probably use some help."

Lefty stuffed another bite in his mouth and mumbled a garbled "I'm not done yet."

Einstein rolled his eyes and hurried to the kitchen. *Even if you were, you'd sit there until the work is done.* The side door opened, and Cookie stomped snow from his boots before he carried in two sacks and set them on the counter. Einstein watched him pull out meat, cheese, and vegetables to put in the refrigerator. When he saw Doc hurry in with a box, he asked, "Need some help?

"There are several more in the van. I'm sure Muscles would welcome another pair of arms."

"How are the roads?"

"Clear, except for the hill. You shouldn't have a problem tonight but drive carefully."

Lefty sauntered into the kitchen after everything was brought in. He started searching through the boxes. "Where are my cartons of *Camels*?" he growled at Cookie.

Cookie glared back, his hands clenched.

Lefty's cold stare turned on Doc. "I said I'd pay him."

"And I told you to quit smoking. Cookie doesn't want the stench permeating his kitchen. The rest of us don't want to smell it either."

Muscles rummaged through the cardboard container he'd set on the table, pulling out coloring books, crayons, some toy cars, and finally a carton of cigarettes. "Here, Geek," he said, throwing it at Lefty. "Smoke outside."

Lefty ducked to avoid being nailed. His lip curled in an unvoiced snarl as he riveted dark angry eyes on each man before he picked up the carton. He ripped it open, pulled out a pack, tossed the box on the counter, and stomped out the door, slamming it behind him. The carton fell to the floor.

Doc raised an eyebrow. "Muscles, he treats you like dirt. Why did you buy him cigarettes?"

Muscles picked up the box and placed it on the counter. "We're partners."

From the doorway, Einstein watched Adolf take quick strides toward the kitchen.

Adolf scowled as he hurried into the room. "Did I hear the door slam? Is something amiss?"

"Not really," Einstein said. "Lefty got angry when told to smoke outdoors."

Adolf shook his head. "You'd think he'd know by now we don't want to be around tobacco fumes." He tapped Cookie on the shoulder. After Cookie turned, Adolf said, "Needles is hungry. Are there any sandwiches left?"

"No, but I'll fix him one."

"If he's hungry," Doc said, "then he's responding well to the medication."

Adolf nodded. "How's Baker doing?" he asked Einstein. "Any problems?"

"No. He's angry, but so far he's kept his cool. He did some exploring, and everything went the way you wanted. However, over the past hour, we've been hearing that chain drag back and forth, stop a few minutes, then start up again."

Adolf cocked his head, listening. "I imagine he is restless. I wonder what he's thinking?" Lefty entered the kitchen, and Adolf waved his hand in front of his nose. "Since it seems you have to smoke, could you at least walk around and air out before you come in? I think, I think I'll keep Needles company while he eats." He picked up the tray and gave Lefty one last look. "Einstein said Baker has been pacing a lot. He could be doing it because he's restless, angry, or he may be plotting something. Take no chances with him. If you hear suspicious noises coming from his room, check immediately."

3

Dan continued to pace with Einstein's words gyrating in his mind—electronic whiz—bomb expert. *These men will stop at nothing to get what they want.* Heart and temples pounding, Dan grabbed the back of a chair. The enormity of what Einstein's words implied increased the gravity of his situation. Dizzy, he slid onto the seat and propped his elbows on the card table, his head against his palms. *Stop. Losing your head won't help matters. God is in control. God is in control.* He repeated this until his heart no longer thudded and his breathing slowed. With a sigh, he sat back and looked heavenward. "And, Lord, I do know You're in control. Please remind me again if I get fearful." *If?* Instinct told him *when* was a better word.

Dan took a sip of coffee, ice-cold coffee. How long had he been pacing this freezing room? He glanced at his watch in amazement—almost two-thirty—over an hour? *Crooksville is probably rejoicing over their ability to rattle me. No more!* Dan took another sip of coffee and stared at the ham-and-cheese sandwich. It looked great, was even made on his favorite bread—rye, but he had no desire to eat. Telling himself he had to keep his strength, he took a bite. Surprised, he took another. Cindy made terrific sandwiches, but this one was fantastic. He polished it off and drank the last swig of coffee. Still thirsty, he rose to fill the mug from the bathroom tap. Stomping feet came running the minute he stepped into the hallway. Lefty sprang around the corner, his .45 drawn. "Where do you think you're going?"

"Should I have yelled, 'Mother may I'?" He held out the mug. "How about some hot coffee?"

Lefty snorted. "Do I look like a waiter?" He gestured Dan toward the archway where Einstein stood holding his gun in readiness. "Baker wants some coffee."

Einstein slipped the revolver under his belt and took the mug. "Decided to finally settle down?"

"I'll bide my time."

Lefty hee-hawed. "Do you expect your mommy to save you?" Einstein joined the laugher.

Dan's brow furrowed over Lefty's off-the-wall comment.

"Was the bogey man after you, Baker? Is that why you kept yelling for your mommy?"

Dan bristled but fought back his anger, refusing to be riled. And no way would he share the nightmare that must have triggered his outburst. He spied the radio on the end table. "Could I have a radio?"

Einstein said, "Why? The Interstate-70 World Series is over."

"Basketball is more my speed. But out of curiosity, who won?"

"The Kansas City Royals beat the St. Louis Cardinals. So, you like basketball. Who do you think will win the championship next spring?"

"The Lakers…with Kareem and Magic Johnson, they're sure to win."

"Not if they play Boston," Einstein said. "That Larry Bird is worth two Lakers. You know what they say, 'One bird in hand is worth two in the bush.'" He laughed.

"Since you're in good mood, is there a radio I can I have?"

"You'd have better odds of standing in front of that fire, but I will get you some coffee."

As Einstein sauntered toward the kitchen, Dan glanced at the cards and chips strewn across the dining surface and asked Lefty, "Playing poker?"

"Yeah. Want to join us?"

"No thanks."

Einstein returned with Dan's coffee. "Preachers don't play poker."

"Too bad…back to your room." Lefty took the mug from Einstein and gestured Dan to turn around. He followed a step behind and waited for Dan to slide onto one of the card table chairs before setting down the coffee and backtracking. From the doorway, he said, "Better stay awake or the bogeyman will get you."

The aroma of fresh coffee helped Dan ignore Lefty's parting remark. He propped his elbows on the table and laid his head on his folded hands. A Bible verse reminded him he should give thanks in all things. The hot coffee seemed the only item for which to be grateful. "And I am thankful, Lord, but I wish I were home. I don't know what lies ahead, but I know You're in control, that nothing can happen to me unless You allow it. Please take care of Cindy and the boys. And please give me courage, Amen."

The strong steaming coffee warmed Dan and bolstered him for a while, but the cold dampness and his idleness soon grated on his nerves. He stood and flinched when the chain clanked against a table leg. *That should bring them to their feet.* He yelled, "Hey, guys, I'm only going across the hall to the bathroom again." No one came.

Dan relieved himself and dragged back to the room. For the first time, the hard bed looked inviting. He settled on it with his back against the wooden headboard, wondering if his car had been found or was it here. It probably didn't take long to figure out the phone call was a hoax, and by now the FBI had been notified. He pictured Cap going head-to-head with the bureau chief, discussing probabilities. *If I can't fathom what I'm up against, how can they?*

His mind drifted back to the day he met Cap. Dan remembered how scared he'd felt seeing this giant hulk of a man lumber into the room and sit across from him. Guilt had plagued Dan. He wanted to bolt to escape answering questions, but when he looked into the eyes of his interrogator, he didn't see hard steely ones ready to convict him. Instead, he saw inquisitive blue ones, willing to listen.

"Did you hate your father?"

"I loved him…even bought him a Christmas gift."

"Take your time and tell me what happened."

When I started sobbing, you brought your chair next to mine and put your arm around me as I unburdened my heart. I love you, Cap. "God, you were so gracious to give me Cap and Amanda for foster parents who would adopt me. Then I met Cindy and now have three boys. Thank you, Lord." Dear sweet Cindy, what was she doing? Surely, Amanda would be at the house to give her encouragement. Dan shivered, pulled the blanket tighter around his shoulders, and decided to lie down.

Mentally, he talked to Cindy. "How would you like to fly to Hawaii? Going anywhere sounds great right now." He closed his eyes and envisioned holding her under the huge avocado tree behind their home. The limbs touched the ground, giving them seclusion. Whenever Cap and Amanda took the boys, he and Cindy often made love under the green canopy. In his mind, Dan embraced her and whispered, "I love you." Dan kissed her honey-brown hair and inhaled deeply to enjoy the exotic fragrance she wore only for him. He groaned in remembrance and slammed his fist on the mattress, shattering the illusion.

Ignoring his headache and the clank of the chain, he riveted his anger on the bolt. He pulled on the links with the ferocity of a pit bull refusing to let go. Behind him, he heard someone say, "Enough, Baker!" Dan continued to pull until his hands were red and smarting, his fury spent. He stared at the bolt, panting hard. "Foolish…very foolish," the voice chided. "Haven't you convinced yourself you can't get away?"

Dan dropped the links and spun around. Two men stood inside the room. "I don't know what your game is, but you'll get no help from me."

The short black-haired man who held a gun bore an uncanny resemblance to Hitler. His dark eyes flashed as his lips curled into a cruel smile. "You'll cooperate…or else." The taller man, holding a satchel, nodded.

"Death threats? For me to live is Christ. To die is gain."

Little Hitler raised an eyebrow. "Baker, I wouldn't expect a man of your profession to say otherwise. No, your weakness won't be fear of death but love and compassion."

His cold calculating tone made Dan stiffen. Was he right? He hated violence. His hands had shed blood once. Never again would he take a man's life. "Must be plenty of loot to bring seven men together," he snapped but winced at a sudden jab of pain.

"How did you come up with that number?" the black-haired man asked, his head cocked.

"Seven used beds."

Little Hitler fingered his mustache. "Ah, yes, you've been exploring." After the two men exchanged amused glances, he said, "Dear me, I have been remiss. I haven't made introductions. This is Doc, and I am Mr. Adolf. You'll meet the others soon." He turned to Doc, a man around forty with dark hair and brown eyes. "Doc, check him over, he's in pain." He gave Dan a mocking smile. "We certainly wouldn't want you to suffer undue stress." His unwavering gun now gestured toward the bed. "Sit," he ordered.

Dan planted his feet. "You're concerned about my health? I'm fine." He glared at Doc. "I need no help from you."

"Sit," Adolf ordered again. The venom of hate shooting from his eyes seemed deadlier than any snake's.

Dan stood his ground a few seconds more before he shrugged and complied. Doc set his bag on the bed, opened it, and took out a penlight. "Look up and open your eyes wide." Dan followed his instructions to look up, down, left, and right. "Now, lean over so I can check the back of your head." Dan jerked when he pressed the lump. "Sorry," Doc said.

"Yeah, I bet."

"He may have a slight concussion," Doc told Adolf.

"Give him a pain pill and escort him to the archway." He opened his jacket and slipped the gun in a holster. "I trust we'll have no more trouble from you. Foolish heroics will only bring grief."

Maybe in your eyes I have been foolish, but any heroics I do won't be.

The two exchanged glances when Dan didn't reply. Adolf said, "Baker, I have the ability to inflict tremendous anguish with no bodily harm to you. Do you read me?"

Dan stood, clicked his heels, and extended his right arm. "Loud and clear, Mein Fuhrer," he said with all the venom he could muster.

Doc stepped between them and stopped Adolf from striking Dan. "Let him have his fun for now. Tomorrow morning he'll sing a different tune."

Adolf's eyes narrowed. "And you will. You'll become as obedient as a circus lion. That I promise." He did an about-face and stomped out of the room.

Dan stared at the empty doorway, wondering how.

"For a minister, you certainly are a belligerent cuss," Doc said. "Is that how you deal with your young people?"

Proverbs 16:32 flashed through Dan's mind. *He who is slow to anger is better than the mighty. He who rules his spirit than he who takes a city.* His mother had made him memorize the verse the first time he'd become angry with his father. She'd remind him of it whenever he lost his temper. Doc's words filled him with chagrin, and his confrontation with Adolf plus his own fears left him drained. "No" was all he could say.

"Let me give you some advice. Don't antagonize Adolf or anyone else. With the exception of Cookie, they're ruthless."

"Cookie?"

"Our chef. You're in for a treat…if you don't cause problems."

"Cookie…cook." Dan rolled his eyes. "Where's Snow White?"

Doc's eyes widened. He laughed, but the laughter sounded forced. "Very funny…seven of us, but we're hardly dwarves." He opened his mouth as if to speak but quickly clamped his lips tight. From his medical bag, he retrieved a bottle.

Was there a Snow White? Dan wondered as Doc unscrewed the lid and took out two tablets.

"Here, take these." When Dan hesitated, he added, "They're only extra-strength aspirin. You can get some water in the bathroom." Their eyes met, and Doc asked, "How come you didn't become a cop like your old man?"

"I didn't want to," Dan said, refusing to divulge more.

Doc raised an eyebrow. "Have I touched a sensitive nerve?" He laughed. "Tell ole doc about it."

Dan grabbed his coffee mug and headed for the bathroom.

"I really did touch a sore spot, didn't I?" Doc watched him down the pills.

Irked at his inability to hide his feelings, Dan said, "Bug out." Instinct told him the man wouldn't let the matter drop.

A smirk spread across Doc's face. He shrugged and pointed toward the archway. "After you. Adolf wants you to meet two more of our little gang."

Little Hitler stood in the archway, watching them approach. "Ah, Baker, so good of you to join us."

As if I had much choice. Dan scanned the huge room, probably more than thirty feet square. He saw two men he hadn't met. One, a tall, muscular, dark-haired man who gave him a mocking smile, reminded Dan of a boxer who had taken too many beatings. The other's appearance made Dan shudder inwardly. Sunken ice-blue eyes glared from a skin and bone face that matched the emaciated body of the young man. He personified death. Dan averted his gaze. "Where are Lefty and Einstein?" Doc was the only one who didn't laugh.

"Busy," Adolf replied. His quirky smile said wouldn't you like to know.

Dan masked an unexplainable jab of fear—the feeling of impending doom. He'd been on an emotional roller coaster all afternoon. Could he survive the next plunge?

The laughter faded, but the three men still wore twisted smiles. Adolf said, "Too bad you can't join in on the merriment, Baker, but alas, if we clued you in, it would spoil our surprise."

Dan fought back his anger. "Merriment at my expense?"

"Sad but true. Dear me, I have been remiss again. I haven't made introductions." He waved his hand toward the muscular man. "This is Muscles."

"Somehow I gathered as much," Dan said.

"And this young man is Needles."

Puzzled, Dan stared until the connection dawned on him. "You're a junkie."

Needles lunged, grabbed Dan's neck with both hands and squeezed hard.

Dan tried to free himself from the man's surprisingly strong grip but couldn't. The chain kept throwing him off balance.

"Enough, Needles," Adolf barked.

Needles let go like an obedient Doberman, but his eyes flashed satanic hatred as he watched Dan gasping. Muscles looked on with smug satisfaction.

"You okay?" Doc asked, checking his neck.

Still fighting for breath, Dan could only yank his hand away, giving him an I-don't-need-your-help look.

"Baker," Adolf said, "I suggest you refrain from using that word again. As you can see, it tends to anger him." He gestured Dan to turn around. "Back to your room...we need to talk." He followed Dan, sat opposite him but didn't speak. His eyes bore into Dan's as if trying to read his mind.

Dan didn't break eye contact but spoke to ease his tenseness. "Does Needles have AIDS?"

"Sad but true."

Dan sensed genuine concern. With the exception of Needles, everyone he'd met was in his forties or fifties. Why was Needles here? Dan studied Adolf's features.

"What are you mulling over?"

"Is Needles your son?"

"What gave you that idea?"

"Your fatherly concern and, except for coloring, there is a resemblance between you."

"Yes, he is my son."

"I'm sorry," Dan said. "Watching a loved one die is hard."

"I think you mean that, but love doesn't enter the picture. His mother kicked him out, and I took him in to keep him out of the gutter." The unemotional statement seemed to indicate the subject was closed. "Now, to the matter at hand, I suggest you keep your cool. Do so, and you'll be allowed to eat the same fine fare we do. We may even let you talk to your wife from time to time. Tomorrow, we'll provide some company...our little surprise."

"You enjoy tormenting people, don't you?"

"Torment...you call this torment? Three hours from now, you'll be eating food fit for a king." He stood. "I suggest you eat hearty."

"What are you guys after? What's my role in this?"

"All in good time, Baker...all in good time."

Dan watched him leave. He knew they would kill him. Why feed him? Did they need him strong over a period of time? Why? He closed his eyes against the nightmare, hoping when he opened them, he'd find himself nestled beside Cindy. Emotionally drained, he stretched out on the bed and listened to the wind and the laughter of men enjoying themselves before he fell asleep. A door slamming awakened him. Dan eased off the bed, walked over to the boarded window, and peered through the widest crack. He saw snow and evergreen boughs. The pink glow indicated a setting sun. If his window faced west, so must the front of the lodge, not that it meant much, but at least he had his bearings.

He turned at the sound of footsteps. A man about his age entered, carrying a tray. He had wavy brown hair and sad brown eyes. "You must be Cookie," Dan said as the man set the tray on the table, turned, and left. Dan wondered why no one had come with Cookie. Maybe they figured he was smart enough not to tangle with the hand that would feed him.

He walked over to the table and stared in astonishment. Adolf hadn't been kidding. The food before him looked equal to any served in the finest restaurant. On the plate lay filet mignon wrapped in bacon, a baked potato blanketed with cheese sauce, and tiny peas cradled in a half shell of golden squash. A slice of warm apple pie lay on another plate next to a carafe of coffee.

Dan hadn't realized how hungry he was until he started eating. When he finished the last bite of pie, he leaned back and sipped the coffee, feeling satisfied. He relaxed a little. When Cookie came to get the tray, Dan smiled. "My hat's off to you. You're a great chef. That meal was fit for a king. How come you're not working at the Golden Palomino or the Black Saber?"

Cookie picked up the tray and hurried through the doorway. Dan wondered at the lack of response. He shrugged. Well, so much for talking with Cookie. With the exception of Doc and Cookie, all seemed like evil-hearted men. Why were Doc and Cookie here—just to serve in their respective professions? That didn't figure. Maybe they had dual roles. Cookie, although uncommunicative, had a kind but sad countenance. Doc appeared to be a genuine MD, being concerned after Needles had choked Dan, and he had stopped Adolf from striking him. No, Cookie and Doc didn't seem to fit in with the rest.

Doc entered a short time later with his black bag. "I must say, you look fairly well relaxed. Cookie's meals do wonders."

"What's wrong with him, and why isn't he working in a classy restaurant?"

"Cookie is deaf. He could read your lips, but he's not very talkative." Doc set his bag on the table. "He did work as head chef for… let's just say at a good eating establishment until he went to prison."

"What did he do?"

Doc grinned. "Poisoned some people he didn't like. They didn't die. He just made them wish they would."

"Poisoned them? Right there in the restaurant? Didn't he realize he'd be caught?"

"He's not particularly bright, but when it comes to food, he's a wizard."

Dan watched Doc open his bag and frowned. "You don't like needles, Baker? It's only a sedative. This will be a nightly ritual, so you might as well get used to it. After all, we'll have business to discuss, and we don't want our 'racket' disturbing you." Doc chuckled at his pun.

"Why am I here?"

"If Adolf wanted you to know, he would have told you. Take off your jacket."

Dan clenched his hands and made no move to comply.

"Baker, I have no patience with stubbornness. You'll only make things harder on yourself. Remove your jacket, unbutton your sleeve, and roll it up." When Dan didn't respond, he yelled, "Muscles, get in here!"

The ex-boxer bounded through the doorway in a flash, licking his lips in apparent anticipation. "Now," Doc said, "would you like a sample of his persuasive skills?"

The sedative represented the lesser of two evils. Dan slowly unzipped his jacket, slipped out of it, and hung it neatly on the back of the chair. Unbuttoning his right sleeve cuff, he turned it back into precise folds while Doc tapped his foot.

"Extend your arm," Doc ordered.

Dan complied but glowered at Doc as the needle pricked his skin. He prayed it was only a sedative.

Doc pointed toward the bed. "Now off to dreamland."

Seething, Dan donned his jacket, walked to the bed, and stretched out, hands clenched.

"Baker, if you think you're angry now, wait until you see what tomorrow brings. Good night."

Dan had little time to contemplate Doc's last words. The sedative pulled him under.

*****

Doc walked through the archway and straight to the fireplace to warm his back in front of the blazing logs.

"Is he out?" Adolf asked.

Doc glanced at his watch. "Give him a few more minutes."

"Are you positive he'll stay under until morning?"

"Are you questioning my skills?"

"Don't get riled. I only want assurance he's not going to hear the bedlam in here when Lefty and Einstein return."

"He won't! What makes you think there will be trouble?"

"Instinct. Is the room ready?"

"Yes."

Muscles's lips drew into a pout. "Boss, how come you let Einstein go with Lefty tonight and not me?"

Adolf curbed his impatience with the ex-boxer who often had complaints. "I didn't want someone with your brute strength involved."

"But Lefty and I are partners."

"And you are good partners in crime, but tonight's operation is one of extreme delicacy. Besides, the second uniform we obtained was Einstein's size."

Muscles shrugged and said no more.

Good, Adolf thought, *he's finally placated.* "Now, I want you to keep your poker game quiet while I finish the letter to Captain Baker.

Captain Baker,

How long your son and grandsons live depends on you and the cooperation of others. By the time you get this letter, you'll know the destructive power of our smallest bomb that is like the one strapped to your son. Others we have are ten times more powerful. We can detonate them from a mile away.

You will see to it that the corporations owning the following chain stores in Orange County are contacted—Quick Stop, More For Less, JR Market, Ware Mart, Shop-Smart, Scott, Peterson, Spend-Less, Ricard, Swifter, ICON, and Market-Place.

Each is to have one million dollars in unmarked one-hundred-dollar bills ready to be delivered to one of their stores. They will be contacted and given specific instructions. *Do not replace the manager.* He will turn this money over to your son who will identify himself with a black card bearing the golden head of a lion. We plan to monitor your son's every move and listen to every word he says. There will be a reprisal if the store does not have the money or if there is an attempt to pass a tracking device to your son.

If the money isn't handed over, a bomb will explode in one of the corporation's stores before the day ends. After one example, I'm sure we'll have no further problems.

Attempts to follow us by any means will be met with reprisal. A few well-placed bombs along the routes we've chosen can easily be set off. Innocent people may die.

To a successful business venture,
LIONS INTERNATIONAL

After he read the letter to the rest of them, Muscles said, "Are we gonna hit all twelve stores?"

"No," Adolf told him. "Only eight. We don't want to be greedy. I'd planned on seven, but Einstein insists his girl should get a million for the risks she's taking."

Doc laughed. "Baker asked if there was a Snow White. Wouldn't he be surprised to learn she works right under his father's nose."

4

S unday evening, from the moment Dan left, Cindy couldn't shake
her foreboding. Every nerve screamed danger, and she couldn't
rationalize away her anxiety. She turned on the TV and watched the
movie *Airplane*, but not even the antics on that film could squelch
her premonition. At eleven o'clock, Cindy watched the news and
afterward picked up a romance novel she had been dying to read
but couldn't find the time. Two pages into it, unable to concentrate,
she tossed the book aside. *Surely Dan won't be later than midnight.
Otherwise he'll call.*

When Jonathan started crying, she rushed to his room to comfort him. He was having a hard time cutting his first teeth. His fret-
fulness while she nursed him took her mind off Dan, but as soon as
Jonathan fell asleep, her worries returned.

Another hour passed—still no word. Cindy emptied the dish-
washer and straightened the house. By two o'clock, she could contain
herself no longer. She phoned the St. Jude emergency room. The
receptionist remembered Dan, relayed what happened, and said he
was probably at another hospital. Cindy contacted each one and gave
them Dan's description. No one recalled seeing him, nor did they
have an injured boy found lying on the sidewalk.

A hoax? Who would pull such a cruel trick, and where was Dan
now? Could he have had an accident on the rain-slick roads? Despite
the hour and the worry it would cause Cap and Amanda, she sat at
the desk and phoned them. Cap would be able to check the accident
reports. When Cap answered on the second ring, Cindy blurted, "I
need your help."

"Easy. Calm down. What's wrong?"

"Dan hasn't come home."

"Take a deep breath and calmly tell me what's happened."

After she relayed the situation and her suspicions, Cap said, "I think you're worrying needlessly, but I'll look into it. Dan probably is at one of the hospitals, but the person you talked to might not have known. As soon as I make a few calls, Amanda and I will come over and stay until Dan gets home."

Cindy tried to convince them it wasn't necessary, but relief washed over her after she hung up. Exhausted more from worry than lack of sleep, she remained at the desk. She studied their wedding picture. Tears clouded her eyes as she thought about how badly she'd treated Dan all day. She hadn't been that obnoxious since the night they'd met.

Cap had asked her, as a favor to him, to attend the police family Christmas dinner and sit at their table. He knew she didn't have an escort and wanted to use her excuse for not attending to convince Dan to come. "We adopted Dan four years ago," he told her. "His parents died tragically just before Christmas, and holidays tend to turn him into a recluse."

Cindy agreed to sit with Cap's family but declined being picked up. No way was she going to be stuck with an escort who might turn out to be a dud. Cap introduced them at the predinner mingle. It surprised Cindy to find this recluse not only handsome but also tall—six feet. At five-feet-ten, she had rarely dated a man she could look up to. Dan's thick crop of brown curly hair made her long to run her fingers through it. But it was his gentle brown eyes and deep dimples that captured her heart. Despite finding the man of her dreams, the moment he offered to bring her a glass of punch, she'd bristled and continued to refuse his every attentive move. *And today, I treated him as if he didn't exist.* Knowing they made up couldn't erase her guilt. Would she ever get a chance to make amends? Cindy laid her head on the desk and cried. "Oh, Dan, where are you?"

The doorbell's ringing brought her to her feet. It had to be Dan's parents. As she hurried to the door, Cindy wiped her eyes, tried to regain her composure, and turned on the porch light. Seeing

Amanda and Cap through the peephole, she threw open the door. "Have you learned anything?" she blurred and stepped aside so they could enter.

"Not yet," Cap said, helping Amanda out of her raincoat. "I left word at the station to contact me here."

The phone rang. Cindy ran to the phone, praying it was Dan so her worries could be put to rest. The caller asked for Cap, and she handed the receiver to him.

"This is Captain Baker." He listened and said, "Please contact me immediately if you have any news of his whereabouts." He hung up and turned to face Cindy and Amanda. "There are no accident reports involving your car. But you're right about a hoax. No injured person has been found lying on the sidewalk." He shook his head, his mouth grim. "I don't know what to think."

Cindy couldn't stem her tears as panic welled. "He's in trouble. I sensed danger before he left. I know something's happened to him."

Amanda put a consoling arm around her. "The Lord will take care of him."

Cindy saw the anxiety in her eyes. Cap looked equally troubled. "What can we do?"

"Wait," Cap said. "Wait for Dan to call. Let's go into the kitchen, and while Amanda makes coffee, I want you to tell me everything you remember."

Seated at the table, Cindy said, "You suspect something has happened too, don't you?"

Cap hesitated to answer as if he had other thoughts. "Cindy, I'm going to ask you something…please don't get angry. Has Dan been under any extra stress? Has he been moody or behaving strangely?"

Indignant at the implication, she said, "I assure you Dan has not had a nervous breakdown. He couldn't be happier with his work and his home life." The minute the words left her mouth, she recalled all that had gone on recently. Was her statement true?

Cap and Amanda exchanged glances as if they sensed problems. In a gentle voice, Amanda said, "What's bothering you? Can you tell us what it is?"

"Oh, Mandy, I was such a shrew. I chewed Dan out last night when he didn't get home for Danny's birthday party. I refused to accept his apology. I didn't even kiss him goodbye this morning or when he came home for dinner. After the kids went to bed, he tried to smooth my ruffled feathers. I continued to chew him out. But we did make up," she emphasized, "just before the phone rang. If only it hadn't."

"I'm sure this has nothing to do with what went on today," Cap said. "Let's discuss this rationally. Maybe you'll remember something that will solve this riddle."

Amanda pushed back her chair. "I'll get the coffee."

Cindy related the story again. They agreed the phone call was either a cruel trick or someone had conned Dan into going to the hospital. For what purpose, they had no idea. An hour passed with no word from Dan, but another call came for Cap. The police had found Dan's car five miles north of St. Jude Hospital, the keys in the ignition, but no sign of him. Trembling at the thought, Cindy said, "Did someone mug him? Is he dazed and wandering?"

Cap's lips pursed together. "I'm going down to the station. I'll have an APB put out. Cindy, try and stay calm. The boys will wake up soon, and you don't want to scare them." He stood and put his hands on her shoulders. "I'm sure Dan is okay. Please, try not to worry. I'll call as soon as I have news."

Amanda said, "We brought both cars, so I'll keep you company for as long as you want."

In their pajamas, Danny and Timmy pattered into the kitchen around seven. Their sleepy faces turned joyous when they saw their grandmother. "Please let me stay home from school, Mommy," Danny pleaded. "Grandma's never here during the week."

Cindy gave in. He only went to kindergarten in the morning. Missing once wouldn't hurt, and he was good at keeping Timmy and Jonathan entertained.

The boys stayed in the kitchen to watch Amanda fix pancakes while Cindy attended to Jonathan who had started crying. She picked him up and patted his back, wondering how to explain Dan's absence to Danny and Timmy. They usually found Dan in the living room. Amanda's being here had distracted them, but Cindy knew it wouldn't be long before they asked where he was. She carried Jonathan to the kitchen and set him in his high chair.

"Mommy, where's Daddy?" Danny asked. "Is he sleeping late?"

"He was called to the hospital and hasn't come home." They accepted her explanation, and she tried to convince herself he'd arrive before they asked again. Her pounding heart said otherwise.

The morning dragged. Cap didn't call until almost noon to tell her the news media had picked up on Dan's disappearance. The evening news carried Dan's picture and asked anyone who might have seen him to contact the police. Cindy had sent the boys to their room to play, but Danny ran into the living room as Dan's face appeared on the screen. "Look, Mommy. Daddy's picture's on TV." He listened and asked, "What happened to Daddy?"

Cindy bit down on her lip. "We're not sure, Danny. Grandpa Cap has the police looking for him. He told me not to worry, and I don't want you to either. Jesus will take care of him."

"Danny," Amanda asked, "do you think your daddy would like some cookies when he gets home? Why don't you and I bake some after dinner?"

"Can we make chocolate chip?"

"Sure."

"Will Grandpa be here for dinner?" he asked.

Amanda glanced at Cindy.

"He didn't say," Cindy told Danny. "Maybe he wants to surprise us." She knew how much Danny loved surprises. What a wonderful one it would be if Cap showed up with Dan.

Shortly after the newscast, the phone rang. Cindy grabbed it, praying it was Dan. It was Pastor Richards, the senior pastor. "Cindy, I just saw the news. I alerted the prayer chain. What else can I do?"

"Nothing. Cap said we'll just have to wait to hear from Dan or from someone who knows what's happened to him."

"We can come over and wait with you and the boys."

"That's not necessary. Amanda's here. I'm trying to keep things as normal as possible. I don't want to scare the boys."

"I understand, but call if you need us for any reason."

When Amanda carried in a platter of fried chicken and a bowl of mashed potatoes, Cindy hurried into the dining room. Seated, she kept the blessing short and tried to keep apprehension out of her voice when she asked the Lord to bring Dan home soon. Finished, she managed to smile. "Danny, I think your idea of making chocolate chip cookies is great. Daddy loves them as much as you do."

His face puckered. "He likes fried chicken too."

Amanda said, "I made plenty so he and your grandfather can have some later."

Cindy had barely finished eating one piece when she jumped up to answer the phone. As soon as she hung up, one call after another came. Teenagers, concerned members and people she hardly knew wanted to help. Cindy told each person to pray. What else could she say when that was all she could do? Only God can help Dan, she thought in despair.

After the next call, Amanda said, "Let me answer from now on. Come sit down and finish before you drop."

"Mommy, can I have some more milk?" Danny asked.

Cindy nodded like a mindless robot, retrieved the milk jug from the refrigerator, and emptied it into Danny's glass.

"That's all I get?"

"I want some," Timmy said.

Cindy stared at the container, wondering how it could be empty so soon. "We don't have anymore. I can make some powdered milk, or you can have apple juice."

Both frowned.

"I'll run to the store and buy more." Amanda volunteered.

"Can I go?" the boys chimed.

"No," Cindy said. "You haven't finished dinner. If you want to help make cookies to eat, you need to clean those plates." She turned to Amanda. "You're a dear for going. I didn't think about checking our supply." Jonathan's head lay on the high-chair tray when she returned from walking Amanda to the door. "You boys finish eating while I put Jonathan in his crib."

Cindy had no sooner laid him down when the doorbell rang. She dashed to the front door, turned on the porch light, and peered through the peephole. When she saw two police officers, Cindy threw off her usual caution and opened the door. The men flashed IDs. Before she could look at them closely, the taller one said, "Mrs. Baker, Captain Baker sent us to bring you to the hospital."

Cindy gasped. "Dan's hurt? How badly?"

"Nothing serious, but the captain knew you'd want to see him right away."

"Mrs. Baker, just now went to the store for milk. She should be back in a few minutes. What happened?"

They shoved their way inside, throwing her off balance. One clapped his hand over her mouth before she could scream. The other shut the door, pulled a bottle and a cloth from his pocket. Cindy struggled but couldn't break free from the powerful arm that held her as the shorter man unscrewed the top from a bottle, poured liquid onto a cloth, and the instant the other man removed his hand, he pressed the rag against her face. She had no time to scream. Pungent fumes stung her nose and eyes. Her knees buckled. She heard Danny yell, "Let me go!"

Voices called to Cindy from the depth of darkness—vague, jumbled words. She fought to lift herself from the mind-numbing blackness. "Wake up," she heard and tried to open her eyes. The lids seemed weighted.

"Cindy, please wake up!"

Desperation and urgency edged the words. *Amanda?* Cindy forced her eyes open and tried to bring the blurred image into focus. She blinked again and again until her vision cleared. Her tongue rolled around in her mouth before she could finally say, "What...?"

"Someone chloroformed you. You're in the emergency room."

Sudden panic pushed the last veils of fog from Cindy's mind. "The boys," she screamed, sitting bolt upright. "Amanda! Where are they?"

*****

"I'm sure glad you thought of giving those kids a dose of the stuff you gave their mom," Lefty said, "or they'd still be kicking and screaming their heads off. That bigger one kicked me so hard I almost back-handed him."

"It's a good thing you didn't. You might have killed him. That wouldn't have set well with Mr. Adolf," Einstein said.

"We'd still have the other brat. Baker would never know."

"Oh, but he would. Remember, his old man's a police chief, and he'll be having contact with him."

Lefty shrugged. "Yeah, guess you're right, but I don't like having those brats around."

"Shouldn't bother you. You don't have to take care of them. That's Cookie and Doc's job."

Einstein drove to a secluded area where they had stashed his station wagon. "We'll leave this car among those trees so it's partially hidden. While I wipe it clean, you put the kids in the back of my wagon and cover them with a couple of blankets."

Lefty finished his task and climbed into the passenger seat to wait for Einstein. When Einstein took his place behind the wheel, Lefty said, "What do you think the boss is going to do to the brats after he kills Baker?"

Einstein shrugged and started the engine. "Who cares? They're just kids."

After they entered the freeway, Lefty said, "Is it fun making and planting bombs?"

Einstein laughed. "I get a big bang out of it…kind of like play-ing god. I get to decide when and where someone's going to die."

"Me, I'd rather shoot a gun…that way I know for certain who's going to die."

"That's too simple. I like the mystery, the element of surprise, and the chaos that follows."

As they neared San Bernardino. Lefty said, "I'm hungry. Can we pick up burgers someplace? We've got the brats covered with blan-kets. No one will see them."

"Okay." Einstein pulled off at the freeway exit before the one that would take them to the mountain road. He saw a fast-food place and drove up to the take-out window. Within ten minutes, they'd ordered and were back on the highway. Lefty wolfed down his two burgers before Einstein finished his one. Both crunched fries while the car snaked up the winding road. Einstein dropped a fry and glanced down to retrieve it while steering with one hand around a curve. Black ice sent the wagon into a whirlwind spin. Disoriented, Einstein managed to keep the car from careening out of control, but the back end clipped a tree before he could straighten and stop. Only the heavy blankets prevented the boys from being tossed about, but Danny's right shoulder banged hard against the side.

Disgruntled, Einstein grabbed a flashlight and leaped out of the car to survey the damage. The station wagon's right rear side was smashed, but not enough to keep them from continuing.

"Sure glad you didn't hit that tree head-on," Lefty said. "We sure wouldn't want to be caught out here with those brats."

Einstein shook his head in disgust. "All because of a stupid French fry. If you hadn't made me go get burgers, this wouldn't have happened."

"Hey. Don't blame me," Lefty bellowed. "You're the one who dropped the fry. You're the one who's supposed to be the ace driver."

"Get in. Let's scram before someone comes." Cursing his luck, Einstein gripped the wheel. White knuckled, he stayed alert as he drove back to the hideout. Stopping in front of the lodge, Einstein told Lefty, "Be careful on those slippery porch steps." Opening the station wagon's tailgate, he said, "You grab the kid that kicked you, I'll get the other." After they hauled the boys out by their ankles, they tossed them across their shoulders as if worth no more than a sack of manure but held the porch railing as they climbed the stairs.

*****

Adolf heard the men arrive, and he, Doc, and Cookie hurried to the door. Adolf asked Doc, "Are you sure Baker's out so he won't hear the bedlam when they bring the kids in?"

"Positive," Doc said, opening the heavy walnut door and holding back the screen.

Lefty and Einstein didn't bother to stomp snow from their boots as they tramped into the living room. Einstein gazed at Adolf and said, "You look surprised."

"How did you manage to get them to sleep?" Adolf asked. "I thought they'd be crying their heads off."

"Both were kicking and screaming before we left the house," Einstein said, "but a dose of what we gave their mother quieted them."

"You half-baked moron," Doc growled. "You could have killed them."

"They're breathing," Lefty said.

Doc took the pulse of the younger boy before he checked the older one.

"Are they okay?" Adolf asked.

"They seem to be, but I want to examine them thoroughly." Cookie helped Doc carry the boys to the bedroom."

Adolf scowled at Lefty and Einstein. "For your sake, they had better be okay."

"Hey, they didn't even wake up when we hit the tree," Lefty said.

Adolf stiffened. "You did what?"

"I skidded on black ice," Einstein said.

Lefty chortled. "He dropped a fry."

"Shut up, blabbermouth!"

"You weren't supposed to stop anywhere."

"I was hungry," Lefty said in defense. "We didn't get a fancy dinner like you guys."

Adolf fought to control his temper. "Einstein, I sent you with Lefty because you have common sense...at least I thought you did. You knew the roads were slick. You should have been paying attention. How hard did you hit the tree? Did the kids get hurt?" Lefty glanced at Einstein and shrugged. "You incompetents! You didn't check?" Both men stood sullen and mute. Adolf threw up his hands and dashed to Doc's room. "Are the boys all right?"

"You look upset. What's wrong?"

"Einstein hit black ice and struck a tree."

"Help me get their clothes off and check them more thoroughly."

They didn't see any sign of injury on Timmy, but Danny's right shoulder had turned red. "I think it's only bruised," Doc said. "But that arm will probably bother him tomorrow."

"Is there any way we can keep this from Baker?"

"Are you kidding? The boy's old enough to complain plenty, and Baker's going to have even more reason to be furious."

"Can you give him something so he won't feel his shoulder aching?"

"I'll not chance giving the kid an injection. When Baker finds out, I'll try to make him realize we never intended for the boys to get hurt."

"That's the best you can do?"

"Yes."

Adolf rounded the corner of the doorway, shaking his head.

5

While the sun rose Tuesday, the sedative Doc gave Dan started to wear off. Groggy, he heard Danny and Timmy sobbing in the next room. "Cindy," he mumbled, "the boys are crying." Gradually becoming more fully aware of his surroundings, he realized he wasn't home. Bewildered, Dan listened. The muffled sobs came again. Trying not to jar his throbbing head, he pushed himself upright and leaned against the headboard, his heart pounding. All remained quiet. *Is that sedative playing tricks on my mind?*

He remembered Adolf's words: "Tomorrow, we'll provide some company...our little surprise." Dan gasped when he heard Danny scream, "I want Mommy." He rolled off the bed to his feet hardly hearing the clanks of chain or feeling the explosions in his head. Like an apparition, Muscles appeared, his feet planted to block Dan's access to the hall. A jeering grin spread across his squat face. Dan fought the urge to slam his fist against it. "Where are they?"

Muscles hee-hawed. "You really want to take me on? Can't do that now. Maybe later?"

Adolf came up behind Muscles, tapped his shoulder, and gestured the ex-boxer to enter ahead of him. Muscles hurried in and stood to the side as Little Hitler sauntered into the room like an arrogant man proud of his accomplishment.

The boys' persistent sobs unnerved Dan. He raised his clenched hand. "What have you done to my family?"

Adolf grasped his wrist. "Easy, Baker, your wife and baby are home. No harm has come to them. We only kidnapped Daniel and Timothy."

Dan's face contorted with rage. "Why? Why have you kid-napped us?" His heart ached as he listened to his sobbing sons. "They're scared. Let me go to them. I promise I won't try anything."

"We know you won't. That's why they're here. Cookie and Doc will take good care of them. We're not heartless. In fact, you'll have all day to play with them. Enjoy it. You'll be too busy later to see them much." He pulled a key from his pants' pocket and handed it to Muscles. "Remove the chain. We don't want to alarm Baker's kids." After Muscles unlocked the padlock, and Dan kicked the chain away, Adolf said, "A bit testy this morning?" His eyes narrowed in warning. "Follow me."

Dan wanted to race down the hallway and barge into the room. Instead, he fell into step behind Adolf like the obedient circus lion the man claimed he would become.

Adolf pointed to Dan's shoes sitting in front of the door. "Put those on. We don't want your kids asking why you're barefoot."

Dan jammed his feet into them and bent to tie the laces, his heart hammering with impatience as Adolf knocked. When the door opened, it took all Dan's willpower not to thrust Adolf and Doc aside to reach Danny and Timmy. They sat on the bare mattress, wailing. "Daddy," they cried, rolling off the bed and running into his out-stretched arms.

Their terrified sobs continued.

Dan hugged and kissed them, fighting back his own tears. How could he comfort and reassure them when he too was frightened? "Are you okay?" he asked around the lump in his throat.

Danny sniffled as he nodded. Timmy clung to Dan's neck. Looking bewildered but calmer, Danny asked, "Where's Mommy?"

"She and Jonathan are home." Dan prayed they were all right. How could these men manage to kidnap his sons without Cindy putting up a valiant fight?

"Where are we?" Danny asked.

Dan knew he had to push aside his fear and anger so he could concentrate on helping his sons cope. "We're in the mountains. We're going to be here awhile. Pretend we're having a vacation."

Danny's eyes widened with disbelief. "Without Mommy and Jonathan?"

"This is a pretend vacation." When he stood to face Adolf, Timmy tightened his arms around Dan's neck. Could his son sense his anger?

"Very tender scene, Baker. You may stay here with them. Cookie should have breakfast soon. Doc will keep you company, and of course, Muscles will be right outside." He put his hand on the doorknob. "Don't make the mistake of thinking Doc's soft just because he's a doctor." He laughed. "Have fun today."

Dan wanted to cram the laughter down his throat, but with his sons' lives in jeopardy, he surrendered all thoughts of heroics. After the door closed, he glared at Doc. "I thought doctors cared for people."

"I care. I don't enjoy seeing children frightened or their father being used. But I need the money to set up a clinic out of the country where I can help people. I can't do it here."

"Why?"

"What's it to you?"

"Don't I have the right to know your motives, the motives of all of you?"

"I served my time, but no town in the USA wants a doctor with a record."

"What did you do?"

"I almost killed my wife's lover when I came home and found them in bed. Would you want me doctoring your kids?"

Dan ran his fingers through Danny's hair while he mulled over Doc's question. "I'm sorry your wife was unfaithful, but in God's eyes, murder or attempted murder is never justified, neither is what you're doing now. As to your question, if my kids do need medical help, I expect you'll do your best."

Doc snorted. "Thanks for the confidence, but keep your preaching in church where it belongs."

Dan would have liked to expound on that subject, but a knock ended the conversation.

Doc flung open the door. Cookie, carrying a large tray, cast Doc a concerned glance as if he sensed Doc was upset.

"Boys, this is Cookie," Doc said with a smile. "I think breakfast is ready."

Cookie shrugged before he grinned and winked at the boys. "Are you hungry?" He set the food on the card table and lifted the lid from a platter to reveal a heap of steaming pancakes. Danny ran to the table, and Timmy squirmed to get out of Dan's arms.

"Thanks, Cookie," Dan said, setting Timmy down.

"For what?"

"For making things appear more normal."

The boys fiddled with their forks but made no move to spear a pancake. Dan knew they were waiting for him to pray.

Laying a hand on Dan's shoulder, Cookie whispered, "I'll take good care of them." Before Dan could reply, he hurried from the room. Dan slid onto a chair, thankful for one seemingly decent man among these criminals.

Doc, sitting across from him, dug into the pancakes. "You've got your boys well-trained."

Timmy and Danny glanced at Doc before they grabbed Dan's hands.

Danny's brow furrowed. "Isn't he going to pray?"

Dan shrugged and bowed his head. "Lord, we thank You for the food You've provided even in the midst of our enemies. We ask for Your divine protection over us and for Cindy and Jonathan at home, Amen."

He poured melted butter and warm syrup over Timmy's pancakes and cut a few bite-size pieces before he cast a side-glance at Doc who scowled. "Straight out of the Bible, Doc, 'You prepare a table before me in the presence of my enemies.' And earlier, David says, 'I will fear no evil.' Do you men realize what an adversary you're contending with?"

"Shut up, Baker."

"Whatever you say." Having the Psalm come to mind calmed Dan, but he was still worried about Cindy. Should he question the boys now? No, it would be better to wait. Maybe he could take the boys to the bathroom. Timmy still needed help. Had these scoundrels taken into consideration the needs of a three-year-old?

"Doc, do you have some pull-up diapers? You and Cookie have babysitting duties, so you might as well be prepared for the worst. Timmy will tell you...if you ask him...if he needs to urinate, but he'd rather mess his pants than sit." Doc's stunned, disgruntled scowl assured Dan he'd be allowed time alone with Timmy in the bathroom, and probably Danny too.

When Cookie came to collect the dishes, Doc said, "When Lefty goes into town to do the laundry, have him pick up some pull-up diapers for Baker's kid."

"Size large," Dan added. He saw Timmy's screwed-up face. "Doc, do you want to take him, or should I?"

"You do it."

Danny said, "I have to go too."

Doc opened the door and told Muscles to escort them to and from the bathroom.

Under Dan's gentle questioning, Danny told his father what had happened. "After Mommy fell, they put a rag on my face. It smelled awful. I felt sick when I woke up here, and Timmy threw up all over the bed. Doc had to take everything off. And my shoulder hurts."

"Did you fall on it yesterday or bump it against something?"

"No."

"Let me have a look." Danny whimpered when Dan helped him out of his shirt. He saw a reddened area that looked ready to turn purple. "Did this hurt at all yesterday?"

"No."

If his son hadn't injured his shoulder at home, it must have happened after he was kidnapped. Had they chloroformed him and tossed him into the car like a sack of potatoes? Seething, Dan's anger exploded the minute he returned to the room. "How could you? You're a doctor! Too much ether or chloroform could have killed my sons! What happened to my wife? And Danny has a badly bruised shoulder. Was he tossed in the trunk like a rag doll, or did one of you use him for a punching bag?" He shook with rage. Timmy and Danny started crying, making Dan angry with himself for raising his voice and scaring them.

Muscles barged into the room; his gun drawn. "Trouble, Doc?"

Dan knelt to protect Danny and Timmy.

"Everything's under control," Doc said. "Baker's upset about his kids being put under." He shooed Muscles out and closed the door. "For what it's worth, I was angry too. The plan was to gag and tie them, but they started screaming. No one hurt him intentionally. Einstein's car skidded on black ice, and the back end hit a tree. Danny must have been thrown against the side. Einstein didn't bother to check to see if the kids were hurt. He and Lefty just hightailed it out of there before someone came. Adolf and Cookie were angry too."

"What about my wife?"

"She should be fine. I didn't want to see her get hurt. That's why I came up with the idea of using chloroform."

"For your sake, she had better be." Dan fought to control his turbulent emotions—anger, fear, and frustration. He bit down on his lip as he hugged his sons. "I'm sorry I scared you. Everything's okay now."

Drained, Dan continued to hold them until they calmed. He had to make the most of today, but his mind seemed numb, unable to cope.

Doc drew back the drapes. "Hey, that looks like a deer."

"Where?" Danny cried and dashed to the window. Timmy raced after him.

Dan was sure Doc had dreamed up the deer, but Danny and Timmy's faces pressed against the glass said differently. When Dan viewed the doe lapping water from a rivulet, he quietly repeated one of his favorite verses from Psalms. "As the deer pants for the water brooks, so my soul pants for You, O God." He put an arm around each boy. "Water can quench a person's thirst, Doc, but only God can quench the longing in a person's heart. Do you think that doe being there is an accident? I don't. God knew what I needed. What do you need, Doc?"

"A breath of fresh air," he growled and yanked the drapes tight. "I'm going into town." He pointed to a cardboard box on the floor. "There are playthings in there."

Danny and Timmy started pulling items out. "No trains?" Danny said.

"And you're not going to get any fancy railway systems," Doc said.

"All they want is Thomas and Percy," Dan explained when he saw Doc's brow furrow in puzzlement. "They're trains from a cartoon show. I could draw a track on paper, and the boys would be content for hours."

"Hours?" Doc said. "Where can I find them?"

"Most any place with a good toy selection."

Doc told Muscles to have Cookie come to relieve him. As he left Cookie in command, he said, "Don't let Baker's preaching get to you."

Had his words upset Doc? He'd only quoted a few verses. How would Cookie respond? Cookie turned his back whenever Dan mentioned anything remotely connected to God. Dan gave up and concentrated on playing with his sons. After Doc returned, Dan remained quiet on spiritual matters. "Show, not tell" seemed a better policy.

At dinner, as he had at lunchtime, Doc respected Dan's "grace" time.

Cookie had fixed hamburgers and fries. The boys' eyes lit up when they saw one of their favorite meals and devoured every bite. Afterward, when Dan finished reading to them, he noticed their eyes growing heavy and said, "Time for prayers." He knelt beside them while they said short prayers and tucked them into bed. He kissed each on the forehead, said goodnight, and mustered the best smile he could. Adolf had said he'd be too busy to see them much. "Lord, I dread leaving them. Please protect my sons."

Doc summoned Muscles who hurried in and escorted Dam back to his room, but didn't shackle him. Used to hours of warmth, Dan shivered. "What now?" he asked.

"You'll see."

Dan wondered if it mattered knowing now or later what torment lay ahead. He regarded Adolf as the master of deceit and evil tactics. For some reason, the opening lines from an old radio show came to him. *What evils lurk in the hearts of men? Only the Shadow knows.* "Well, Lord, You know, and I've got to keep trusting in You."

Dan didn't have to wait long. Adolf came in and asked Muscles, "Any problems?"

A puffed-up grin spread across his face. "Not with me. He's too scared."

Adolf studied Dan a few minutes. "You've done pretty well. Continue to keep your cool, and maybe we'll let you talk to your wife, but not tonight. Tonight, you'll talk to Captain Baker at the station." He handed Dan a sheet of paper. "Look this over. Get it in mind and stick to the script."

Dan read the paper and raised an eyebrow. "What if he won't go for it?"

"He will. You're his son, and those cute boys are his grandsons. When you see him, you will give him these instructions when I tell you." He showed Dan an envelope and pocketed it. "All he has to do is follow them, and who knows, we might let you live."

Fat chance of that. "And my sons?"

"They'll be returned to their mother."

"What are you guys after?"

"Just a little money you'll be fetching for us."

A little? You have enough people to rob Fort Knox. "How do you know my father will be at the station?"

Adolf laughed. "Guess we'll have to chance it."

Dan was positive Adolf would leave nothing to chance. Was there an inside man or a woman? Snow White?

Muscles pulled out a red bandanna and handcuffs. "Now, boss?"

"Yes." He gave Dan a warning glance. "Are you planning to balk?"

Dan shrugged. "What's the point?" Before Muscles could wrench his shoulders, he put his hands behind his back.

"He's too scared to resist," Muscles said as the cuffs snapped shut.

He blindfolded Dan, gripped his arm, and guided him through the lodge.

Outside, Adolf said, "The steps are steep and slippery." He grasped Dan's other arm, and both held onto him.

Snow crunching beneath Dan's feet confirmed his suspicions they were in the mountains. Which range? San Gabriel? San Bernardino? The wind whipped through his jacket. He shivered in the below-freezing night air as they descended a rocky pathway. When they reached level ground and stopped, Dan heard a car door open. "Step high," Adolf said. "Muscles, get in back."

Dan raised his foot and found the floor of the vehicle. Was he climbing into a truck? Seated, he heard the rear door slide open and shut. *A van?*

Adolf closed his door and said, "You're going to talk to your father at the station. Keep it short and stick to the script."

Traveling down the rutted, winding gravel road told Dan they were well off the beaten path. His mind clocked up about fifteen minutes before they reached a paved road, then another twenty before they stopped. Adolf said, "I'm dialing now. Remember your script. Do not deviate from it. No tricks, or your sons will never see their mother again." He dialed and held the phone so Dan could talk.

When Cap answered, Dan said, "Don't ask questions. I need to give you an envelope with instructions from our kidnappers. I will call you tomorrow morning before eight to tell you where to meet me. Leave immediately. They'll be watching. Come alone. We're okay, but the boys' lives are at stake." He added, "Take care of Cindy and Jonathan."

Adolf grabbed the phone and shut it off. "That wasn't in the script, but I'll let it slide. Now back to the hideout for your fitting."

"A what?"

"Dear me, I have been remiss again. I forgot to tell you. Never mind, you'll see shortly."

What now in this drag-it-out-wear-me-down game? Dan wondered. He knew he wouldn't like it.

After Adolf reached the hideout and stopped, he said, "You've been awfully quiet. What are you thinking?"

"I'd like to see my sons."

"Before your fitting? Not possible. And afterward, they might wake up and get frightened at seeing you in a foul mood. That might give them nightmares. You, on the other hand, will be sedated so that won't be a problem. Will it?"

Dan knew instinctively Adolf wanted his words to make him angry. The blindfold kept him from seeing the man's face, but he envisioned the cruel mocking smile. Refusing to be riled, he said, "What if I'm not in a bad mood?"

Muscles hee-hawed. "You will…"

"Shut up, Muscles. Get out of the van and help Baker."

While they guided him up the incline, Dan wondered what Muscles might have revealed?

Inside the lodge, Muscles removed the blindfold and handcuffs. Carrying a box, Einstein sauntered out of the back living area and led the way to Dan's room. Muscles shackled Dan and leaned against the wall, his eyes gleaming with keen interest as if he were waiting for the entertainment to start. *And I have star billing. Brace yourself, Daniel. Don't overreact.*

Einstein set the box on the table.

"Is it finally ready?" Adolf asked.

The bomb expert nodded and rubbed his hands together with glee.

"Then get started."

Dan's knees grew weak when Einstein opened the carton and pulled out an ominous gray plastic box about five inches square fastened to what appeared to be a man-sized harness.

"Take off your jacket," Adolf ordered.

Staring at the contraption, Dan tried to convince himself he was wrong.

"Baker, I gave you an order."

Dan glared at all three men while he pulled down the zipper tab.

Muscles let out his obnoxious laugh. "Look at his face. He knows what it is…figured it all out by his self."

Einstein held the harness in front of Dan and grinned. "Let's try it on, Preacher."

Dan leashed his anger and submitted to being fitted to a harness that wouldn't have controlled a mad dog but would curtail him. Would they use the device to end his usefulness? At least it would be quick.

Einstein opened the leather straps, positioned the box in the center of Dan's chest, pulled the straps together in back, and padlocked them.

"Well, Muscles," Adolf said, "we didn't need you after all. Baker's finally learning who's pulling the strings." He laughed. "Or maybe I should say straps."

Too drained to speak, Dan stood mute as a lamb being sheared.

"No questions, Baker? No comebacks? Einstein, I believe your brilliance has dumbfounded him."

Einstein flipped the key to the small padlock securing the harness. "Want out, Baker? What if I lost this key? Someone could cut the straps?" He shook his head. "I wouldn't advise that unless they know the code to defuse the bomb." He tapped his head with his forefinger. "I've thought of everything. You can show this to the captain tomorrow before our demonstration."

Dan's rage turned on Adolf. "You told me…"

"That you were to give him the envelope and drive away. Dear me, I must have lied. You will be meeting your father at the old abandoned stone house near Yorba Linda. You know the place…the one where five people were murdered?" Dan nodded. "Your father needs to witness the power of our small bomb that is like the one strapped to you. It has enough power to demolish, oh let's say…a fair-sized store."

Probably a bank, Dan figured. What would blowing up a bank or store accomplish? What were they after? Did they really need him? How could he foil their plans and not bring harm to his sons? If he blew himself up, he'd be sacrificing their lives too.

"What are you thinking, Baker? Let me see if I can guess," Adolf said. "You're trying to figure out how to detonate that bomb and foil our plans without harming your kids."

Dan stiffened. How could his thoughts have been so apparent?

Adolf laughed. "Look at his face. I was right." Adolf's eyes bored into Dan's with deadly seriousness. "Now let me give you something to consider. How would you like it if I let my son play with your sons?"

However remote the chance might be, Dan recoiled at the thought of his boys getting AIDS. Adolf's threat was not an idle one. Dan knew until he could come up with something to foil their plans; he had better appear defeated to lull Adolf into a false sense of security. Dan let his shoulders slump and closed his eyes.

"Einstein," Adolf said, "let our young preacher out of that rig. He looks tired. Muscles, go get Doc. It's Baker's bedtime."

As soon as Einstein slipped the harness off, Dan picked up his jacket and started to put it on.

"Leave it off," Adolf ordered. "Doc will be here soon with your nightly injection." He gave him a mock salute. "Goodnight, Baker… pleasant dreams."

When Doc entered with his bag, Einstein picked up the box and sauntered out. Doc closed the door.

Dan trembled as he sank to the bed. "Are the boys all right?"

"They're fine. And the sedative will help you recover. You're shaking like a leaf."

"I'm cold."

"More like scared half out of your wits. Where's your trust in God?"

"I'm resting in His arms right now. I'm exhausted and scared, but I know the Lord will carry us safely through this ordeal."

Doc looked thoughtful while he readied the injection.

Dan removed his shoes and rolled up his sleeve. When the needle entered his arm, he said, "Trust Him, Doc. Right now, you're freeing me from tension, but my relief is nothing compared to what you'd feel if you asked God into your heart and allowed Him to free you from the burden of sin."

Doc threw everything back into his bag, grabbed the handle, and stomped out of the room.

*****

Doc warmed his hands in front of the fire.

"What are you scowling about?" Adolf asked.

"You would have to nab a preacher. I don't like it!"

"What's your beef? He was gentle as a lamb tonight."

"Lamb my foot! Ever see a caged lion turn? He will. Mark my words. He'll take everything you throw at him, but if he gets the chance…watch out."

"He won't take the chance. Our bomb demonstration will show him we mean business. He'll know before he fetches the money from the first store that one wrong word or false move from him, or the police interfering, will bring death and destruction."

Doc shook his head. "I don't like it."

"Just do your job. I can't help it if Captain Baker's kid turned out to be a preacher. Captain Baker cost me fifteen years in the slammer, and he'll rue the day he testified. Because of him, I wasn't there for my son. Needles and I will get our revenge. You will enjoy slowly killing the preacher, won't you, son?"

Needles's ice-blue eyes took on a strange glow of eagerness as he nodded.

"Now, down to business. The stolen cars that we will be using will have car phones. Don't make personal calls. These are only to be used between us in the cars. Keep conversations short. Do not use our nicknames. Use your designated number to identify yourself. I'm number one, Einstein, two, Doc, three, Lefty, four, Needles, five, Muscles, six. Muscles, I decided you should drive one of them since Einstein or Doc will be riding in the car with Baker. So study your map well. Do you have any questions?" When no one spoke, he asked Einstein. "Do you have the bomb in place for tomorrow's demonstration?"

"Yes."

"Are we finished?" Lefty asked. "I need a smoke." After Adolf nodded, Lefty hurried outside but came back five minutes later. "It's cold out there. Einstein, I thought you said the weather man predicted clear skies for the rest of the week. Guess what? It's snowing."

6

Wednesday morning, Dan awakened to a cold silent room, his thoughts as gloomy as the blackness pressing in around him. He dreaded leaving his sons. He thought about the day's agenda. Tense and plagued with foreboding, Dan tried to shut his mind to his predicament and go back to sleep. He couldn't. What time was it? He debated getting up and turning on the light. When Timmy and Danny started calling, Dan rolled out of bed but sat on the edge to wait for pain and dizziness to ease.

Doc flipped on the light, already dressed. "Good, you're awake. I thought your head might be hurting." He handed Dan two tablets. "You can get some water in the bathroom."

"Are Danny and Timmy all right?" Dan grabbed his shoes and slipped into them.

"Yes. I told them you'd be in soon. I left a disposable razor and a comb on the sink ledge. When Cookie gets back this afternoon, you'll have clean clothes."

"And the boys? They need some, and snowsuits so they can play out back. Doc, they need some fun to make this ordeal more bearable."

"I agree, and I know Cookie would enjoy playing outdoors with them." His hand gestured toward the door.

"Do you have the key to the chain lock?"

"No, Muscles does. He'll be here by the time you're ready. I've got to get back."

Dan wondered how he could make himself presentable after days and nights in the same clothes. He closed the bathroom door and studied his mirrored reflection. *I look as crummy as I feel.* Shivering the minute he removed his jacket and shirt, Dan did a quick body-and-hair wash with water as hot as he could stand. He grabbed a can of deodorant from the shelf, sprayed his armpits and the underarms of his stinky shirt before putting it back on. Dan sniffed. *At least now the kids won't hold their noses.* Finished, he flung open the door and stopped short of crashing into Muscles who stepped back, gun drawn. "Sorry," Dan said. "Maybe you shouldn't stand so close. Can't you give a guy some leeway? I'm not about to bolt."

Muscles regarded him with wary eyes before he slipped the gun under his belt, pulled a key from his shirt pocket, and after giving Dan a warning glance, knelt to remove the chain. "Go to your brats. Boss says we leave in one hour."

Dan nodded. While the ex-boxer followed close to his heels, Dan vowed, *I will not let my sons see my anger or my disheartened spirit.* When Doc answered his knock, Dan gave him a smile and a broader one to his sons running to him. "How are my boys," he said, hugging and kissing them.

Timmy giggled. "Your nose is cold."

"So are my hands." Dan playfully slipped one underneath each boy's shirt. They squealed and squirmed as his palms touched their warm tummies.

"Daddy," Danny asked, "can you draw a track for our trains?"

"There won't be time this morning, and I don't know what's planned for this afternoon."

Doc strolled toward them. "If your father can't, I will." Dan heard someone tap on the door, and Doc said before he opened it, "Must be Cookie."

After Cookie set the tray on the table, Danny asked, "Can you eat with us?"

Cookie smiled and cuffed him playfully on the chin. "Not today, Champ, I need to serve breakfast to the others. If you eat all your oatmeal, I'll fix you a special treat later."

After breakfast, Dan had no time to play with his sons. "I'm counting on you boys to obey Doc and Cookie."

"Why can't we go with you?" Danny asked.

"I have work to do."

"Can you bring Mommy and Jonathan back?"

"It's too cold for Jonathan. Besides, this is a pretend vacation for us."

Danny's face puckered. "I don't like pretend vacations! I want to go home. I don't like these men."

Son, Dan thought, I don't like this anymore than you do.

A pounding at the door distracted Danny. Muscles hurried into the room. "Time to go, Baker," he said in his gruff voice.

The boys pressed close to Dan, their upturned faces wide-eyed with fright. "Please don't leave," Danny pleaded. Both began to cry.

Dan knelt and encircled them with his arms. "I have no choice," he said over the lump in his throat. "I love you, but I have to leave. Please, no more tears." Their crying persisted as they clung to him. His anguish over seeing them so scared left him powerless to give comfort. He took a deep breath to regain his composure. "What special treat do you suppose Cookie has for you today?"

They shrugged, but tears continued to roll over their cheeks.

Doc held out a box of tissues to Dan and gave him an understanding smile bordering on sympathy.

Dan pulled out two tissues. "No more tears," he said in a soft but firm voice. "Dry your eyes and blow your noses. Doc already said he would draw a track for you, and Cookie promised a treat. He might even find snowsuits so you can play outside. You'd like that, wouldn't you?" After they nodded, he said, "You'll have more fun here than with me. Now give me a hug and kiss."

In the hallway after the door closed behind him, Muscles said with scorn. "You're too soft. You should've slapped 'em, told 'em to shut up."

"And have them turn out like you?" Dan faced him squarely, braced for a blow.

Muscles clenched his hands but didn't strike. "Back to your room," he snarled.

Adolf and Needles awaited them. "What took you so long?" Adolf asked.

"Baker's brats raised a fuss."

"They're frightened," Dan said. "If they're treated well, they'll lose their fear and cause no more problems."

"You'd better be right."

Einstein sauntered in, carrying the box he'd brought the previous night. Envisioning the man-controlling harness, Dan's heart sank. "You don't like my creation?" Einstein said. "I'm crushed." He laughed and set the box on the table. "You know what else my little bomb can do? Listen. If I hear anything I don't like, or if Adolf gives the word…" His hands pantomimed an explosion. "Boom!"

The antics disgusted Dan as much as they frustrated him. How could he possibly pass information to Cap now?

Adolf said, "Your sons' lives are in your hands. One false word, and I will let Needles play with them. He especially likes little boys, and I'll make sure no one is there to rob him of his pleasures."

The previous night, Dan hadn't realized the full implication of Adolf's threat. Horrified, he stood mute.

"Too angry to speak? Good…you understand me clearly now, don't you? I didn't think you did last night. Take off your jacket and get wired."

Dan bit down on his lip, feeling more contempt for Adolf than he had for any man. After Einstein lifted the bomb out of the box and held open the harness straps, he raised an eyebrow. "You look fighting mad. Are you going to balk?"

Dan fought to bring his anger under control. He wanted to lash out at everyone in the room. Instead, in silent submission, he put his arms through the harness straps, but his heart pounded so hard, he wondered if it would trigger the bomb. Could the device detect anger and fear? He slipped back into his jacket.

Before he zipped it, Adolf held out the sealed envelope. "Put this in the inside pocket. There's a phone in the car. I'll give you instructions and tell you when to give the envelope to Captain Baker." He cocked his head to one side. "Do I detect a ray of hope? Let me squelch it. We'll be using stolen cars. I've taken every precaution."

Dan pulled up the zipper tab. The bomb pressed against his heart, making him stiffen. He wanted to crawl into bed, go to sleep, and awaken in another century or another world.

Needles suddenly started beaming an idiotic smile of self-importance and came toward him. Dan's skin prickled as if every pore feared infestation of the man's disease, but he stood firm. Needles was only a mindless junkie, a man to be pitied not feared, but Dan scowled when Needles drew handcuffs and a red bandanna from his rear pocket. He jangled the cuffs and said, "Hands behind your back."

Dan offered no resistance to being handcuffed and blindfolded, but when Needles pulled the bandanna too tight, Dan fought the urge to kick him.

"Let's go," Muscles said. He grasped Dan's arm to lead him.

Before they left the room, Dan heard Adolf tell Needles, "Stop antagonizing Baker."

Dan felt a blast of cold air when Muscles opened the front door. "It snowed again last night. The steps are slippery, but I'll keep hold of you."

Dan could feel ice under his shoes and was thankful for the man's firm grip while they descended. At the bottom, Muscles continued to guide him while their feet shuffled through four to six inches of fresh snow. Danny and Timmy would love playing in it. Last winter, he and Cindy had taken the boys to Santa's Village, and afterward they'd gone sledding. He wished the boys had their snowsuits so Doc or Cookie could take them outside to slide down the steep hill in back. Dan desperately wanted them to look back on this as if they had been vacationers, not prisoners. He was positive God would save them but longed for his sons to be free of fear. Dan didn't want nightmares to plague Danny and Timmy. "Please, Lord, let them look upon this as an adventure." *And if you die?* The thought blasted Dan harder than the icy wind. He looked heavenward. "Even then, Father."

Behind him he heard clomping footsteps. "Needles," Adolf ordered, "slide the van door back so Muscles can put Baker in."

"I want to do it," Needles said.

"No. You get in afterward, and remember what I told you."

Dan envisioned Needles's scowl.

"Muscles," Adolf continued, "you sit in front with Einstein. Lefty, you'll ride with me."

After Muscles aided Dan into the van, he forced him to lie face down on the floor.

Muscles got out, and Needles climbed over Dan. Once settled, he started pressing the heels of his boots into the small of Dan's back.

And he's not going to antagonize me? Fat chance.

"I'm sure glad it quit snowing," Muscles said.

Einstein said, "The forecaster who predicted clear skies all week must have been drunk when he looked at the weather map. Now we're supposed to have intermittent showers in the valley." He started the van. "At least it's nice for now."

As soon as the car began moving, Needles jabbed Dan in the ribs with the toes of his boots. The senseless act angered him. The ride was tortuous enough without the insane prodding. The gutted road bounced the van like a jackhammer, jarring every bone in Dan's crammed-in, contorted body. His insides churned. His head throbbed. Needles chuckled every time Dan tried to change position. A thought kept running through Dan's mind. Was the bomb for real? Would all this bouncing cause it to explode? A morbid thought, but if the bomb wasn't that sensitive and only Einstein could trigger it, maybe Dan could put that fear to rest.

When the road became smoother and straighter, Dan gave an inaudible sigh. He switched his thoughts to the ordeal ahead. Would Cap tell Amanda and Cindy he was meeting Dan? He hoped not—they might get frightened and call the police. Would Cap come alone without tracking devices? His worries created all kinds of scenarios. Would Doc or Cookie even try to protect Danny and Timmy? So absorbed with foreboding thoughts, he didn't even realize they were slowing down on a dirt road and stopping. How long had the ride taken? As Muscles transferred Dan from one van to another, Needles stepped on his back as he climbed out and climbed back in. Dan wasn't sure how much longer he could curb his anger. About twenty minutes later, they ascended a winding gravel road and stopped. Einstein said, "We're here. Too bad you don't have raingear. Looks like the clouds are ready to burst."

"What are we waiting for?" Dan asked as Needles dug his boot heels in the small of his back.

Muscles laughed. "Getting tired of Needles needling you? We're just waiting for Mr. Adolf's instructions."

Adolf's voice sounded on the phone. "Einstein, take Needles with you. Muscles will get Baker out."

The van door slid open, and Needles scooted over to the side and carefully stepped over him. *Adolf must be watching.* Muscles waited a few minutes before he grabbed Dan by his belt and hoisted him out and to his feet. After he removed the handcuffs and blindfold, he pointed to a shiny new, '85, black VW. "Sit," he ordered, opening the door. "There's a phone on the dash. Pick it up and listen."

Muscles closed the door as soon as Dan was seated. Before he could pick up the phone, Adolf said, "Comfortable? Now for the fun part...as soon as you see your father, you will get out and meet him. You can show him the bomb and even tell him how many men he's up against, but not our names or the fact our hideout is in the mountains. If you decide to do otherwise, all it takes is one shot before you can even get the words out, and five guns are aimed at him. Oh, we don't plan to kill him, only make it harder for him to walk."

"I get the picture."

While Dan waited, he studied the old stone house, supposedly once owned by the mafia. Ten years ago, five men had been murdered there, and rumor had it more lay buried on the twenty-acre parcel. Sniffing dogs found none, but no one wanted to buy the place. Orange and avocado trees once gracing the landscape now stood lifeless, surrounded by weeds, wild blackberries, and other brambles. They have plenty of places to hide, Dan thought.

*****

Tuesday night after Cap received Dan's call, he told everyone he was going to take Wednesday morning off but did not give a reason. As he drove home from the station, his mind replayed the phone call. Dan's voice had cracked when he said to come alone—the boys' lives are at stake. Cap knew he'd get chewed out but decided to keep the matter private until he knew what they were up against.

He parked in the driveway and dashed into the house before a sudden downpour could drench him. The minute he entered, Amanda said, "Any word?"

He shook his head, slipped out of his damp jacket, and hung it on a wall tree along with his hat before he kissed her. "How are you and Cindy coping?"

"We're keeping busy. I'm glad you insisted she and the baby stay with us. She's upstairs nursing Jonathan. We're both worried sick. Whoever chloroformed Cindy must be ruthless." Her eyes searched his. "You know something, don't you?"

"Only that Dan and the boys were kidnapped." Cap headed for the kitchen. "I need a cup of your good coffee." He poured himself a cup and sat down at the table. By the time Cindy joined them in the kitchen, Mandy was ready to dish up dinner. Cindy looked so exhausted, Cap scrambled to his feet and rushed to her side.

Cindy blurted, "Any word?"

"Not yet. Come sit before you collapse."

Mandy set a plate of food in front of Cindy. When she shook her head, Mandy said, "You've got to eat something."

"How can I eat when I don't even know if Dan, Danny, and Timmy are alive?"

Cap had debated about telling them anything, but their despondent faces convinced him he had to give them hope. "I want you both to know Dan and the boys are okay. Dan told me so. The kidnappers had him call. I'm to meet him tomorrow morning so he can give me instructions. I'm taking the morning off. When the call comes, I must leave. Don't ask questions and don't contact the station," he said firmly. They stared at him as if questions were exploding in their minds, but they refrained from asking as they picked at their food.

When the phone rang, Amanda rose to answer it. "I hope it's not another reporter."

Cindy said, "Beside concerned friends, half a dozen reporters have called. We've told them…no comment and hung up."

Amanda returned to the table. "Another church member will be praying for us."

Cap said, "As far as reporters being a concern, tomorrow should be better. The FBI chief has informed the media you cannot be interviewed. You are in seclusion and under police protection. Cindy, starting tomorrow morning, a squad car will be parked out front to keep the media away and escort you if you go anywhere."

"Cap, do you really believe that's necessary?"

He shrugged. "Maybe…maybe not, but it can't hurt." The ten o'clock news confirmed what he had told them, and Cap felt better about their being alone when he was gone.

Wednesday morning shortly after breakfast, the call came for him to meet Dan. "I've got to leave," he told Amanda and Cindy. "I'm not sure when I'll get home, but I'll call as soon as I can." He embraced Mandy, kissed her, then gave Cindy a hug. "Look, everything's going to be fine. God assured me of that before I fell asleep." He grabbed his hat and jacket. They followed him and looked so frightened he gave them his best reassuring smile. Before getting in the car, he said, "For dinner, I'd like fried chicken with all the trimmings."

*****

Dan climbed out of the car the minute he saw Cap coming up the driveway and met him. Cap gave him a hug then reared back and stared at Dan's chest. "Yes, it's a bomb."

Still looking stunned, Cap said, "Are you okay?"

"So far. We need to sit in the car. Answer the phone when it rings."

Cap answered the phone, and Adolf asked, "Did you come alone?"

"I said I would. I have no tracking devices on me, and there are none on the car. I only came to get your instructions and hug my son."

"Which you already did. And, yes, it's a bomb harnessed to your son. Show it to your father." After Dan did, Adolf said, "I think you

80

realize now how important it is to follow our instructions. Now, we're going to give you a little demonstration. This bomb is our smallest. I want to see what it can do. Walk over to the rock wall opposite the house. You should be safe behind it. After the demonstration, your son will stay put, and you will walk back down the driveway to find your car. Baker, search your father as soon as you get out. Toss his keys, gun, and any weapons on the car seat and walk to the wall."

As they walked, Cap asked, "You okay?"

"What do you think?"

Cap gave him a hug. "Hang in there. Can you tell me anything?"

"There are five men out there with guns aimed at us. Two more are at the hideout with Danny and Timmy. They're being well-cared for and will be returned to Cindy when this is over. That's all I can say."

The sky opened up before they reached the wall. Both turned when they heard two cars leave, and Cap said, "Looks like I'll be soaking wet before I find my car." Behind the wall, he said, "I judge the distance to be about one thousand feet between us and the back of that house. If they intend to demolish it, we'd better be ready to duck for cover."

Dan stared at the ominous black sky surrounding the old stone house. Lightning flashes highlighted it like a prelude scene to a Hollywood horror flick. He jumped when a clap of thunder resounded followed by a convulsive explosion rocking the ground. They dove and covered their heads as debris struck the wall. Dan felt his heart thudding against the bomb. When the dust settled, he rolled over and sat up, pressing his back against the wall. His father stood and offered him a hand. Dan waved him off. He didn't want to see the destruction he equated with his own.

Cap reached down again; his gaze sympathetic. Dan grasped his hand and allowed Cap to assist him to his feet. "Are you okay?"

"What do you think?"

Cap sent Dan a reassuring smile. "You're my Daniel. I know your strength."

Dan didn't feel strong. His legs felt ready to buckle. He handed Cap the envelope, and he said in a choked voice, "Take care of Cindy and the boys for me. Thanks for all you've done."

Cap put the envelope under his jacket and retrieved a picture of Cindy enclosed in a clear sandwich bag. "Maybe this will help you cope." He placed his hands firmly on Dan's shoulders. "Hang in there, son. God has given me assurance you, as well as the boys, will get home."

Dan couldn't stem his tears. "Thanks, Cap," he said, gazing at Cindy's picture before he slipped it into his pocket.

"Hang in there," Cap said again before he turned and started down the road.

The minute Cap rounded the curve in the long driveway, Needles jumped out from behind some bushes, pointing his .45. "Too bad your old man has a long walk before he finds his car. He'll be wetter than you are."

"Don't rile me. There's nothing I'd like better than to make mincemeat out of you."

"You really want to try something? Your sons are awfully young to die." His lip curled. "Walk." He pointed to where Muscles and Lefty stood in their raingear.

Dan had averted his eyes from the house; now he had no choice but to view the wreckage. Cap had not reacted nor said anything about the rock-strewn clearing where stone lay beside stone. He was wise, Dan thought as he shuddered, translating the scene to one of human carnage.

Needles jabbed the gun in Dan's ribs. "Get moving."

Dan needed no more prodding. He took quick strides toward the two men.

Lefty held out his hand. "Give me whatever your father gave you."

"It's only a picture of my wife."

"Give." After Dan did, Lefty said, "Wow, she's a knock-out."

Muscles grabbed the picture. "Hey, Needles, it looks like he hooked himself a winner."

Needles laughed. "I bet you guys could sure get your money's worth in her bed."

Dan slammed his hand into Needles's jaw, sending him flat on his back. Before the junkie could get up, Dan straddled him, his fingers encircling the scrawny neck.

Muscles's gun bashed Dan's head. The ex-boxer rolled Baker off Needles. The junkie lay stunned, and his legs buckled the minute Muscles helped him to his feet. "I'll carry him."

Lefty knelt to check Dan. "Good thing he's alive. Get to the van. We're late." He hoisted Dan over his shoulder and hurried after Muscles who had Needles buckled in the front seat by the time he reached the van. They had Dan cuffed and blindfolded but heard the blare of sirens as they put him behind the back seat.

*****

At the rendezvous area, Adolf paced beside his car until he saw the van. He hurried over to it as Lefty climbed out. "You're late," he bellowed.

Lefty pointed to Needles. "Problems."

After Lefty explained, Adolf's eyes rolled. "Where's the picture?"

Lefty handed it to him. "I retrieved it after Muscles dropped it."

Adolf pocketed the picture and glared at his now-conscious son. "I told you not to antagonize Baker. Go sit in my car. Lefty, put Baker in the van."

At the hideout, Adolf helped Needles to the couch in the living area while Lefty carried Dan to his bed. After Muscles secured the chain, they returned to the warmth of the fireplace.

Doc straightened after examining Needles. "His jaw's broken. No doubt about it."

Adolf paced the room, scowling at Muscles and Lefty. "Am I surrounded by incompetents?" He glared at Needles. "And you… you've been taunting people all your life. I told you not to antagonize Baker. I hope you've learned something from this. Doc, what can you do for him?"

"He needs to be X-rayed. I can't do much except give him morphine."

"Do it. Keep him comfortable. Broken jaw or not, he's going to do his part. As for the rest of you, our errand boy seems to have more gumption than we gave him credit. Back off. Is that clear?" Their eyes narrowed, but they nodded. "Now, Doc, let's check on Baker. For your sake, Muscles, he had better be okay." Adolf stomped from the room with Doc close behind.

After Doc examined Dan, Adolf said, "Will he be functional?"

"He may have had a slight concussion earlier after Muscles mugged him. Now there's no doubt in my mind he has one. Will he be functional?" Doc shrugged. "I'll know more when he comes to. Do you have a backup plan?"

"No. Everything rides on Baker. Revenge may be my primary objective, but believe me, I want that money as much as the rest of you." Adolf headed for the door.

"Before you leave, help me get Baker out of his soaked clothes."

"Let him sleep in them. I need to help Needles."

"Don't let anger cloud your reason. Do you want Baker to get pneumonia from this freezing room? Who is more important right now…him or your son?"

7

Wednesday morning, panic seized Cindy while she and Amanda watched Cap drive away to meet Dan. Would he return, or would he disappear like Dan? She knew Amanda must be having fearful thoughts. Despite all the crime scenes she had witnessed as a police officer and the knowledge anyone can fall victim, she found it hard to believe this was happening. *God, these men are ruthless. Stop them. Don't let them destroy my family!*

Amanda continued to stare into space. "First, Dan, then the boys. I just don't know. I...just don't know what to think."

"Should we call the station?"

Amanda shook her head, her face drawn but her voice calm. "Cap told us not to. We will wait until we hear from him."

"How can you stand waiting that long? I'm already crazy with worry."

"Because I've done it often enough. Cap's asking for fried chicken was his way of telling me not to worry because he wasn't worried. This morning, I sensed he was almost eager to get that phone call so he could meet Dan. Could this be a ploy to harm him? I don't think so. Whatever Dan told him last night assured him he'd be okay. If he doesn't call or isn't here by dinner time, I'll check with the station."

Their attention was drawn to a car coming down the road and parking across the street. Amanda said, "That must be this morning's officer assigned to protect you from reporters."

Cindy recognized the officer. "That's Earl." She rolled her eyes. "Amanda, I really don't think this is necessary." No sooner had she said this when a TV station truck rumbled toward the house and pulled to the curb. Before it stopped, Earl was out of his car to confront the driver, ordering him to move on and not come back. Earl stepped on the curb and watched them leave. Cindy went to him and said, "Thank you, Earl. I really didn't think they'd be bothering me."

"I'm glad I arrived before they did. Sending them away before they set up is easier than having to send for back-up to get rid of them and the crowd they'd gather." Unexpectedly, he gave her a hug. "We'll find Dan and the boys and bring them back to you. Try not to worry." He went to Dan's mother and put his hands on her shoulders. "Cap told me to tell you not to worry either. He's a wise man and a great captain to work under." He turned and hurried across the street.

Amanda watched him climb in the car. "I'm glad he was here. I never dreamed they'd try to get to you so soon. I think we're safe for a while. Let's go inside."

For a while, they sat at the table, going over Scriptures to quiet their hearts. When Jonathan started crying, Cindy scrambled to her feet. Amanda stood. "I'll change Jonathan and rock him to sleep. You're exhausted. Why don't you lie on the couch and at least rest?"

Cindy shook her head. "I'll take care of him. I've got to do something."

She hurried up the stairs to Jonathan's crib in the Baker's spare bedroom—once Dan's room. While she changed the baby, she glanced around. Not one reminder of Dan remained. Picking up Jonathan, she gazed out the window giving her full view of the backyard where roses still had blooms. She envisioned Dan strolling plant to plant to find a perfect flower. "Your daddy used to bring me a rose for every date." The moment she said *daddy*, Jonathan cocked his head and stared at her as if asking, "Where's Daddy?"

Cindy kissed his forehead. "I don't know where Daddy is, but I'm sure he's thinking about us just like we're thinking about him. He wouldn't want us to worry." *That's impossible.* She gave a deep sigh. *I really should go back to the living room and stay with Amanda. We need to bolster each other.* Instead, she continued to gaze out the window. *Less than two weeks ago, Dan and I sat at that patio set and ate barbecued chicken with Cap and Amanda.* Cap had wanted to take videos of

Danny and Timmy using the new tire swing he had hung in the huge apple tree. Jonathan, sitting on her lap, had bounced with excitement while they watched. "Your father had so much fun pushing Danny and Timmy." Mentioning the boys' names made Jonathan's face pucker. She hugged him. "You miss them too, don't you?"

Cindy knew he would probably enjoy watching the videos but realized she wouldn't be able to bear viewing them. Her eyes turned skyward, seeing rain clouds as foreboding as her darkest fears. Tears misted. "Lord, why are you allowing this to happen to my family?" Thoughts of how she had treated Dan Sunday assailed her. They had barely made up before he was called away. *There's so much I wanted to say. Now I can't.* Heavyhearted, Cindy returned to the living room with Jonathan and collapsed in the swivel rocker.

Amanda looked up from reading her Bible. "Are you okay?"

"Before we were engaged, I remember Dan telling me that he liked my gumption, my ability to take on criminals. Today, I sure don't feel strong. I wish Cap would call to let us know what's happening."

Amanda turned on the TV to watch the twelve o' clock news. "We have breaking news. Around ten-fifteen this morning in Yorba Linda, an explosion rocked the area, demolishing the old stone house once owned by the mafia." He continued talking while pictures showed firemen hosing down a house.

Amanda pointed to the left corner where a drenched police officer was talking to the fire chief. "I'd swear that's Cap."

"Amanda, you can't possibly be sure…his back is to us, and why would he be there?"

"I have no idea."

"Now, to what we reported yesterday about the Sunday disappearance of youth pastor, Daniel Baker. Apparently, he was kidnapped. Monday night, two men dressed in police uniforms forced their way into his home, chloroformed his wife, and kidnapped their sons, Danny age five and Timmy age three." Pictures of Dan, Danny and Timmy filled the screen as he continued. "If you see them or have information, please contact the police or this station. There has been no mention of a ransom, and the police are not commenting, nor are they allowing us to interview Mrs. Baker. No reason has been given, but she is under police protection. We will keep you informed on the strange circumstances surrounding this kidnapping."

Amanda turned off the TV. "Except for the explosion, that broadcast was the same as yesterday. "I hope Cap calls soon. I'll fix lunch while you change Jonathan."

Cindy was changing Jonathan when the phone rang. She finished and carried the baby downstairs. "Was that Cap?"

"Yes. He'll be here for dinner, and that was him on the TV. He'll fill us in when he gets here. He's all right and said Dan told him he and the boys are okay. The boys are frightened but are being treated well."

"What are the kidnapper's instructions? What is Dan up against?"

"Cap wouldn't tell me, but said not to worry…just keep on praying for God to answer our prayers soon."

While Amanda went grocery shopping, Cindy tried to read but stopped and stared out the window at the pouring rain. Would she ever see Dan again? Twelve years ago, she wouldn't have given him a second thought if he'd dropped out of sight. It seemed ages since she'd apologized at the police picnic for her attitude at the Christmas dinner. When she fell in love with him, his actions showed he loved her, but he wouldn't say the three little words she longed to hear.

Shortly after Dan graduated from seminary, he invited her to visit his stepsister and see her new baby girl. Afterward, they would buy fried chicken and have a picnic on the beach—his treat. Cindy was positive he would propose. It amazed her as she watched Dan holding his new niece. She saw him in a different light. Most men with newborns looked reluctant and uncomfortable, but love and tenderness radiated from Dan's face as he cradled the tiny girl, stroking her wispy fluffs of golden hair and kissing her forehead.

That afternoon, when she and Dan walked on the beach, Cindy said, "You really like babies, don't you?"

"Of course." He picked up a few shells and heaved them into the waves.

Taking courage, she asked, "Have you ever been in love?" He picked up another shell and tossed it, then another. "Dan, what's wrong?"

"I can't afford to fall in love," he said, staring into the waves.

"Love doesn't need money."

"I can't allow myself to fall in love."

"Why?"

He turned to face her, his eyes filled with sadness. "You know the Bakers took me in after my parents died. You know I killed my father."

The anguish in his face wrenched her heart. "And?"

"How do I know what genes I carry? My father was abusive and violent, especially when drunk."

"Dan, when I watched you cradle that baby today, I knew you'd make a wonderful father." Cindy remembered holding her breath, wondering how he'd react.

Dan looked stunned, moved his head side to side with disbelief, and stared at her as if too overwhelmed to speak.

"Please don't be afraid of marriage," she added, praying he wouldn't be offended by her boldness. She saw the wall he'd built around himself crumble brick by brick. He closed his eyes a moment as if drained by its very destruction. Slowly the lines furrowing his brow disappeared. His eyes misted as he bit down on his lip. Cindy wanted to engulf him in her arms, but the next step had to be his.

He gave a half-laugh, half-cry and opened his arms to her. "Help me out. What do I do now? I've never been given a proposal. Do I kiss you first, or do you kiss me?"

Cindy wished she could kiss him now. "Dear Lord, please protect Dan, Danny, and Timmy. Bring them back to me."

When Amanda returned, Cindy helped her put the groceries away and told her, "Shortly after you left, Earl drove away, and his replacement parked two doors up. I feel well protected from reporters." After Amanda put items in the refrigerator, she asked, "Are you fixing fried chicken for dinner like Cap asked?"

"No, he deserves his favorite…beef stroganoff."

"Are you trying to butter him up before we deluge him with questions? He'll see right through you."

"Of course, he will, but we're going to curb our impatience and at least let him try to relax for a few minutes."

Cap came home on time, and Amanda put her arms around him and kissed him. "While you change and wash up, we'll put dinner on the table."

"I don't detect fried chicken."

"That's right. I fixed your favorite meal…beef stroganoff."

"Thank you. I promise I'll fill you in after dinner."

While he ate, Cap asked how their day had been and if Jonathan's two bottom teeth had come in yet. They told him about Earl and the TV station truck.

Amanda removed his plate, refilled his coffee cup, and took her seat, her expression stern. "Now, tell us what we want to know. What happened when you met Dan? If the kidnappers want money from us, how much and what are the instructions? And, Cap, I recognized you at the explosion site…you were soaking wet. Why were you there? What happened today?"

Cindy studied Cap's face as he leaned back in his chair and stared out the window, his expression guarded as if he were mulling over what to say. Or was he wishing she hadn't asked? He took a sip of coffee and gazed at the window.

"Cap?" Amanda said.

"I'm sorry. I was thinking about that TV broadcast. I saw it at the station after I changed into a dry uniform. It's remarkable that you recognized my drenched backside from that short clip. By the way, I dropped my uniform off at the cleaners to be pressed. Remind me in the morning to pick it up on my way to the station."

Amanda gave him a stern look. "Cap, why were you at the explosion site?"

Cindy suddenly knew why. "You met Dan at the old house, didn't you? What happened? Why did it explode?"

Amanda gasped. "She's right. I can read it in your eyes. Tell us what happened. Tell us everything."

Cap shook his head. "You know I can't, and what I do say goes no further than this table."

"We both know that," Cindy said.

After Amanda nodded, Cap continued. "Yes, I met Dan at the old house. The explosion demonstrated how they intend to keep us from tailing them. While we watched, one of them drove my car away along with my gun. By the time I reached the fire chief, I was drenched. I can't tell you about the instructions or what they want, but it's not money from us."

Cindy's hand flew to her mouth as she stared at Cap in horror. "They took the boys to force Dan to get money. They'll kill them."

"Cindy, don't start thinking like that. Yes, Dan's in a tough spot, but God is still in control. And believe me, every law enforcement agency will be working on this to free them." Cap closed his eyes a moment then stared out the window, his face drawn.

Amanda reached across the table and laid her hand over his. "Cap, what's wrong? Can you tell us?"

He sighed. "Sometimes I'd like to kick myself for being so stupid, but this has nothing to do with the present situation. I have a confession."

Amanda blurted, "What did you do?"

"Not what I did, but what I stupidly thought before I met Dan today. This will upset both of you, and I apologize. In defense, I want to say I've seen too many bizarre crimes committed by people considered model citizens."

When he hesitated, Amanda said, "Go on."

"Cindy, I know you were chloroformed. Despite this, I had to consider the possibility that Dan had dreamed up this whole scheme to make it appear something had happened to him, but in actuality, he was running out on you and taking the boys with him. That's why I asked you if he was under stress or acing differently."

Shocked, Cindy blurted, "Dreamed up? How could you even think him capable? He would've had to hire men to chloroform me and kidnap his own sons." Her heart pounded with rage. "He'd have to be completely off his rocker."

Cap raised his hands in front of his face. "Whoa…simmer down."

Looking equally upset, Amanda said, "Have you lost your mind. Dan is our son."

His lips compressed, Cap gazed at both of them. "Before you hang and quarter me, let me explain. I know now I was dead-wrong." He waited a moment before continuing. "Look, we all know Dan still has nightmares. When Dan and I had lunch the other day, he mentioned working with a troubled youth who had an abusive father. Last night when he called me, there was no hint of duress in his voice. It remained strong, steady, and business-like, even when he told me to take care of you and Jonathan."

"They probably had a gun on him," Cindy interjected.

"Most likely, but I also ran this by Dr. Kincaid. He mulled over the situation before saying he wasn't a psychiatrist, but he had treated several patients who were depressed and had done bizarre things, and that it was possible Dan's counseling had triggered something."

"He agreed with you?" Amanda's face registered disbelief.

Cap shook his head. "He told me what I suspected was ridiculous because Dan loves the Lord."

Amanda said, "You of all people should know how much he depends on God, so how could you think him capable of doing such a violent act?"

"I'm a police officer. Sometimes my head takes precedence over my heart. Mandy, I've seen too many good people commit violent acts, even Christians. But I apologize to both of you for voicing my negative thoughts. I should have kept them to myself and not upset you. Forgive me?"

Amanda placed her hand over his. "Of course, I do. You were being honest with your feelings the way it's always been between us, and should be."

He took a sip of coffee and gazed at Cindy.

Cindy wasn't sure what to say. "Cap, I can't do otherwise. I love you and Amanda, but next time…"

"Use my head and get all the facts first?"

She smiled as she nodded.

"Cap, you should get to bed," Amanda suggested.

"I want to watch the ten o'clock news first."

After Cindy helped Amanda clean up the kitchen, she checked on Jonathan before she joined Dan's parents.

Cap turned on the TV. Again, the breaking news was the explosion, but the broadcaster gave the history of the old house and the mafia. "The police are not commenting on the bombing, but those of us who remember the violent mafia acts can't help but wonder if a new organization might be responsible."

After a commercial break, the newscaster repeated the same story they'd heard earlier about Dan and the boys but emphasized that Cindy was under police protection. "We tried to interview her today, but an officer made our crew leave."

Cap turned off the TV, and Cindy asked, "Are you really shielding me from the reporters, or do you think I'm in danger?"

"No, you're not in danger, nor will you be. Amanda will be free to come and go, but you will have a discreet escort. We want the media to believe you need protection."

Amanda said, "You don't like reporters, do you?"

"It's not a matter of like or dislike. I don't trust them. Too many times they cause more harm than good by speculating, making people jump to the wrong conclusions before all the facts are in...like mentioning the mafia and leaving that fear in people's minds."

When Jonathan started bawling, Cindy rushed up the stairs to the crib and patted him on the back. "Shh, it's okay. Mommy's here. Close your eyes and go back to sleep." His crying lessened, but his body gave little jerks with a few remaining sobs before he finally relaxed. His forehead felt warm. Was he getting sick, or were his teeth bothering him?

When Cindy returned to the living room, Amanda asked, "Is Jonathan okay?"

"I think his teeth are bothering him, but I was able to pat him back to sleep."

"Maybe you should turn in too...try and rest while you have the chance."

"I don't think I could sleep. I think I'll read."

"Cindy," Cap chided gently, "Dan wouldn't want you worrying like this."

"What am I supposed to do? Go out and party?" Cindy snapped. "I'm sorry, but it's so frustrating not knowing what he's up against."

Cap sighed. "Our faith is really being tested. As I told Dan, hang in there." He stifled a yawn and sank deeper into his recliner.

Amanda rose from the couch and put an arm around him. "You need to get to bed."

He gave her a sleepy grin. "Before I conk out here?" He brought the chair upright and lumbered to his feet. They stood gazing at each other as if communicating their thoughts with eyes reflecting the deep love they shared before he kissed Amanda and said, "See you in the morning." He stopped by the rocking chair and gave Cindy a reassuring smile. "God will take care of them. If I didn't believe that, I'd never fall asleep." He kissed her on the forehead and with broad shoulders squared, he walked down the hallway.

Cindy watched him leave, knowing, despite his worries, he truly did believe God had complete control over the situation. She glanced at Amanda who looked as if she couldn't decide whether to stay or follow Cap. "Why don't you go on to bed? I'll be fine."

"I think I'll stay up a while. It will be hard to sleep with so many thoughts going through my head."

"You're as worried as I am. I keep praying and praying for God to stop these men and bring Dan, Danny, and Timmy back to me. I know it's in His timing and that His will be done, but what if He says no?"

"Cindy, He loves us and wants what's best for us. Don't let the devil plague you with doubts. I can't begin to tell you how many times God has protected Cap."

"Aren't you afraid of that one phone call?"

"Of course, I am. I dread it, but I know God will carry me through whatever happens."

"How can you stay so strong? I'm a pastor's wife. Why don't I feel strong?" Cindy couldn't stem her tears.

Tears misting, Amanda hurried over and put an arm around her. "Oh, my dear sweet Cindy, you're so very young. You haven't been tested as much as I have." She gave Cindy a hug and a smile. "Believe me, by the time you raise those three boys, you'll have strength beyond measure." She handed Cindy a tissue. "Now wipe your eyes and go to Jonathan. I hear him crying."

"Thanks, Amanda. I love you."

"And I you."

Cindy listened to Jonathan. "Amanda, he never sounds that miserable unless something's wrong." They rushed upstairs. Jonathon lay in his crib, trembling with fever.

Amanda felt his forehead. "Poor little tyke, he's burning hot." After Cindy took his temperature, Amanda said, "You call Dr. Kincaid while I cool Jonathan down in the tub."

While Amanda carried Jonathan to the bathroom, Cindy phoned Dr. Kincaid's exchange, hoping he was on call. He was not only their family physician but also a trusted friend and godfather to the boys.

Dr. Kincaid called her back a few minutes later. "What's his temperature?"

"One hundred four…I'm staying with Cap and Amanda. He'll probably be all right, but…"

"You know I'll come over. I'll be there in a few minutes."

Cap hurried into the bathroom, tying his robe. "What's wrong?"

"Jonathan's sick," Cindy said.

"I'll get dressed and warm the patrol car."

"I already called Dr. Kincaid, and he should be here any minute."

Amanda finished bundling Jonathan in a large towel and handed him to Cindy. "Let's go downstairs to wait."

When the doorbell rang, Cap said, "That must be Dr. Kincaid now. I'll let him in."

Amanda told Dr. Kincaid she had cooled Jonathan down under tepid water, and he seemed better.

"Good. Lay him on the couch so I can check him."

Jonathan lay still until the doctor pulled the towel open, then he perked up and started kicking.

Cindy saw the baby's legs go still. "Watch out," she cried, tossing the doctor a diaper, but he had already replaced the towel. "Did he get you?"

Dr. Kincaid chuckled. "After raising three boys, I've learned to be quicker than any p-shooter." He waited a few seconds more before he examined Jonathan. "How long has he been fretful?"

"He's been crying a lot for two days. I think he's cutting teeth, and I think he misses Dan and the boys."

"Well, we won't have to take him to the hospital. Both ears are inflamed."

"No wonder, he's been cranky," Cindy said.

Jonathan reached for the stethoscope and began to babble. Dr. Kincaid picked him up and kissed his tummy. "You gave everyone quite a scare, young man." He handed the baby to Cindy. "I think the crisis is over. I'll give you some samples of medication to use now and write a prescription."

In the living room, worry lined Dr. Kincaid's face when he settled in the armchair across from Amanda and Cap. "I heard the news on the radio. Are Cindy and Jonathan now in danger?"

"No," Cap said. "She's being protected to keep reporters from hounding her. We now know why Dan and the boys were kidnapped." He sighed. "Dr. Kincaid, I was way off base when I confided in you yesterday that I thought Dan might have gone off the deep end. This is in confidence. Criminals kidnapped Dan, then the boys, to force him to do something. That's all I can tell you."

Dr. Kincaid's eyes clouded with sadness. "I've taken care of Dan since he was four. And his mother was my patient before she married. I suspected her husband of abusing her, even asked outright, but she vehemently denied being beaten, told me if I didn't quit making false accusations, she'd find another doctor. I suspected Dan might have been beaten as well." He shook his head. "I recall the summer he worked in my office, doing cleaning. He was fifteen. I caught him rifling through my narcotic's cabinet I'd left open while I answered the phone. I remember his face...so much guilt written on it when I confronted him. Dan lamely told me he needed something for his headache. When I asked him if he was hooked on drugs, he emphatically said he'd never taken any. Call it premonition, ESP or God telling me, but I knew in my heart he'd been beaten. I asked Dan to take off his shirt so I could examine him. He bolted, ran out the door, and never came back. I didn't see him again until that fateful Christmas." Anger filled Dr. Kincaid's eyes. "Now Dan is going through more torment, and your whole family is suffering." He slammed his fist against his palm. "God will avenge all of you."

8

Explosions in Dan's head shocked him awake. Nausea followed. He rolled off the bed to make his way to the bathroom, but his legs buckled. He dropped to all fours, too dizzy and miserable to care. When a hand touched his shoulder, he looked up. "Doc, I'm going to be sick."

Doc lifted him to his feet, helped him to the bathroom, and held his head while he retched.

Dan didn't remember Doc helping him back to bed. He must have passed out. How long had he been unconscious after Muscles knocked him out? He glanced at his watch, but the numbers blurred. At the sound of footsteps, he turned toward the doorway. The slight movement brought knife-like stabs, making him groan and shut his eyes against the pain. The light flipped on, and he saw Doc hurry over with a glass of water.

"Take these," Doc said. "They're codeine." He gently raised Dan's head so he could swallow the pills. After he checked Dan's condition, he said, "I told you Muscles was itching for you to get out of line. That was a stupid move on your part. You fared a lot better than I expected, but you do have a concussion. Get some rest. I need to relieve Cookie so he can finish dinner."

"How are Timmy and Danny?"

"Full of energy. After Cookie returned from town, we took them outdoors to play in the snow. They enjoyed sliding down the hill."

Dan sat up, his hands against his temples. "Without snowsuits?"

"Relax. They had snowsuits." He eased Dan back down. "At a Goodwill store, Cookie bought snowsuits, boots, and mittens as well as everything else they needed. He got them at the same time he purchased items for you...even the blue flannel pajamas you're wearing." Dan glanced down in surprise as Doc continued, "You'll find clean trousers and shirts in the closet and underwear and socks in the bureau drawer."

"Adolf approved?"

Doc snorted. "He could care less how you'll look, walking into a store." Doc chuckled. "However, he did help me undress you after I pointed out you'd end up with pneumonia if you slept in wet clothes in this freezing room."

Dan fingered the pajamas. "Cookie bought everything?"

"We both did."

"Thanks, Doc, for caring and thank Cookie for me. What are the boys doing now?"

"They're helping Cookie make chocolate chip cookies. Danny said they were your favorite, but I doubt if Adolf will let you have any."

"Because I slugged Needles?"

Doc nodded. "Muscles told Adolf Needles was kicking you in the van and stepping on your back every time he got in or out. For what it's worth, Adolf chewed his son out royally. Lefty told him about the picture and gave it to him."

"Do you think I'll get it back?"

He shrugged. "Just because he chewed Needles out doesn't mean you're off the hook. I suggest you don't ask...wait until he cools down."

I don't think that will ever happen. "Are the boys okay?"

"Yes. Both have been asking for you. I told them you weren't feeling well. They begged to see you, so I showed them you were asleep."

"Some sleep," Dan mumbled. "What time is it?"

"Did your watch stop?"

"The numbers are too blurry to read."

"It's almost three."

Dan slowly moved his head in disbelief and winced. "I hope the codeine takes effect soon."

"I thought about giving you morphine, but I only have enough for Needles to keep him comfortable. You broke his jaw." The doctor cocked his head as if waiting for a comment.

"You expect me to say I'm sorry?"

"Maybe not to me, but you'd better apologize to Adolf. Yes, Needles has been antagonizing you, but aren't Christians supposed to turn the other cheek?"

Dan could only say, "I'm not perfect, Doc," and closed his eyes.

"I'll check in on you later."

Abruptly awakened by footsteps, Dan's hand doubled as his eyes flew open. "Oh, it's you," he said in relief as Cookie set a tray on the table. "I thought someone was sneaking up on me. It's a good thing you weren't closer, or I might have…"

"Hit me?"

"Not if I'd known it was you, but I'm so edgy I might have struck out on impulse and looked later."

"Bad nerves. Maybe my soup will help." With an arm around Dan's back, he eased him into a sitting position and adjusted the pillow they'd finally given him. He felt warm and realized two heavy blankets covered him.

Grateful, Dan settled against the headboard while Cookie retrieved the tray and set it on his lap. One whiff of the steaming soup brought on an attack of queasiness. "Take it away."

Cookie whisked the tray off Dan's lap. "You gonna get sick? You look green."

Dan took a few deep breaths. "I think I'm okay now."

"I'll leave the soup. Maybe you can eat later."

After Cookie left, Dan stared at the wooden rafters a few minutes before he gazed at his hands. "Lord, forgive me," he prayed as he reflected on how close he'd come to killing Needles. "Forgive me for feeling so much hatred. Don't let Adolf take his anger out on Timmy and Danny."

Doc rushed into the room. "Cookie said you couldn't eat. Are you feeling worse?"

"Only my conscience, Doc. I blew it today. I wanted to kill Needles. I haven't been that angry since I killed my father." Dan stiffened when he realized what he had inadvertently said.

Doc's mouth dropped open. "You killed your father? Captain Baker isn't your father?"

"He and Amanda adopted me."

Doc's eyebrow shot up with interest. "Tell me about it."

"You heard enough," Dan said, mentally kicking himself. "Go have your fun...tell the others how the supposedly good preacher is really a murderer."

"I may be greedy, but I'm still a good doctor and adhere to the doctor-patient code of ethics. I'd really like to hear how you ended up being adopted by a cop." Doc grabbed a chair and set it next to the bed.

Dan closed his eyes and debated sharing his innermost pain.

"If you're not up to it, that's okay."

"It's not that so much, but talking about it still hurts. Doc, my dad beat my mother to death on Christmas Eve. Two weeks earlier, we tangled. I got the worst of it, but I deserved my thrashing. I only had my permit and stupidly drove home from a party drunk and cast slurs at him...told him I was a better driver drunk than he was sober."

"Not too smart. I wondered how you got the marks on your back. I saw them when I took off your soaked T-shirt."

Dan gave a slight nod in grim remembrance. "On Christmas Eve, I went caroling with the church youth group. I came home and heard Mom screaming in the bedroom. How long Dad had been beating her, I don't know. I barged in and lunged. He managed to get his hands around my throat. I remember groping for the desk paperweight, but I don't remember hitting him."

"Sometimes we block things out, or maybe you were close to passing out."

"I don't suppose it matters," Dan sighed. "He's dead. When Captain Baker questioned me, he asked if I hated my father. I said, 'I loved him, even bought him a Christmas gift.' Cap noticed the red marks on my throat and realized I'd been fighting for my life. He took me home to spend Christmas with his family. The love I saw between him, Amanda, and their two girls overwhelmed me. The Bakers became my foster parents and adopted me on my eighteenth birthday. It was a wonderful present, but I received an even better one because of them."

"What was that?"

"Salvation through Jesus Christ. I'd always gone to church with Mom. I assumed I was a Christian, but I learned from Cap that I personally had to ask God to forgive me for my sins, thank Him for dying on the cross for me, and ask Jesus to be my personal Savior. I've never regretted the night I turned my life over to God."

Doc scrambled to his feet. "Well, that's an interesting saga. I'd better get back to your sons."

"Doc, I want to see them."

"I'll try to get Adolf's okay. It all depends on whether or not Adolf is still angry about your strangling his son."

"Doc, please protect my sons from Needles."

Doc's lips drew into a grim line. "I heard about Adolf's threat." Laying a hand on Dan's shoulder, he said, "Cookie and I detest their lifestyle. We won't let either of them touch your boys."

Dan stared at Doc, his mind reeling under the impact of his words. *Their lifestyle? Father and son?* "Both?" he blurted as panic seized him. He fought to breathe after Doc nodded.

Doc gripped his shoulders. "Look at me, Baker. Get hold of yourself. Adolf will be here shortly."

With effort, Dan managed to take a few deep breaths and calm down.

"Tell me now. Where is your God? I thought you trusted him."

Dan hung his head before he gazed at Doc, searching for the right words. "I'm only a man, Doc. I don't have superhuman strength. Sometimes I fail miserably like trying to kill Needles or letting fear get the best of me, but even though I fail, God won't fail me."

"Forget God. Cookie and I will protect your sons. You just do your part and get our money." As if it were a done deal, he grabbed his bag and strode from the room.

Dan heaved a sigh. "I blew it, Lord. No sooner do I share my testimony when I counteract it by buckling under. Forgive me. Give me the right words to reach Doc and Cookie, and the others too. My trust is in You, Lord." Putting the matter in God's hands helped him relax. God would protect Danny and Timmy—maybe by enabling Cookie and Doc or some other means.

A few minutes later, Adolf strode into the room, his scowl so fierce, Dan offered a quick prayer. "Lord, show me how to appease his anger." *A soft answer turns away wrath.*

"I hope that display of temper was worth it, Baker. It cost you more than the loss of a decent meal. We were going to let you talk to your wife tonight."

"I'm sorry I broke Needles's jaw. I can take a lot of physical and verbal abuse, but I won't stand slurs about my wife."

Adolf raised an eyebrow. "Are you sorry about trying to kill my son...my one and only son?"

Fear gripped Dan's heart. *Eye for an eye?* He gazed at Adolf's face. Why wasn't it livid with rage? "I'm sorry about that. I was too angry to realize what I was doing. I asked God to forgive me, and I'm asking you too."

Adolf laughed. "For what...trying to kill that worthless piece of meat? His loss means nothing to this operation. Yours means everything."

What manner of man is he? Adolf studied him a few minutes, making Dan wonder what he was thinking or plotting?

"For a preacher, you have guts. Care to switch sides, join me in another business venture I have in mind, more money in it than you'd make in fifty years? By the way, how did you enjoy sitting in that brand-spanking new '85 VW...much better than the beat-up one you drive. With the money you'd be getting, you could have your pick of vehicles."

"Money can't buy peace of mind. No, I think I'll stay on God's side." Dan wondered how long they had been watching him and his family's movements.

"Then nothing's changed. Tomorrow you start fetching money from a few stores."

"Not banks?"

"Too much security...stores have lots of customers."

Dan laughed at the bizarre scene he envisioned. "I'm going to be robbing customers?"

"Don't take me for a fool. Right now, if your father's carried out our instructions, twelve corporations are scurrying to have money ready for us. I'll contact each and tell them which store. They'll have one hour. Lefty will drive you there. You'll go in to the manager's office and bring the bundle out. An uncooperative corporation will have an explosion mess to clean up in one of their stores. I bet you shop at all of them…Ware Mart for bulk items, ICON for clothing and appliances, and Ricard for prescriptions. We also have bombs planted to detonate if we're tailed."

"That's why you gave the demonstration." Dan tried to bring under control the anger rebuilding in him. "You've chosen stores because they'll be full of people."

"That's right. You may not spot us, but we'll be watching your every move and listening to every word you say. Do you think the police will interfere with so many lives at stake? Your side considers each life precious. To me, people are expendable."

"Even Needles?"

"Like your God, I'd willingly sacrifice my own son." His mouth curved into a cruel smile. "Goodnight, Baker. You'd better eat your cold soup. You'll need your strength."

Dan stared at Adolf as the evil man turned to leave. Had he just witnessed a manifestation of Satan? He shuddered as icy fingers clawed his spine. A tomb-like chill pervaded the room. His head no longer throbbing, Dan rolled off the bed and shivered. He had to wait for dizziness to pass before he could walk to the closet to find his jacket and shoes. After he put them on, he paced the room. How could he thwart Adolf's plan? How could he lead the police to this hideout? Surely, any information he could pass would help pinpoint the area and, maybe, by relaying the descriptive nicknames of the gang, the police might be able to identify them. Maybe they'd served time in the same prison. But he'd be wired, and he had no writing material. Doc watched him constantly whenever he was with the boys. Maybe he could snatch a crayon. But paper? No way.

Dan racked his brain for the solution as he paced like a caged animal. The codeine had reduced the pain to a dull ache, but walking made his head throb again. He sat down on a folding chair, propped his elbows on the table and laid his forehead against his palms. He stared at the cold bowl of soup. A gum wrapper lay crumpled beside it. Who had tossed it? Cookie? Doc? Adolf? *Gum wrappers.* No one took notice of them. The crooks had taken his wallet but not his change. He remembered having one dollar and eighty-five cents in his trousers. He went to check his damp ones in the closet. The coins were still there. He had to take the chance, buy gum at the first store, find a way to write down information, and convey to a manager the importance of the wrappers he'd drop. *Dumb. Your idea doesn't have a prayer of a chance.* "Lord, help me think of something better." No other ideas came to him. Could he cause a delay without putting Danny and Timmy in danger? Maybe he could work the head injury to his advantage. Dan was still in a quandary when Doc entered.

"How are you feeling? Doc asked.

"My head still hurts, but my stomach's settled down."

"You didn't eat."

"I'm not really hungry."

"Worried about your kids?"

"Yes."

"Well, they're doing fine…gorged themselves on spaghetti while I ate Cookie's specialty…beef stroganoff."

"Doc, I need to see them to reassure them I'm okay."

"To reassure yourself, you mean. Muscles will be in shortly. I'd advise you not to do anything foolish. Adolf may not be so gracious next time."

Muscles sauntered into the room to unshackle Dan. His beam of satisfaction clearly showed pride and pleasure over his ability to inflict pain. Dan fought the urge to slam his fists into the man's jaw like he had Needles's. Muscles hee-hawed. "You look like you wanna take me on. I'm shakin' in my boots." They stared at each other with mutual hatred. Muscles broke eye contact, gave Dan a warning glance before he leaned over to remove the chain. "Go to your brats."

Dan hurried down the hallway. Doc had said the boys were fine, but they didn't act like it when he walked through the doorway. Both ran to him crying, "I want to go home."

Dan pulled them close. "I'd like to leave too, but we can't."

"Why?" Danny asked.

"Son, these men are criminals. They want money, and they're forcing me to do what they want." Dan glanced at Doc who looked up from his book, seemingly undisturbed by Dan's comments.

"But...but criminals are bad," Danny said. "Doc and Cookie are nice. Why won't they let us go?"

Dan tried to hold his frustration in check. How could he explain enough for them to understand but not frighten them? "They're nice, but they're still criminals. They want lots of money. They'll continue to be nice as long as we behave ourselves. Climb into bed, and I'll tell you a story."

On the bed, Danny said, "Can you sleep with us? You have your pajamas on."

"I wish I could, but I need to return to my room." Dan sat between them on the bed and recited the story of Daniel in the lion's den. Afterward, he said, "Daniel wasn't afraid because he knew God had control of the whole world, even the lions. And we shouldn't be afraid even though we're in a den of criminals. God will protect us. Remember that while I'm gone tomorrow. I should be back in time to have dinner with you."

He knelt with them as they prayed and kissed them after they climbed back in bed. He couldn't say goodnight. Anguish filled his heart. *Heartache, fear, and anger, are these the only emotions I will ever feel again?* Dan couldn't bear to leave his sons. After the boys settled under the covers, he stretched out beside Danny who snuggled close.

"Hold me," Timmy said, scrambling from underneath the covers and crawling over Danny to sit on Dan.

Danny struggled to toss off the blankets. "I want to be held too."

"Stay where you are, and, Timmy, get back underneath the covers. I'll sit between and put an arm around each of you."

"Please sleep with us," Danny said.

"I can't, but I will stay and rest awhile." Peace came over him and an overwhelming sense of love. "Lord, thank You for reminding me all is not black. Peace and love are from You. Nothing can take them permanently from me." He managed to smile at Doc who looked up from reading his book.

"Don't get too comfortable," Doc said. "It's almost your bedtime."

Dan gazed at his sons who lay content and would soon be asleep. He too felt relaxed. *Oh, how I wish I could sleep with you. I really wish we were home.*

Muscles barged into the room, the door banging against the wall.

Dan sat bolt upright, wishes and peacefulness shattered by the jarring noise and his bawling sons who threw their arms around his neck. Doc dropped his book, jumped to his feet, and yelled, "What is all hellfire wrong?" Dan pulled the boys to his chest and hovered over them.

"Nothin', I just came to get Baker."

Doc rolled his eyes. "You half-baked moron, look what you've done. You've upset all of us. It will take Baker half an hour to calm his kids. Get out, come back in thirty minutes and tap lightly on the door before you come in." Muscles stood wide-eyed as Doc pointed to the door. "Out!"

Muscles backed toward the door and scurried away.

Nerves shattered, Dan sat trembling, his heart pounding as the boys cried. He pulled his sons closer, kissing each to calm them.

Doc rushed over to him. "You okay?"

"I think I had my senses jarred loose."

"I can relate to that. I thought maybe one of Einstein's bombs was destined to explode."

Danny cried out, "Daddy, sleep with us!"

Before Dan could answer, Doc said, "He can't. He has to get up early tomorrow, and I don't want him disturbing you. I'll make sure Muscles won't scare us again. Try to go back to sleep."

Dan kissed each on the forehead. "Everything's okay now," he said, but they continued to gaze at him with fearful faces. After nightmares, he often quieted them with a song, so he started singing "Jesus Loves Me." They snuggled back under the blankets and closed their eyes—at peace. But he found it harder to finish the last verse. Tears welled. *Oh, God, protect my boys.*

Doc tapped him on the shoulder, his eyes reflecting empathy. "Muscles will be here soon. You don't want him to see you like this."

Dan gazed at him in wonder. "It would bother you to watch him gloat, hear him crow like an obnoxious rooster?"

"I guess that does surprise you. For what it's worth, I don't like associating with the likes of him or Lefty."

"And the others?"

Doc shrugged. "Necessary evils. I understand what you're feeling, and I don't like one man tormenting another." His eyes went steely. "However, that doesn't change a thing. I need that money."

"And if I cooperate?"

"Cookie and I will protect your sons and make sure they get home safely."

What if Adolf hears him talking like this? "I take it your room isn't bugged."

He smiled. "Cookie and I don't take chances. We make sure it's clean."

Their conversation helped Dan regain his composure before Muscles tapped very lightly on the door. Trying not to disturb his sons, he scooted off the bed.

Muscles stood gazing at Doc, still looking thoroughly reproved.

Doc gave him a nod. "Much better…just remember what you've learned." He turned to Dan. "As soon as Cookie comes, I'll be in to sedate you."

"I could use some codeine too. My head aches like crazy."

Doc's eyes gestured toward Muscles. "So does mine, and he didn't even lay a finger me."

Not missing Doc's comment, Muscles's lips tightened, but he said nothing then or while he escorted Dan back but gazed at him with hatred, shackled him, and stomped to the doorway. He turned to glare once more before he stormed out.

Stretched on the bed, Dan waited for Doc, his throbbing head again making him queasy.

"You look miserable," Doc said when he hurried into the room.

"Right now, I'd like to trade my head in for a new one…my stomach too, for that matter."

Doc laughed.

"You sure lost your empathy in a hurry."

"Sorry, but for some reason, that sounded ludicrous coming from you. Codeine should have you feeling better soon."

Dan gave a slight nod and winced. When Doc handed him a glass of water with the pills, he downed them as if pure ambrosia.

"You purposely told the boys that story tonight, didn't you? Are you expecting a miracle?"

"Why not? Daniel of old got one."

"Even for a preacher, you certainly are naive."

"Don't make the mistake of equating faith in God with naiveté, Doc. There's a vast difference."

"Shut up and roll up your sleeve."

*****

Doc walked under the archway and warmed his hands at the fireplace.

"How is he?" Adolf asked.

Doc turned. "His head aches enough to make him queasy, and he's experiencing some dizziness."

"Is this going to cause problems?"

"The codeine should keep him functional."

"Will his attitude stay under control?"

"He'll do what he's told. He loves those boys."

"Good. Now, let's get some shut-eye. I want to leave at four o'clock tomorrow morning...beat the rush hour traffic into Anaheim."

"When did you decide that? You should have told me. The sedative I gave Baker won't be worn off."

"He can sleep in the van."

9

E arly Thursday morning, Cookie poured round after round of coffee to go with the scrambled eggs and bacon.

Needles sucked coffee and broth through a straw.

"You should probably pick up some protein drinks and more straws," Doc told Adolf. "It's a good thing I picked some up for Baker's kids. Better take some along."

Adolf nodded. "I want to go over the plan one more time before we leave. Doc, you'd better get Baker up and moving." After Doc left, he said, "Do you all have your disguises?" They nodded. "Put them on after we go over details."

*****

Slaps across Dan's face made him wince and carried him back in time to age five. "No more, Daddy," he cried until the slapping stopped.

Someone shook his shoulder. "Baker, snap out of it. Wake up! It's Doc."

Dan's mind advanced to age twelve. "I fell, Dr. Kincaid. Honestly, I did. My father wouldn't hurt me."

"Baker, wake up!"

Steam wafted across Dan's face. He smelled coffee, opened his eyes, and saw Doc, but his dream-like state of mind lingered, leaving him confused.

"Drink some coffee," Doc urged.

Dan swallowed a mouthful of the hot liquid and closed his eyes.

"No," Doc said. "You've got to wake up." He put the mug to Dan's lips.

The urgency in Doc's voice made him sip more. "Are the boys okay?" he asked, blinking, barely able to keep his eyes open.

"Your sons are fine…still asleep."

Dan let the lids close. "Sleep."

"No," Doc said again and pulled him upright.

Groggy, Dan stared at Doc. "I wish you'd make up your mind, first a sedative, now coffee." He sipped more. The teeth-cutting bitterness penetrated his fogged brain. He drew back.

"Drink it. All of it."

Dan took more sips until he emptied the mug. "That's the worst coffee I've ever tasted."

"Sorry for the rude awakening, but Adolf decided to start earlier. If you want to eat, you need to get up now." He retrieved Dan's clothes from the closet and underwear from the bureau drawer. "Shower and get dressed. Cookie will be here in ten minutes. We leave in thirty."

The minute Dan stood, he winced and put his palms against his throbbing temples.

"I'll give you some codeine before we leave." He handed Dan his clothes. "Get going." He followed Dan into the hallway, pointed to the bathroom door but headed for the living area.

"Wait. Aren't you going to remove the chain so I can shower?"

"No, Muscles will take the chain off and put it back on. I have to eat breakfast. I'll be back by the time you finish yours."

Muscles passed Doc in the hallway, hurried to Dan, and unlocked the padlock. "I'll be right outside the door. Be quick. I have to get back."

Dan laid his clothes on the counter, slipped out of his pajamas, took a short shower, and dressed. The minute Dan stepped out of the bathroom, Muscles secured the chain, ushered him into his room, and hurried away.

A ham-and-cheese omelet awaited him. Before he sat down to eat, he retrieved the coins from his damp trousers and put them in the dry ones. He now had money to buy gum, but he still thought it was a dumb idea, and he had nothing to write with. At the table, he said a short prayer for the food and asked God to give him a better idea and calm his nerves. Despite his apprehension and headache, Dan devoured his meal, washing down the last bite with a perfectly brewed cup of coffee. He barely finished before Doc entered. Compelled to check on Danny and Timmy, he said, "Doc, I want to see my sons before I leave."

"More assurance? They're asleep."

"I know that, but I need to see them."

"You'll have to be quick about it." He undid the chain and followed Dan.

The night light glowed softly across their peaceful faces. Dan knelt and prayed for their safety. Before he rose, a small chunk of crayon under the bed caught his eye. He snatched the purple stub and jammed it into his pocket before he stood. He heard a light tap on the door, and Cookie entered.

"All yours," Doc mouthed. In the hallway, Doc handed Dan four pills. "Get some water from the bathroom faucet and take two tablets now. Put the others in your pocket for later." He followed Dan and said after Dan downed them, "Adolf and Einstein will be here shortly."

Dan wished the codeine were a sedative. He preferred induced sleep to the daylight nightmare awaiting him. Einstein equated bomb. Back in his room, Dan asked, "Does Adolf really believe the police will stand quietly by while I retrieve the money?"

"Hardly, he's planned for all contingencies."

Einstein sauntered in with Adolf close behind. "Can you imagine, Baker, what a bomb planted on the Interstate can do...or in a market?"

Dan glared at them. "If you kill anyone, you'll lose my cooperation."

"What about your sons?" Adolf asked with a smug look.

Dan kept his cool. "You're going to kill us anyway."

"You? Yes." His mouth twisted into a sadistic grin. "Your sons? I think they'd make a rather nice present for Needles, something to bring him pleasure during his last days. After that, if they're not infected with the HIV virus, I'll take them."

Dan lost it. Shaking with rage, he cried out, "God will never allow that. My sons belong to Him. You may think you can do as you please, but God will only allow you to go so far. And I draw the line at seeing anyone die."

Doc put a restraining hand on his shoulder. "You've said enough."

Dan yanked the gripping hand off and stared at Doc. "You're no better than the rest of them. If you don't change, you'll burn in hell too!"

Adolf looked unperturbed. "Daniel, the lion-hearted, it really is too bad you can't be bought." He waved toward Einstein. "But enough talk. Harness time."

Dan submitted to the heart-racing ordeal and quickly donned his jacket. Adolf handed him a black business card with yellow lettering. The words *Lions International* stood out boldly beneath the golden head of a snarling lion. "What's this for?"

"Identification…the corporations have told their managers to give the briefcase to the person bearing this card. We've threatened to explode a bomb in one of their stores if the managers divulge the transaction to anyone, call the police, or interfere in any way."

"And you really expect the managers to stay mum? I can think of a dozen ways your scheme can fail."

"And I've planned for every one of them. On the chance you might be recognized from your picture appearing on TV, I bought a navy stocking cap to make you less distinguishable." He took it from his back pocket and handed it to Dan. "You will keep this on at all times."

"What happened to my baseball cap?"

"Lefty took it. He likes the Angels too." He extended his hand. "Give me the card."

Dan slapped it in his hand. "What if I lose the card?"

"I guess we'll have to assume you've given this plus information to the manager and…" His hands flew up in the air. "No more store…all because of your carelessness."

"You make me sick!"

Adolf laughed. "Sick? Is that the best you can do? Come on. Try. Damn me to hell."

"From where I'm standing, I'd say you're already playing with fire."

"And you'd love to watch me burn, wouldn't you?"

"Yes." Standing face-to-face, Dan steeled himself for a blow as their eyes locked in mutual hatred. To his surprise, Adolf broke contact.

Looking thoughtful, Adolf tapped his finger against his lips. "You know, I bet you're counting on the cops watching us. I'm sure they have every store covered, but they know what will happen if they try to tail us or pass you a tracking device."

Mimicking Adolf, Einstein's hands flew apart, but he yelled, "Boom."

Adolf rolled his eyes and continued. "Do not talk to anyone except the manager. Einstein will give you directions to where he will be. Do not enter his office. He will be instructed to keep the door wide open. Take the briefcase he hands you and come straight back to the car. Now, we need to leave. Einstein, cuff him."

Einstein pulled handcuffs from his back pocket. Dan didn't balk, but he dreaded the grueling trip down from the mountains. "Who's riding with me?" he asked, praying it wasn't Needles.

"Why do you care?" Adolf asked.

"I just don't want your son sitting in back with me."

"Ah, yes. Muscles told me about yesterday, how my son antagonized you. No, you won't have to worry about Needles…for now." He smiled his sadistic smile and shrugged. "Later? Well, Needles is in a lot of pain, and he really needs release from his anger. Holding one's anger in is not healthy. Is it, Doc?"

Dan glanced at the doctor and saw the man's lips drawn tight. Einstein's Cheshire grin indicated he looked forward to watching whatever Needles planned to do.

"You know, Einstein, I don't think Doc likes what we consider entertainment. And, Baker, you look positively ill. I do believe you get the point of this whole conversation."

"That you're going to let Needles kill me when my usefulness is over? I've known you were going to kill me from the beginning."

"But how...aren't you the least bit curious as to how Needles will do it? There are so many ways to make a man suffer a slow agonizing death."

"Have fun. Play your little games. You know, for what it's worth, how I live is more important than how I die."

"Ah, yes, Daniel, the lionhearted. We'll see how brave you are when the time comes."

Dan saw a flash of anger in Adolf's eyes as he turned to Einstein. "Blindfold him."

He wondered if his not cowering had upset Adolf. Behind the blindfold he prayed, "Lord, please give me Daniel's courage to face death. Don't let Adolf and his son get the satisfaction of seeing me afraid."

"Muscles," Adolf called, "stay with Baker while the rest of us get ready."

Dan heard the others leave. Muscles led Dan to the bed and sat next to him.

"What are we waiting for?"

"You'll see when your blindfold is off."

"Are you going to be driving me around today?"

"No, Lefty is."

"Is everybody going?"

"All but Cookie...he has to sit with your brats and cook dinner."

In the van, Dan again mentally clocked up about fifteen minutes of twists and turns on the rutted gravel road before they hit pavement. No longer jostled, he relaxed. The purring tires became a lullaby.

The van crunching to a stop on a dirt road jarred him awake. The door slid back, and Muscles said, "Time to wake up." He grabbed the back of Dan's belt, lifted him out, and gripped him under the armpits to help him to his feet and walked away.

Handcuffed and blindfolded, Dan stood alone with the cold misty air swirling around him. Days ago, the cold air would have bothered him, but hours spent in a freezing room had changed his perspective. Would it rain today? He hoped not. That might ground helicopters or force them to fly lower and be spotted sooner. He listened as the van drove off, followed by three more vehicles. The gang had taken great pains to make sure he didn't see them. Were they traveling in their own cars to and from the hideout? Adolf had said they would be using stolen ones. Where were they stashing theirs? *And where am I now?*

Approaching footsteps grated against gravel. "Ready to go to work?" Einstein asked, removing the blindfold. The lights from a sedan revealed a white-haired lady standing in front of him. He wore a black skirt, hose, flat-heeled black shoes, and a black raincoat. "Do you like my disguise?" Einstein's voice quivered, matching that of an elderly woman.

Dan shrugged. "Not bad," he said but knew he'd been fooled. "I thought Lefty was driving me around."

"He's waiting in the car. Adolf says you'd like to foul up our whole operation. Is that right?" He cocked his head and studied Dan.

"What could I possibly do? You hold all the cards."

"That's right, and I'll be sitting right behind you. Should you decide to jump out, I can detonate that body bomb anytime I wish… maybe wait until you reach a crowd of people. But you won't try anything, will you? You love your kids." He grinned. "I'm looking forward to counting all that money."

Somehow I will foul up their whole scheme.

Einstein gestured toward a late-model blue Buick. "Get in front."

"Still handcuffed?"

"I guess I should take those off, might attract attention doing it at the market."

Rubbing his wrists, he walked toward the car. A gray-haired man with a neatly trimmed mustache sat in the driver's seat. "I must say you two look well-matched," Dan said as he took his place next to Lefty and fastened the seat belt. The strap pressed the bomb into his chest, making his heart race.

He glanced at his watch, six-fifteen. They'd left after four. The amount of time it had taken for the trip was no help without sounds and smells. What a rotten time for him to have fallen asleep. Dan gazed around. Where were they? Would the crooks use this area again? Doubtful. Twenty minutes later, they reached Santa Ana Canyon Road in the Anaheim Hills area. Lefty took the on-ramp onto Interstate 55. He exited at Chapman and drove to Scott's, a twenty-four-hour market in Orange. Though early, he saw plenty of cars in the parking lot. Dan hoped the police had the market and the surrounding streets covered. What if they tailed him? The scenario his mind played made his stomach queasy.

"Okay, Baker," Einstein said, "in you go. The manager will be in back in the glass-encased office to your left. We'll be watching and listening. No tricks."

"You guys left me some change. May I buy a couple of packs of peppermint gum to settle my stomach?"

"I'll do it," Einstein said. "Give me the money after we get out."

"You're going in with me?"

"Of course, and I won't be the only one watching you."

Inside, they parted ways—Dan going to the left, Einstein toward the check-out stand.

As Dan approached the glass window, he saw the man stiffen—his eyes widened with fear the closer he came. Dan tapped on the window and pressed the card against it. The manager opened the door. "I believe you have something for me."

"I'll get it for you."

A sudden attack of queasiness hit Dan when he saw the brief-case. He started taking deep breaths.

"Are you all right?" the manager asked.

Dan nodded. "I just need gum to settle my stomach."

When he headed for the car, his fingernails indented his palm as he gripped the heavy briefcase, as if his life depended on it.

Einstein stood by the rear door and smiled like a sweet old lady. "Open the door for your mother and give me the briefcase." After Dan did, he said, "And the card." Dan fished it out of his pocket and slapped it in his hand. "And here's your gum. I bought two large packs...one for you, one for me."

Lefty grinned after Dan slid onto the seat and buckled his seat belt. "That was real easy, wasn't it?" He pulled out of the parking lot before he glanced at Dan, "You don't look too swift. Hey, Einstein, I don't think the good preacher likes his easy job."

"Shut up! I'm counting."

Dan unwrapped three sticks of gum, put them in his mouth, and pocketed the wrappers.

"Lefty," Einstein said, "contact One and tell him Scott's came through."

Lefty picked up the phone and said, One, this is Four…Scott's came through."

Dan started to ask if they were going by numbers now but turned around when he heard the back window roll down. He saw Einstein toss out the briefcase. A truck behind swerved to miss it, and the driver blared his horn. "You'd better be more careful," Dan told Einstein. "People get shot for less than that."

"What happened?" Lefty asked.

"After I put the money in our suitcase, I threw the briefcase out. It almost hit a truck."

"That was an expensive case. Why'd you throw it away?"

"The cops probably had a tracking device in it."

Lefty drove down the road, turned east, and doubled back through a residential area.

Dan fingered the wrappers in his pocket. "Lefty, is there any chance of stopping at a gas station? Doc made me drink too much coffee."

Lefty contacted One and asked him. Dan heard Adolf say, "Not now Four…you're being tailed. Have Baker call them off."

Lefty punched in the number for Cap's precinct and handed Dan the phone. "You heard what Adolf said. Order your father to call the cops off."

Dan told the dispatcher who he was and asked to speak with Captain Baker. When his father came on the line, Dan said, "Don't talk. We're being tailed. Call them off."

Lefty grabbed the phone and added, "Or else."

Dan ignored the theatrics. "Are you all going by number names now? Is Adolf paranoid?"

Einstein said, "Not paranoid, just cautious."

I think the man has a serious mental problem—a dangerous one.

*****

Adolf smiled at Needles. "I told you it would work." He contacted Lefty. "Drive around a while longer. Five said the one car he spotted tailing you has turned around and left, but we want to make sure another hasn't taken its place."

Ten minutes later, Adolf called again. "The way's clear, but we'll keep tabs on the situation. Take the freeway to the next store as planned. Yes, you have time to stop at Burger King. Don't let Baker go in alone and remind Two he's now a woman. The rest of us will monitor the area."

Adolf laughed when he hung up. "Baker drank too much coffee in order to wake up. He needs a restroom."

Needles opened a tablet and scrawled—I'm hungry.

"Maybe we should keep them company," Adolf said. "I'll get you a milkshake." He followed Lefty but drove around the block and parked out front near the fast-food restaurant.

10

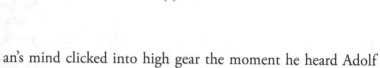

Dan's mind clicked into high gear the moment he heard Adolf give Lefty permission to stop at Burger King. What was the most valuable information he could pass? *I won't have a whole lot of space to write on wrappers with a crayon, and at tops, Lefty will give me two minutes. Their descriptive nicknames might help. These guys must have met in prison—that must be the common link.*

Lefty pulled into the parking lot and drove around until he found the closest vacant space. "Here's your pit stop, Baker." He followed Dan inside, ushered him into the men's room, and stood outside the cubicle. "Don't take too long."

Dan smoothed a wrapper and used his thigh as a table—too soft. He placed the paper against the bumpy wall. He managed to write Leader-Hitler look alike, but it was barely legible. Chancing Lefty wouldn't hear, he used the metal door and printed *H's Son, AIDS.* The soft waxy crayon still proved a poor substitute for a pen, but at least the words were neater. The third paper said *Einstein-B-exp.*

Lefty rapped on the door. "You okay?"

Dan knew the crook wasn't concerned about his health—only the passage of time. He flushed the toilet, folded the wrappers, and jammed them, along with the crayon, into his pants' pocket. "I'm fine." He opened the door and kept his right hand partially closed to hide the smudges of purple before he washed. *I sure hope this dumb idea works.*

Lefty gestured him into the hallway and told Einstein, "Keep an eye on him while I go."

When Lefty came out, Einstein said, "You watch Baker now. It's my turn."

Dan recalled Adolf warning him to remember he was dressed as a woman, but Lefty didn't remind him. This could prove interesting, Dan thought, when he saw an approaching man stop and stare at seeing a woman enter the men's room. Lefty's eyes widened with realization. The man resumed walking toward them but stopped a few feet away and gazed as if unsure of what was going on. Without hesitation, Lefty said, "Sorry." He shrugged and opened his arms as if he were helpless to do anything. "She's senile."

With furrowed brow, the man took a step backward. "I can go later." His tone suggested he wanted no part of this threesome. He did an about-face and hurried toward the order line.

Dan wanted to yell, *Come back. Things might get more interesting when the old lady rejoins us.*

The minute the man was out of earshot, Lefty said, "You enjoyed that, didn't you?"

"Watching you squirm? Of course…I wish the guy had stayed."

He wished it more when Einstein came out cursing, "These damn panty hose. I'm not wearing them tomorrow." And Dan enjoyed hearing Lefty lambaste the bomb expert, but the respite from the seriousness of his situation didn't last long. He still needed to find a way to delay them. "Can we get something to eat?"

Lefty shook his head. "Adolf motioned me to take off."

When Dan cocked his head in puzzlement, Lefty grinned, making Dan wonder how he could have missed seeing Adolf.

In the car, Lefty chuckled, "You didn't recognize Adolf and Needles, did you?"

"No." *I wish I had. Their disguise descriptions might prove useful.* "How are they dressed, perhaps as Mutt and Jeff?"

Lefty leaned his head back and laughed.

Einstein said, "I wouldn't say that in front of Adolf if I were you."

"If they aren't Mutt and Jeff, who are they?"

Lefty said, "Adolf is…"

Einstein whacked him on the shoulder. "Shut up!" He leaned over the seat and eyed Dan with suspicion. "Why do you want to know?"

"Just curious."

"What's the harm in telling him?" Lefty said. "He's going nowhere, and he can't blab to the cops."

"Even so, you keep your mouth shut."

Dan realized with Einstein around he would never be able to con Lefty into letting information slip. What he really needed to know was the hideout's location. He wished he hadn't fallen asleep in the van on the way down. Getting the information to the police tomorrow might be too late. At best, putting together his bits and pieces would take time. Since the crooks had used a rendezvous spot close to the Riverside Freeway, Dan's gut feeling said they were holed up in the San Bernardino Mountains. He laid his head against the seat and closed his eyes. How could he possibly relay all the information on gum wrappers?

"Sleepy?" Lefty asked. "You'll be busy soon."

Dan kept quiet. He didn't want to enter another store, be linked with a gang of crooks, ruthless killers willing to use bombs. Why didn't God act? A bit of Scripture came to him. *My ways are not your ways.* Dan knew God didn't work as man wished, but the knowledge didn't stop him from craving a quick solution.

When Lefty parked in front of Ware Mart, Dan's heart plummeted. His whole being cried—*Don't make me go in there,* but he summoned courage to face what he could not change and opened his eyes.

"Yep, we're here," Lefty said, taking the black card from Einstein and giving it to Dan. "Don't take too long."

After Einstein told him where the office was located, he said, "Knock on the door and press the intercom button. Do not enter the manager's office. He's to keep the door fully open."

A twinge of pain reminded Dan the codeine was wearing off. He fingered the tablets in his pocket but decided against taking them now.

"What are you waiting for?" Einstein said. "Get moving."

The man sounded edgy. Perhaps his nerves weren't as steady as Lefty's seemed to be. Or was Lefty too dumb to get nervous? He and Muscles seemed to be a matched pair—all brawn—no brains.

Dan opened the car door and strolled toward the store. He stepped back from the entrance to allow two women to enter first. The glass door mirrored Einstein standing near the car. After Dan entered, he glanced back and saw Einstein approaching. Did he suspect Dan was stalling? He reached the office door, knocked, and pressed the intercom.

"Yes."

"I believe you have something for me."

The door slowly opened part way to reveal an angry frightened man, looking ready to slam the door in Dan's face. "Any identification?"

Dan showed him the card. "Sir, I need you to open the door wider."

The manager snorted. "You afraid I have the cops in here?" He flung the door back all the way. "I wish the cops were in here to gun you down."

Dan took a fortifying breath. "Do you have the money?"

His clenched hands matched his rage-red face. "No. The courier's stuck in freeway traffic. What now? Are you going to blow up my store for something I have no control over?"

Dan lost it. "I'm not the enemy," he blurted. "I'm being forced to do this. They're holding my kids hostage. I have..." He clamped his mouth.

"What?"

Dan shook his head. "Nothing...forget it."

"Are you going to bomb my store?"

The man looked ready to bolt. Dan knew he needed to cam him. "Sir, I really don't think they want to destroy this store. They only want the money. I'm sure they'll let me come back later if you don't do anything foolish."

"So what are they going to do now?"

"They're probably making that decision while we talk."

"They're listening?"

"And watching. I'd better get back before they get antsy." He slipped his hand in the pocket of his trousers, pulled out the gum wrappers, and gestured his eyes toward them. "For your sake, I hope they'll do nothing." He turned and dropped the wrappers behind him. *I hope you're not too upset to notice these, but please wait until I'm gone to pick them up.*

Dan took long strides through the store and hurried straight to the car. Einstein already sat in back. Lefty started the engine before Dan could get his seat belt buckled. Neither spoke. And Dan wasn't about to break the silence.

"So they didn't have the money," Lefty finally said. "Einstein, which Ware Mart store have you targeted?"

Dan turned. "You can't blow one up! You heard that manager. He has no control over the situation. The courier is tied up in traffic."

"You want Adolf to renege on his promise?" Einstein retrieved from his coat pocket a metal box a little larger than a pack of cigarettes. He grinned and poised his hand above the numbers. "Everything is programmed in here. Now, which store should I choose?"

"No! The money is coming. Let me go back later. That manager was angry and scared. That manager wasn't lying."

"It's Adolf's decision."

Dan breathed a sigh of relief when Adolf told them to forget the store for now, grab a bite to eat, and proceed to Market Place. "And, Baker, I want you to know your pitiful outburst in the store almost touched my heart strings...such a sad predicament you're in." His sarcastic tone changed. "But you almost blew it. It's a good thing you had enough sense not to mention the bomb. But it was good of you to calm the man down. I'll think about having you go back later."

Lefty said, "Too bad, Einstein, you'll have to wait. Adolf must be in a good mood today."

Einstein leaned over the seat and fingered his detonator in front of Dan's face. "I so wanted to use this...maybe later, even if the corporation comes through with the money." He laughed. "Rest easy for now." Still chuckling, he settled back in his seat.

Dan pressed his head against the seat and closed his eyes. Rest was impossible. Thinking about what one of Einstein's bombs could do made his throbbing head feel ready to explode. He didn't want to take the codeine yet. How much would he suffer if he didn't take it? He fingered the tablets but decided to pursue an idea and pretend to be searching.

"What are you looking for?" Lefty asked.

"The medication Doc gave me. I had two pills. Now I can't find them." Silently, Dan asked the Lord to forgive him for lying.

"Maybe they're in your trousers?" Einstein said. "By the way, where's the card?"

Dan retrieved it from his jacket and handed it over. "I'm positive the pills were in there too. Maybe they slipped out when I showed one of the managers the card." He leaned back and searched his pants. "They're not in these pockets either."

"I'll pick up some pain pills at the market," Einstein said.

Lefty pulled into the first fast-food restaurant they saw. The others ordered breakfast items. Dan thought a hamburger sounded better, but after two bites, he set it down. His stomach felt queasy again. He had been casually glancing around from time to time to see if he could spot Adolf and Needles. He couldn't be positive but thought he saw them enter. The younger thin man had dark hair and used crutches. If it was Needles, someone had done a remarkable make-up job. The shorter man appeared taller than Adolf, and his dark red hair looked unnatural. Dan hadn't seen anyone on crutches at Burger King, but he did recall seeing a man with dark red hair. The information was useless unless he could confirm it. "I spotted Adolf and Needles. Their disguises are pretty good," he said, nodding in appreciation. "Where'd Adolf get the platform shoes?"

Lefty blurted, "Doc ordered them."

"You blabber-mouth!" Einstein said, slipping out of character.

"Lay off! He already recognized them."

Gotcha! Now for a restroom.

As before, Lefty stood guard outside the stall. All Dan had time to do was write down Adolf's and Needles's disguises. He could only pray the information would be useful.

Lefty rapped on the door. "Hurry up. Adolf's ready to leave."

"Keep your shirt on." Dan couldn't have hurried if he'd wanted to. He didn't know whether it was nerves, something he ate or the flu, but his insides churned. The acid taste in his mouth suggested coffee as the culprit.

When Dan came out, Lefty said, "You got a problem?"

"Yes." *And I plan to use it and anything else I can think of to full advantage.* "My head's throbbing, and my stomach's upset. I hope it's not the flu."

Back in the car, Lefty contacted Adolf and told him Dan was sick. "No, he's not pretending. You should see his face, and he only ate two bites of his burger." Dan heard Adolf say, "Have Two pick up something to help Baker's stomach and head." The anger in his voice told Dan he'd better be able to convince Adolf, or else. Dan shuddered at what that or else might entail, but he didn't have time to dwell on it. They'd only gone two blocks when Lefty pulled into a crowded Market Place parking lot.

Dan walked as if it were an effort and took his time to reach the office. He saw the manager clench and unclench his hands. *Lord, let him have the money.* The man paled when Dan showed him the card and looked more frightened when Dan told him to leave the door wide open. "Do you have something for me?" Dan asked.

"Yes." His voice quavered, but the words brought Dan a sense of relief. He unwrapped a piece of gum, put it in his mouth, and pocketed the pack. After the manager passed him the briefcase, Dan pulled wrappers from his pants and pointed a finger toward the floor as he dropped them behind him, praying the manager wasn't too rattled to comprehend. He hurried past Einstein, who stood in line to pay the cashier.

After Dan laid the briefcase on the back seat, he took his place in front. Lefty started the car, and as soon as Einstein climbed in, he pulled out. Were they behind schedule?

Einstein leaned forward and dropped a sack on the seat. "Here's something for your head and stomach. Take some now and get yourself in gear." He held out his hand, and after Dan gave him the card, he said, "You were slow. You'd better not be trying to stall."

Dan popped two extra-strength pain relievers into his mouth and used the liquid, store-brand pink antacid to wash them down. There was no question he needed them. As for stalling, he hoped they'd never discover the truth.

Lefty drove through a subdivision until Einstein said, "Contact Adolf and tell him the money's all here."

A thought crossed Dan's mind—*fingerprints. Did Einstein slip up, or didn't I notice him wearing gloves?* He turned and saw Einstein roll down the window and toss out the briefcase. *Rats! No slip ups. He's* wearing *surgical gloves.*

The phone rang, and Dan heard Adolf tell them to go back to Ware Mart.

Lefty turned toward Dan. "I guess Adolf loves money more than bombs."

Einstein grumbled, and Dan envisioned his scowling face, but Dan felt a sense of relief.

In the store, relief also registered on the face of the manager when Dan asked. "Do you have the money?" He handed Dan the briefcase and promptly closed the door.

Lefty laughed. "This is easier than taking candy from a baby and a lot more fun."

The phone rang, and Dan heard Adolf say, "The cops are tailing you again. Make Baker choose which reprisal Two will use."

Dan grabbed the phone. "No bombs! Let me call them off."

"They had their one warning."

"If you kill anyone…"

"I won't be responsible. You will. Where that bomb explodes is your choice." Dan envisioned the sadistic smile on Adolf's face when he added, "Choose wisely."

"I won't do it," Dan yelled.

"My. My," Einstein said. "What a dilemma…so many choices…a manhole on a busy street, a call box on an Interstate, or a mailbox in a shopping center. I know, how about a trash can near a school playground?"

Dan stared in disbelief. "You can't be serious."

"Dead serious." Einstein tapped the numbers on his detonator.

Dan pressed his head against the seat while his heart cried out, *Why God? Why?*

"Which is it?" Einstein asked.

"The call box," Dan mumbled, hoping that would be the least destructive.

"I can't hear you."

"The call box, you son of Satan!"

"Good choice. The explosion's bound to cause a pileup on the freeway. Care to change your mind?"

Dan collapsed, letting his body sag over the seat belt. *Today, you'll get no more help from me.* He knew Einstein would slap his face to bring him around and steeled himself against reacting. The blows came swift and hard.

"He's not moving," Lefty said. "Is he breathing?"

Einstein checked Dan's neck for a pulse "He's alive." After he slapped him several more times, he said, "Must be out cold, or he would have flinched."

Lefty contacted Adolf who told them to meet at the rendezvous spot. Einstein held the collar of Dan's jacket to keep him upright. When the car stopped, he let go. Dan slumped forward. Despite the pain pills, the throbbing in his head had increased. *I need to take the codeine before they handcuff me.* He had to be pain-free in order to concentrate on the sounds and smells on the way to the hideout. When he heard Lefty and Einstein get out, he slipped his hand into his pocket, praying they weren't watching. His position made swallowing difficult, but his saliva increased until he could gulp down the pills. When no one came running, a wave of relief washed over him.

The car door opened. "All right, Baker," Adolf said, pulling him upright, "snap out of it."

Cold water hit Dan's face. He shook his head and sputtered but managed to keep his eyes closed.

"I said snap out of it!"

Dan moved his head back and forth against the seat as if coming around. He opened his eyes and stared past Adolf, hoping to appear confused. He saw Einstein watching.

"Einstein," Adolf said. "Blow up the trash can on the school playground."

Dan stiffened but tried not to overreact. "No bombs," he mumbled. "Let me call them off." He feigned passing out again.

"I already detonated the bomb in the call box. Do you really want me to blow up that particular bomb?"

Dan found it hard to breathe as he waited for Adolf to speak. No verbal answer came. Did Adolf nod or did he shake his head? Was the trash can bait, a trap to trick Dan into revealing he was faking? Dan remained "unconscious."

11

At the rendezvous area, which was again off Santa Ana Canyon Road, Dan remained "unconscious" while they transferred him from one van to the other. Scrunched on the floor, he felt miserable. The pink liquid had settled his stomach, and the codeine eased his headache, but nothing calmed Dan's nerves. Sleep might help, but he couldn't afford the luxury. Too much depended on staying alert. When the even flow of freeway traffic began to dull his senses, Dan concentrated harder. He stuck to the assumption the crooks were holed up in the San Bernardino Mountains and figured they should now be on the Riverside Freeway, heading for Corona.

He'd expected to hear conversation between Lefty and Einstein. Not a whisper reached him. Did they suspect he was awake and listening? He heard a click followed by bits and blurbs from the radio as the dial switched back and forth before it settled. Einstein must have picked the station. Lefty definitely would not listen to classical music, but Dan couldn't picture Einstein enjoying it either. News came next. Dan tensed. Had a bomb gone off near a school? The lead story was an explosion on Interstate 57, causing a chain reaction pileup, seriously injuring two people. A dumpster at an apartment complex exploded an hour later, but no one was hurt.

The radio clicked off. Adolf spoke from the front seat. "Did you hear the news, Baker? No one was killed. Guess you keep on working. Wasn't that the deal you made?"

"Boss," Lefty said, "why are you talking to him? He's out cold."

"Are you, Baker?"

Did Adolf really expect him to answer? Where was Einstein? Rigging more bombs? Adolf probably wanted to keep an eye on Lefty, make sure he didn't let information slip. Maybe he still would if he remained convinced Dan was unconscious. *And I didn't make a deal with Adolf. I delivered an ultimatum.* Classical music resumed— the kind Dan liked. It seemed ironic he and Adolf shared something in common.

"Do you like the music?" Adolf asked. "I don't picture you straightlaced and listening to hymns all day. Perhaps, country western? No, you're too suave for that."

Suave? Dan almost laughed, and maybe that was the point of the one-sided conversation: to trip him up. Blocking out the radio and Adolf's voice, he concentrated on his whereabouts.

"Boss, can I pull off at the next exit and get coffee? I'm sleepy."

"Then I'll drive."

Did Lefty's asking mean they were going through Corona? Lefty pulled to the side of the road, and Dan heard them exchange places. After the van started and resumed speed, Adolf said, "Did you want to stop too, Baker? Need a restroom again?"

"I'd like to use the john," Lefty said.

"We're not stopping."

Okay, Dan thought, we must be in Corona. Dan figured Adolf was headed for the San Bernardino Mountains instead of San Gabriel Range when he stayed on the Riverside freeway instead of turning due north. He'd often traveled this stretch of freeway and knew how long it would take to reach Riverside. He mentally approximated the passage of time.

When he figured they should be close, Lefty confirmed it. "Can't we stop at that gas station? I really need to use the john."

"I'm not stopping."

Adolf exited and eased into traffic on another freeway. Dan pictured Interstate 10. If he got off again soon, they would shortly be in Redlands. When Adolf exited and headed north on another freeway, Dan mentally clocked up the minutes to reach the mountains. Three roads wove through them. Which one would lead to the lodge? Dan concentrated harder. Adolf turned left. A few minutes later, he took a right, followed by another right before he turned left. He switched back and forth until Dan lost all sense of direction and gave up concentrating.

Melancholy crept over him. He thought about the last time he'd been in this area. A year ago, he and Cindy drove to Big Bear Lake for an intimate picnic—a kid-free all-day outing. After a relaxing afternoon, she dropped a bombshell—she was pregnant. Was that when their problems started or was it after Jonathan's birth? Cindy had two Caesareans, and the doctor advised them not to have more children. Her announcement made Dan angry with himself for not taking precautions in case she hadn't. He feared for her safety and worried about the expense. Lack of money was their key problem. She begged him to find a church that not only offered a better salary but also medical coverage. Dan loved his present position and felt needed. He had good rapport with the young people and felt that was where God had called him. Through scrimping, they'd managed to pay the hospital bill for Timothy one week before Jonathan was born. Dan visualized the money he'd handled today—three million bucks. What would he do with that much money?

The road started to wind, and Dan mentally clocked up the time it took to reach the gravel road before he resumed thinking. He fantasized about building his dream house. He wanted to tear down the old house he'd inherited and construct a rambling ranch home on their five acres. *It's foolish to fantasize. I'll never have the money.*

When the van stopped, Dan groaned as if jarred awake and in pain. After Lefty helped him to his feet, he swayed. If Lefty hadn't caught him, he would have carried his pretense to completion and fallen.

Adolf said, "We'd better help him." They supported him up the steps and to his room.

"I need some codeine," Dan said, sitting on the edge of the bed, his head in his hands while Lefty shackled him. Had Muscles stayed behind with Einstein and Needles? Or was everyone here?

"Doc will be in shortly," Adolf said before leaving. "Codeine had better be the answer to your problems. I won't allow anything to foul up my plans." The anger in his voice sent a chill through Dan, making his confidence ebb, but not enough to cancel his own plans. Tomorrow, before he entered the second store, he would pass out. He only had a few minutes to contemplate this when Adolf returned with Doc and Einstein.

After Einstein removed the bomb and carried it from the room, Adolf said, "Doc, I want to know if he's faking."

Doc raised an eyebrow. "Are you?"

"I feel better now. I'm no longer dizzy or queasy."

"But your head still hurts?"

"Yes." And it did, even though he'd taken the codeine less than two hours ago.

"Check him thoroughly, Doc. And I mean thoroughly."

Adolf stomped out of the room, and Doc said, "You'd better not be pulling a fast one." After examining him, he said, "You know without an X-ray I can't verify how serious your concussion is, which well may be the source of your problems. If you're faking, you're doing a good job. But you won't be able to lose the codeine tomorrow. Einstein will carry it and dole it out. We have too much at stake. Do you read me?"

With his shoulders slumped and his eyes half closed, Dan tried to convince Doc he was miserable. "Now may I have some codeine?" He downed the medication. "I need to see Danny and Timmy, but I don't want them seeing me like this. Maybe if I can rest all afternoon, I'll feel better. Could they eat in here tonight?"

"I'll see." From the doorway, Doc said, "It's lunchtime. Would you like Cookie to fix you a sandwich?" After Dan shook his head, Doc said, "I'll close this so you can have a peaceful rest."

At least he'd fouled up Adolf's scheduled heists for today. Would he be able to do the same tomorrow?

Sleeping sounded great, but right now he had a job to do. *Thanks, Doc, for shutting the door. Now I won't have to keep glancing over my shoulder at the slightest noise.* If he heard footsteps or the jiggle of the doorknob, he'd have time to hide what he was writing. He eased off the bed and quietly stretched the chain behind him as he crossed the room to the table. He retrieved the packet of gum and the purple crayon from his trousers. Seated, he pondered how much to convey on the fewest wrappers possible. Dropping too many could prove dangerous. Except for the hair, Einstein resembled the scientist. Within ten minutes, he finished, satisfied he'd done his best. One clue understood was better than none. The throbbing at his temples told him he'd used his brain enough. He really did need sleep. He relaxed the second his head hit the pillow.

Dan awakened with a throbbing headache. Surprised to have fallen asleep, he stared at his watch in disbelief. He'd slept the afternoon away. He heard the boys' bedroom door close and recognized Doc's footsteps in the hallway. When he sat up, he put his hands against his temples and was glad to see a glass of water in Doc's hand.

"I knew you'd be hurting when you woke up. I'm glad you were able to rest. Both times I checked on you, you were snoring. Adolf agreed to your request. You can eat dinner with your sons in here and without me."

"What about the chain? The boys don't know."

Doc withdrew a key from his shirt pocket and removed the chain. The bolt was embedded next to the dresser, and Doc was able to shove most of the links behind. "Maybe they won't notice. The dresser should block their view since the card table is in the corner. I'll go get them."

Too surprised to question this sudden break, Dan could only nod. After Doc left, Dan gazed heavenward, his eyes seeing only the rafters, his heart the realm beyond. "Thank you, Lord, for making me feel better and for softening Adolf's heart so I can spend time alone with my sons. It bothers me that I have to keep up this pretense. It probably won't faze Timmy, but Danny's quick to notice when someone's not feeling well. He's so tenderhearted. I don't want him to worry. Please let him only see that I'm tired."

He wished he didn't have to cut short what few precious minutes he'd have with his sons, but convincing the gang now was imperative if he wanted them to believe his passing-out-act tomorrow. Dan wondered about Adolf's change of heart. Why would he let the boys eat in here without Doc? *Because my room is bugged, and he wants to listen.* Alert to this possibility, Dan planned to monitor his words while they ate. He relished being unchained and alone with them.

Did Adolf trust him not to grab the boys and bolt? *No way. On the remotest possibility I had a chance, where could I run? How far would I get with seven mad dogs on my heels? Adolf will never give me a chance. He'll have his guard dogs on patrol.* He pictured Lefty stationed at one end of the hall, Muscles posted at the other. "Lord, I know what lies ahead for me. Still, I must cause a delay to give the police time. If Adolf discovers what I'm doing, he'll be angrier than he is now. Please let him take his wrath out on me. Please protect Danny and Timmy." He recognized Doc's quick footsteps in the hall. The boys burst through the doorway with Doc gripping their hands, trying to restrain them.

Dan dropped to his knees with outstretched arms. Doc released the boys. "I do believe they missed you."

Kissing each, Dan said, "And I've missed both of you."

Danny looked up. "Are you okay? Doc said you weren't feeling well."

"I'm fine," he said, hugging him.

His five-year-old gazed deeply into his eyes. "Are you sure?"

"Yes, Danny, my sweet tenderhearted son, Daddy wasn't sick, only tired." When he picked up Timmy and stood, the three-year-old nestled against Dan's chest and smiled with contentment. Dan kissed his forehead. "No father could love his sons more than I do." He glanced at Doc.

The man's eyes glistened with moisture. "Cookie will be here soon."

Dan held the boys' hands while he said the blessing. Afterward, he looked up to see Doc gone and Cookie hurrying in with a tray of covered plates.

Danny lifted his lid first. "Goody, spaghetti and meatballs."

"Thanks, Cookie, you know my boys pretty well."

Cookie grinned. "They requested it…said it was one of your favorite dishes too. Doc told me to bring in the heater. I'll be right back."

Dan welcomed the warmth. He'd adjusted to the frigid room but silently thanked Doc for being considerate.

Danny stopped devouring his spaghetti. "We had fun today. Cookie took us outside to slide down the hill. He said he'd try to have someone buy us a sled."

The boys talked excitedly, relating what they had done all day with Cookie. Pleased they were being well-cared for, he relaxed and listened. He wanted to romp and roughhouse with them but settled for telling them a story.

When Doc entered, Dan hugged and kissed each boy. "I'm a little tired. I'm going to let Doc take you back and get you ready for bed."

"Daddy," Danny said, "can we go to Santa's Village with Mr. Adolf and his son? Cookie wouldn't let him take us today. He said we needed your permission. Mr. Adolf promised he'd take us day after tomorrow. Can we go?"

"Please, Daddy," Timmy begged.

Over my dead body. The bitter truth hit him. Adolf planned to kill him and take his sons. He stared at Doc, too overcome to speak.

"You boys will be home," Doc said. "You know, I bet your grandparents would love to take you."

Danny beamed. "Would they, Daddy?"

Dan nodded, fighting anger, fear, and frustration.

"Are you okay?" Danny asked.

"Just tired. I'm glad you'll be home soon." He knelt and drew them close. "I love you with all my heart."

"Why are you sad?" Danny asked.

Dan managed a wink and a faint smile. "Because you'll get to see Mommy before I will. Tell her I love her."

Danny's face puckered. "When will you get home?"

"I'm not sure." He embraced them, his heart shedding the tears he held back. "Don't forget to say your prayers." Fearing he would break down, he rose quickly and gave Doc a nod.

"Your father needs to get some rest. Run along and choose a story for me to read. I'll be there in a minute." The boys dashed down the hallway. "Train book," Timmy said. "No, the one about…"

Dan's chest constricted as he stared at the empty doorway. Helpless to protect his sons, he bit down on his lip. *Lord, I can't stop*

Adolf. I can't stop him from doing vile things to Danny and Timmy. Only You can.

Doc gestured him across the hallway into the bathroom and shut the door. "This room isn't bugged."

Dan trembled. Doc gripped his shoulders and squeezed until Dan winced. The pain snapped him out of his morose state, but he couldn't stop shaking.

"I promise your sons will come to no harm. Cookie and I may be crooks, but we do have principles. You do your part and get that money, and we'll make sure they get home."

"Even if I'm dead?"

"Yes." Doc shook his head sadly and said gently, "Now back to your room." Doc followed him and picked up the heater.

Adolf burst into the room. "Why isn't he chained?"

"I was going to check on the boys and come right back."

"Give me the key."

Doc forked it over and hurried out. Dan started breathing hard. His hands balled into tight fists. Adolf chuckled. "Something wrong...nerves a little taut? You look as if you'd like to kills me. But you won't raise a finger, will you? You know I'd make good my threat. Do you think Doc and Cookie can prevent me from letting Needles play with your sons?" He leaned against the door frame and laughed. "Too angry to speak? Santa's Village really got to you. I probably won't take them there, but we will visit wonderful places all over the world. They'll be well educated and have many pleasurable experiences. Different strokes for different folks." He laughed again. "Come on, boil over. Strike out. Let me unleash Needles."

Dan regained his composure. Adolf had been listening and visualizing his torment. Now he had come to taunt. "You make me sick."

"Can't you ever come up with something better than that? Come on. Damn me to hell." When Dan said nothing, Adolf said, "We'll see what tomorrow brings." He remained in the doorway, turning the key over and over.

Why doesn't he come in and shackle me?

"Your sons didn't notice the chain...how thoughtful of Doc to hide it."

Muscles rushed into the room, and Adolf tossed him the key he'd been fiddling with. "Chain Baker."

He was waiting for Muscles. He's afraid I'll attack him. Dan stood still, ignoring the click of the padlock around his ankle. He watched Adolf walk to the closet where clothes hangers now hung on nails. He lifted a shirt off of one and trousers from another and draped them over his arm. At the dresser, he opened a drawer but took his time before grabbing clean underwear for Dan. Why? Dan shifted his weight. What kind of a game was Adolf playing?

Was he looking for something? Did Adolf now suspect Cookie and Doc of treachery since they hated his lifestyle?

"These should do quite nicely," Adolf said, holding up a long-sleeved maroon shirt and navy trousers. "You do want to look your best tomorrow." He laughed. "Maybe I should loan you a white tie. But then, no one is going to see it under your jacket." He gave Dan a mocking smile. "You could wear it for dinner tomorrow night. Did I mention we're having a Thanksgiving feast? I know it's early, but you won't be around to have one later." He took the clothes and draped them over a chair, taking time to smooth a few wrinkles. "Muscles, I don't think I needed you to stay after all. Baker has really learned to control his temper. Needles will be so disappointed. Maybe Baker will be edgier tomorrow night. I do hope Needles's plans won't spoil his last feast." He gave Dan a mocking salute. "Sleep well."

Dan fought clenching his hands until the two men left. His temples pounded. He needed to vent his anger or go mad, but he refused to give Adolf or anyone else cause to laugh if they were listening. Dan beat the air with his fists in silent rage and sank to his knees in exhaustion, his head on the floor. In despair, he cried out to the Lord. Relief came—God's assurance he and his sons would be home soon, that the gang's triumph would be short-lived.

When Cookie came in to collect the dishes, he stared in surprise. "You seem calm. Doc said you were breaking down. He thought Adolf might have pushed you over the edge."

"He almost did, but I have a wonderful God who's given me peace and assurance that He's in control, that my sons and I will be home soon. I know you and Doc are committed to this racket, and

I'll have to trust God to deal with you later, but I want to thank you both for taking good care of Danny and Timmy."

Cookie shrugged, gathered the dishes, and said before leaving, "The boys made Doc kneel with them while they said their prayers."

Doc never mentioned a word about it when he came to give Dan the sedative. Dan studied the man's countenance, hoping to catch a glimpse of anything to show Doc's concern about his spiritual condition. He toyed with the idea of bringing up the matter. *Maybe it will be better to let the boys' prayers soften Doc's heart.*

Doc set his black bag on the card table and opened it. "You okay?"

Dan nodded. "Cookie told me you thought I was close to losing it. I guess I was. Adolf's saying he was going to keep my sons and raise them in his lifestyle did send me into a tailspin. But God is good, Doc. He's given me the assurance Adolf will not lay one finger on my boys."

"What about you. Is God going to save you?"

Dan shrugged. "That's up to Him. I don't want to die. I want to grow old with Cindy, watch my sons become men and play with my grandchildren. My plans may not be His plans."

"You're not afraid of Needles slowly killing you?"

"I'd be stupid not to be. I hate pain. Right now, my head aches like crazy. The torment Needles could inflict gives me the hereby jibes. But he can only stop my heart. He can't destroy my soul. Death is victory, not defeat."

"Do you expect me to say bravo?"

"Hardly, I know you're committed to this scheme, but I can't stop wishing otherwise."

Doc rolled his eyes. "Want me to bring you the wishbone after dinner tomorrow?"

Dan managed a chuckle. "If I thought that would answer my prayers, I'd gladly pull that wishbone with you."

"Take off your shoes and roll up your sleeve. I need to rejoin the others."

After Dan did so, he said, "I take it I have to sleep in my clothes tonight."

"That's right. Adolf didn't give me back the key."

Dan studied the doctor's face while he injected the sedative.

"What are you thinking, Baker? You'd better not be plotting some way to foul up our plans. Let me make one thing clear. Money is my god." He grabbed his bag and hurried out.

Dan glanced at his watch—seven-thirty. The sedative lasted eight hours, which meant the gang planned to get another early start and hit each store quickly. His last thought was—*I've got to give the cops more time.*

A throbbing headache awakened Dan Friday morning. When the light flipped on, his hand flew to shield his eyes. He winced. Doc entered with a glass of water. "I figured you'd be hurting." Dan sat up to gulp down the tablets as Doc, unlocking the padlock, said, "The bathroom's empty. Adolf is in a hurry."

Dan eased off the bed, feigning dizziness. "I guess I'd better help you." He grabbed the clothes Adolf had laid over the chair and assisted Dan to the bathroom. "Want me to stay?"

"I'll be fine."

"You're sure?"

Dan nodded.

As soon as the door closed, he went into high gear. Before he stripped, Dan flushed the crayon and unwrapped gum down the toilet and placed the folded wrappers in the clean trousers. In the shower, Dan soaked in the luxury of being warm and clean. Dressed, clean-shaven, and hair combed, he was ready before Muscles pounded on the door, saying, "You've got ten seconds to come out."

Dan made it in five.

Muscles followed Dan, but didn't chain him. He sat at the table to keep an eye on Dan while Dan ate. Last night, despite his hunger, Dan had left most of his food. His stomach growled, and his mouth watered at the sight of the heaping plate of pancakes, but he only ate half of one. Muscles had stayed in the room to keep an eye on him, and Dan was positive the ex-boxer would report the fact to Adolf.

Muscles glanced at the pancakes. "Not hungry?"

"My stomach's still queasy."

The ex-boxer grabbed the plate, rolled the cakes up with his fingers, swished them in the syrup, and finished Dan's breakfast before Einstein entered. The customary routine followed—bomb, handcuffs, blindfold.

Lying face down in the van, Dan blotted out what might lie ahead. He wondered how Cindy was holding up. If he didn't make it, he knew she would manage. She was bright, attractive, and friendly. Whenever they went with Cap and Amanda to a police social function, men enjoyed talking to Cindy. Was he jealous? Yes, especially after Jonathan's birth when she became zealous about trimming her figure.

Dan tensed when someone turned on the radio. The bomb explosion on the freeway was again mentioned. Two people were sent to the hospital. Dan's hands doubled into fists. "Lord, why don't You act? Why are You putting me, my family, and innocent people through this torment? Strike Adolf and his cutthroats down! If I weren't handcuffed, I'd take care of these two."

Like you tried to kill Needles?

The words slammed his mind like Muscles had slammed his skull. The van grew stifling. Dan's chest constricted. Gradually, his breathing became easier. What had happened? Had the heat of his anger caused him to hyperventilate? Or had God caused it to remind him he'd become a pastor instead of a police officer because he never wanted to kill again? "Lord, forgive me. I feel so frustrated, so helpless. Give me strength and courage."

At the rendezvous area when the blindfold was removed, Dan saw Lefty and Einstein wearing the same disguises. Today's car was a silver-gray station wagon. A handicap plaque hung from the rearview mirror.

"Would you like to open the door for your mother?" Einstein asked in a falsetto voice.

Dan turned his back and climbed into the passenger seat.

Einstein said, "You're not very sociable this morning…nervous about this being the last day of your life?"

Was it supposed to be? Would it still be, even if he passed out to stall for time?

"Not even talking to your own mother," Einstein continued, "my, my, how disrespectful."

When Lefty took the Harbor Boulevard exit, Dan realized this was home turf. As a teenager, he'd worked as a box boy for Peterson's. Was Lefty headed there? Would Mac still be the manager? Mac had been the greatest. Whenever Dan felt depressed, he could count on Mac to say or do something to snap him out of it.

Dan took a fortifying breath when Lefty pulled into the small shopping center and parked in a handicap spot in front of the market Dan knew so well. "Okay, in you go." Lefty handed Dan the card. "Don't be slow. We have lots of territory to cover."

Before Einstein could tell him where the office was, the phone rang, and Adolf said, "I learned the manager will be at check stand 2. Apparently, he is helping out while his office is being painted. I don't like this, but we'll continue as planned. Baker, I will be close by."

A wave of panic hit Dan—Adolf would be watching. How could he pass the information now?

"You heard Adolf," Einstein said and hiked his thumb toward the market.

Dan made a change in plans as he strolled to the entrance. He saw Mac behind the counter and prayed he wouldn't acknowledge him. When he walked behind stand 1, he saw someone watching—Adolf in a different wig, but he didn't cancel his plans—just prayed his idea would work. His and Mac's eyes met briefly as Mac placed a closed sign on the counter. Dan withdrew the wrappers from his jacket pocket and pretended to slip—his right foot sliding forward, his arms flying across the counter to keep from falling. He dropped the wrappers behind the counter. "Whew," Dan said as he straightened. "You'd better have someone clean up this floor."

Mac said, "I will, sir. Are you okay?" After Dan nodded, Mac said, "Were you planning to make a purchase?"

"No, but I believe you have a briefcase for me."

Mac immediately looked alarmed. "Any identification?" After Dan showed him the card, Mac studied it and gave it back. He retrieved a briefcase and laid it on the counter but said, "You'll have to sign for it...store policy." He put a piece of paper in front of Dan that said we need the information from the first wrapper. He wrote quickly and laid the pen down. Mac angrily said, "And the date." As he pointed to the paper, his hand lowered, brushed Dan's, and slipped a disc under it. Dan enclosed three fingers around it, picked up the pen and awkwardly scribbled and put the disc in his pants' pocket before he grabbed the briefcase.

Outside, Einstein glared at him when he handed over the brief-case and card. Lefty said nothing as Dan slid onto the passenger seat, but Einstein ordered him to drive to the Shell station. "Mr. Adolf has some questions to ask Baker."

When Lefty pulled into the station and stopped, Dan saw Adolf waiting by his car. "Get out," Lefty said.

Adolf pointed to the restroom, and Dan had a sinking feeling when Muscles followed and waited outside. Adolf said, "What did you write on the paper?"

"The information the manager requested."

"You didn't put down the location of the hideout?"

Dan shook his head. "I don't know where the lodge is."

"Did he give you anything?"

"Why would he? I only came for the briefcase."

"Instinct tells me he did. Let's make sure. Hang your jacket on the door hook and raise your arms while I search your shirt."

Dan rolled his eyes. "How could he give me something? You were watching the whole time."

Adolf finished and glared at him. "Now strip...shoes, socks, everything."

Dan's spine prickled. While he stripped, Adolf searched his jacket, even under the lining when he discovered an open edge. Dan tried not to react. What would Adolf do when he found the tracking device in the pocket of his pants? He shivered in the damp room, too alarmed to be disgusted or embarrassed. At least he'd gotten rid of the incriminating gum wrappers. He cringed when Adolf searched his trousers and found the disc.

"Well, well, well. What do we have here? So, the manager did give you something. Get dressed." Adolf walked him to the car and told Einstein, "Pick out a target to blow up after Baker calls in and tells his father there will be another explosion because they tried to pass Dan a tracking devise. And, Baker, another stunt like that means your kids lose, and Needles wins."

Lefty handed Dan the phone. After Dan relayed the message, he pressed his head back and closed his eyes praying that Mac's store would not be destroyed or Mac hurt. He groaned in frustration.

"I suppose you'd like us to believe you're still having problems?" Einstein said.

"I could care less what you believe." He crammed all the weariness and misery into his voice he could. "Could I at least have some codeine?"

Einstein snorted. "No...not after that stunt."

"Then just let me rest." The confrontation with Adolf shattered Dan's nerves. He knew the chance he'd be taking if he kept to his original plan, but he had to do it, if only to end today's activities. He pressed his palms against his temples and moaned.

Lefty contacted Adolf and told him Dan was really hurting and that Einstein wouldn't give him any codeine. *Good, at least I've convinced someone.*

Einstein leaned over the seat and took the phone. "He'll live," he told Adolf. "The store is only a few blocks away. After he returns with the money, I'll give him the pills."

Lefty parked in front of Quick Spot, a convenience store. "Okay, Baker, do your thing."

Dan looked around in pretended confusion.

Einstein handed Dan the card and said, "Out."

Dan opened the door and held onto it for support. He stood motionless; his eyes closed.

Lefty emitted a low snarl. "Get moving. It's not that far."

Dan shot him an angry glance and let go. He took five steps and made a vain grab for the car fender before he collapsed.

Car doors opened and slammed. A hand gently patted his cheeks. "Danny boy, wake up. It's mother."

Someone said, "Call an ambulance."

"No need," Lefty interjected. "Help me get him into the car. It will be quicker if we take him. His doctor's only two blocks from here."

Dan went limp and hoped they wouldn't drop him. He couldn't believe Lefty was smart enough to think that fast. He'd better not underestimate the man again. Dan continued his unconscious act at the rendezvous spot while Muscles cuffed and blindfolded him. He heard Einstein tell Muscles to ride with Lefty, that he was going out to breakfast with Snow White.

During the ride to the hideout, Dan thought about Einstein's words. Who was Snow White? How did she figure in—police mole?

When the van stopped, he pretended to come around but acted groggy. After Muscles and Lefty assisted him into the lodge, Adolf bellowed, "Bring Baker in here."

The anger Dan read in his voice made his heart freeze.

12

All day Thursday, Cindy and Amanda had listened to every radio and TV news broadcast. Two explosions had occurred in the morning but not in the afternoon. Cap had called to say he would be there by seven for dinner. The minute they heard his car in the driveway, they hurried to the front door.

Cap shook his head in amusement when he entered. "You two look like…"

"Like eager beavers?" Amanda said as he hung his hat and coat on the hall-tree. She kissed him. "Any news?"

"How about letting me change and wash first while you get dinner on the table…okay?"

They nodded, and Cindy gave him a hug. "Are you sure we don't look like vultures?"

Cap chuckled. "The thought did cross my mind, but I like beavers better."

She and Amanda gave him a few minutes at the table to eat and relax, then they looked at each other as if on cue.

Cap grinned. "Okay, my eager beavers, I'll tell you what I know, but it's not much more than what you've heard on the news. So far, the media knows nothing about the extortion scheme. Law enforcement has refused to comment on the bombings. If the news media finds out and connects the two, they'll have a field day."

Cindy blurted, "Are Dan and the boys all right?"

"As far as we know, yes." He gave them a warning glance. "And I don't need to tell you anything else I say goes no further from this table. Dan retrieved money from three stores this morning. The

146

bombings were warnings for us to back off or else. So far, no one has been killed."

Amanda said, "There were no explosions this afternoon." Her eyes reflected Cindy's same fears when she asked, "Is Dan finished getting money for them? Are he and the boys in greater danger now?"

"No," Cap said emphatically. He reached out and laid his hands over theirs. "This gang wants a lot more money. We don't know why they quit today, but it does give us more time."

Around nine, Cindy carried Jonathan upstairs to put him to bed. She tucked the covers around him and patted his back until positive he lay peacefully in dreamland. He'd been restless while nursing, as if he sensed her tenseness. She hurried back to the living room to see Cap switching the TV to the ten o'clock news. The newscaster recapped the featured story about the bombings.

The broadcast over, Cap let down his recliner. "Think I'll turn in."

Amanda, sitting next to Cindy on the couch, patted her hand. "Don't stay up too late, dear child."

Cap chuckled as Amanda stood. "Cindy, get used to it. The longer you stay here, the more she'll mother you."

Cindy jumped up and hugged her mother-in-law. "Don't you ever stop." She gave Cap a scolding look. "Mothering me is one of the ways she shows love."

Cap's hands shot up in defense. "No offense intended. I was only stating a fact."

Cindy hurried to his side, gazed up at his rugged features, and grinned. "A gal can always use some fathering too."

Cap nodded before he threw his bear-like arms around her and kissed her cheek. He stood back with his hands on her shoulders, his eyes shimmering with tenderness. "The smartest decision I ever made…" He glanced at Amanda. "Let me rephrase that. The second smartest decision I ever made was to invite you to sit with us at that Christmas dinner. Did Dan ever tell you I chewed him out royally for being so chauvinistic that night?"

"He did, and I told him I wished my mother had been there to see my behavior. She would have turned me over her knee."

They exchanged warm smiles before Cap said, "God has been good to you and Dan. And," he added with deep conviction, "He will take care of him and the boys." He gave her a reassuring hug and whispered, "Don't stay up too late, dear child."

She watched them exchange loving smiles before they left. No woman could have better in-laws, she thought.

An hour later, Cindy climbed into bed. Exhausted but too tense to sleep, she propped her pillow against the headboard and stared at the sparkles in the white plaster ceiling. Had it only been five days since the thugs had kidnapped Dan, and four since Danny and Timmy were torn from her? How often had she heard people say "It's been an eternity since I've seen you." To her, this was an eternity.

She glanced at Jonathan sleeping peacefully in his crib. What if she only had him to see her through the rest of her life? The morbid thought made her heart cry out, "Please, Lord, bring my family back to me." She tried to push depressing thoughts aside and rest in the knowledge that God was in control.

Cindy studied the bedroom—Dan's old room. Amanda had done a masterful job of turning it into a gorgeous guestroom. Being surrounded by beauty should have lifted Cindy's spirits, but no trace of Dan remained. She longed to be home where she could feel Dan's presence, but staying in the old house, among five acres of orange and avocado trees, would be scary. They didn't have a watchdog, couldn't afford to feed another mouth. Dan wanted the boys to have a German shepherd. His salary barely paid for essentials. His dream was to tear down the Spanish-style stucco house and build a rambling ranch one.

Since Cindy saw this as an impossible dream, she never tried to thwart it. She loved the old-world charm of their home—the arched doorways, the living room's walnut-beamed ceiling. The living room as well as their bedroom had French doors accessing the courtyard. And no way could they destroy the huge rock fireplace with its two-inch thick obsidian mantle. Dan's grandfather had gathered the rocks from all over the United States. Cindy did understand Dan's feelings about the house. He'd grown up there, and the place still held haunting memories. When Cap and Amanda became his foster parents, and later after they adopted him, they made sure he didn't lose his only inheritance, despite his not wanting it.

Cindy had assumed, when she and Dan married, they'd move into the house right away. He refused. "How do you expect me to live in the place where my father killed my mother and I killed him?" Practicality won out when Dan accepted the youth pastor position in the small church only a mile away. Moving brought nightmares. One night she rolled over and realized he wasn't in bed. She found him sitting on the couch, sobbing.

After Danny and Timmy were born, fun times began to squeeze out bad memories. Dan laughed more, and his sons brought out his mischievous side she'd never seen, as if for the first time he could relax and be the child he'd never been allowed to be. Good memories—she and Dan had oodles of them. *If he brings up tearing down our old house, I'll remind him of what he'll also be destroying.*

On a positive note, Cindy fell asleep only to awaken an hour later sensing danger. After tossing and turning the rest of the night, she sat bolt upright in bed around daybreak. The premonition came so strongly that something major was going to happen today; she poured her heart out to the Lord, pleading for protection for Dan, Danny, and Timmy. She tried to go back to sleep but couldn't. She started thinking about why she had become a police officer. It wasn't the excitement that had drawn her but the need to make a difference—try to stop criminals and help victims.

When she was eighteen, God had allowed evil to befall her family, allowed them to be victimized, but He had used the situation to turn around the life of a young man.

Her parents owned a hardware store, and Cindy had caught their teenage employee stealing. Her father gave him another chance but fired the young man when he was caught again with his hand in the cash register. In retaliation, the kid threw a pipe bomb through the window, injuring her parents. Showing remorse during his court appearance, he said he'd done it on impulse. At a juvenile correctional camp, a counselor led him to the Lord. That young man went into the ministry and became a missionary in Indonesia.

The world needed more men like Dan and that counselor. *And I need to learn how to cope and not nag. I need to get back on the police force where I can again make a difference.* She wouldn't be able to do that until Jonathan was older. Right now, she would have to learn to be more patient.

Cindy fell back to sleep only to be awakened half an hour later by Jonathan's cries. After changing her little one, she nursed him, hoping he'd fall asleep. He didn't. He loved having cereal. Maybe a full tummy would make him drowsy. After a restless night, she couldn't face keeping up with his infant demands.

In the kitchen, still half asleep at the table, Cindy offered Jonathan the last spoonful of cereal. Amanda strolled into the kitchen, looking refreshed. She and Cap had risen around four, and Cindy had heard Cap leave at five. He'd started working longer hours after Dan was kidnapped. Amanda buttoned the cuff of her long-sleeved floral shirt. "Why don't you let me feed Jonathan? You had another bad night, didn't you?"

Cindy nodded and gazed at Amanda with admiration. "How do you do it? You rose hours before me but look as if you could spend all day shopping."

Amanda laughed. "I don't think I'm quite up to that, but I could take care of Jonathan while you go back to bed."

"Thanks for the offer, but I don't think I could sleep."

Amanda put an arm around her. "I know you're worried. I am too, but we have to trust God to take care of Dan and the boys." Her eyes reflected love and faith, but the care-worn lines in her face seemed deeper. "I really wish you'd lie down," Amanda said.

"When Jonathan falls asleep, I'll try to rest."

Around eight-thirty after nursing, Jonathan grew drowsy, but she continued to rock him and watched Amanda in her recliner reading her Bible. *I'm a pastor's wife, and I never seem to have time for meaningful daily devotions.* She stifled a yawn. Amanda closed her Bible. "Why don't you go lie down?"

Cindy nodded, carried Jonathan to his crib, and covered him with a blanket, tucking it securely. Oh, to be able to sleep like a baby—so at peace—no worries. Cindy's fears descended the moment she stretched out and closed her eyes. Like vultures, they dropped to claw and tear at her mind. Her premonition Dan was in danger had robbed her of rest last night. Now she sensed immediate peril. Her heart pounded. "Lord, help him. What's happening? Will I ever see Dan again? Will I ever be able to ask his forgiveness for all the words I threw at him in anger and frustration?"

A vision came. She saw a hunting knife flickering in the sunlight as a shadowy figure made slashing motions. Dan's image flashed, smeared in red. Cindy screamed. Jonathan started bawling. Amanda rushed into the room. "What's wrong?" She glanced at Cindy before picking up Jonathan. "Shh, it's okay." Sitting on the edge of the bed, she asked over the baby's crying, "What's wrong?"

"Dan! He's hurt. I saw him covered with blood!"

"You were dreaming."

"I wasn't asleep!"

Horror replaced the concern on Amanda's pale face as she rocked Jonathan to quiet him. When he fell asleep, she put him in the crib and embraced Cindy. "We mustn't give in to our fears. Dan's told me that your premonitions usually have validity, but...but I know God will take care of him and the boys. Maybe Dan won't be unscathed when God brings them back to us, but they will be home soon. God gave me that assurance while I prayed."

"I want so much to believe that. There's so much I need to tell Dan."

When the baby whimpered, Amanda said, "Let's go down to the kitchen where we can talk without disturbing Jonathan."

While Amanda set two mugs on the table and poured coffee, Cindy tried to put her thoughts into words. How much should she tell Amanda? Had Dan mentioned their problems? Probably not. Amanda took the seat across from Cindy and stirred her coffee as if waiting for Cindy to begin. "I...I need to ask Dan to forgive me," Cindy said. "I've been a shrew lately. I guess ever since Jonathan was born." As she thought back, she realized she'd begun to nag Dan right after she'd conceived Jonathan.

Amanda reached across the table and patted Cindy's hand. "Don't be so hard on yourself. Taking care of three little boys would tax anyone, and I don't think you've recovered your strength since Jonathan's birth."

"I wish I could blame it on that, but I can't. It's just that…" Cindy didn't know how to say it other than bluntly. Would Amanda understand, or would she take offense? "Dan never has time for me except in bed." The loving concern she saw on Amanda's face gave her courage to continue. Her words tumbled out. "I try to be a good pastor's wife. Every day I work hard to keep the house neat, the kids and me presentable, and make sure homemade goodies are on hand in case anyone drops by. Dan manages to be home by six so we can eat as a family, then he romps with the kids until he has to go to a meeting or to counsel someone. Sometimes he doesn't get home until after midnight. He's not only a teen and family counselor but he's become chief visitation pastor because he's always willing to step in when others can't."

Cindy's tongue crept between her teeth as she fought back tears. "Amanda, I've tried to be patient. Really, I have. Dan's heart will always be pure as gold, but I'm becoming resentful."

"Have you told Dan how you feel?"

"No."

"Why not?"

"How can I? He has enough pressure. My feelings aren't important. I've just got to learn how to deal with my frustrations."

Amanda shook her head. "Cindy, communication between man and wife is crucial to a good marriage. Life wasn't easy for me when Dan came to live with us. He had so many hang-ups. He blamed himself for his parents' death. His self-esteem was nil. I tried to be patient and loving. I bent over backward not to put stress on him. The girls resented Dan's not having to live under the same rules Cap and I set for them. I became extremely frustrated. And I didn't tell Cap. I didn't want to put more stress on him."

"But you learned how to handle the situation."

Amanda shook her head. "I exploded at the dinner table. I don't even remember what set me off, but I lashed out at everyone… unleashed my frustration like a mad pit bull. Once, I verbally started shaking my family by the throat, I couldn't stop. Cap carried me to our room, set me on the bed, and held me until I calmed down."

Cindy couldn't believe what Amanda had shared. She'd never heard her utter a cross word. "You're making this up."

"I wish I could say yes, but I can't. A Christian marriage counselor helped us. We learned how to communicate, how to confront in love…confront without attacking."

"And you think I need counseling?"

"You need to tell Dan how you feel. A man's priorities should be God first, wife and family second, work and others third."

"Are you implying that Dan has his priorities mixed? I can't buy that. I'm just being selfish about sharing him with too many people, people he can help. I need to learn to be more patient."

"Until you explode? Talk to Dan. Explain how you feel. Let him find balance." She rose. "I'll be right back." She returned with some books. "Look through these. They're on the art of communication."

Cindy carried them into the living room and thumbed through one. The pages blurred as tears filled her eyes. In her mind, she saw the bloodied image of Dan. But she didn't sense pain. Was he dead? She rose quickly. *I've got to get out of the house, do something—anything but sit and think.*

Grocery shopping for Amanda helped her endure the slow passage of time. When she returned, she noticed the stroller missing. On the kitchen table, Cindy found a note from Amanda saying Cap was coming home to take a nap, so she decided to take Jonathan to the park. "Drive over to the park. We'll go out to lunch."

After Cindy put the food away, she grabbed her purse to go meet Amanda. When she heard Cap pull into the driveway, she opened the door for him. "How come you're home?"

"To get a little shut eye. Things appear to be at a standstill."

"Is Dan okay?"

"As far as we know. Amanda told me about your premonition."

"Reality, Cap. I've never had a sensation so strong. Dan's hurt."

"Then you know more than we do. When he entered Peterson's market, the manager said he seemed fine and managed to pass information. When he arrived at the next market, I want to stress here that I think Dan is stalling for time to give us a chance to work on the information he left."

"What happened?"

"He appeared to pass out. Two gang members carried him back to the car and drove off. All we can do now is wait."

"Wait? Oh, Cap, I'm scared. What if Dan is really hurt?"

He shook his head. "He was fine earlier. I'm positive he saw his chance to slow the gang down and grabbed it." He put his hands on her shoulders and looked deeply into her eyes. "We wait. We have to trust God and Dan's good sense." He kissed her forehead. "Now go meet Amanda, have a good lunch, and try not to worry. I'm going to take a nap. After you return, I'll tell you both the latest." He opened the door and pointed. "Your escort will follow."

*****

Cap watched Cindy drive away. How much should he tell them? He couldn't tell them about the failed attempt to pass a tracking device to Dan, nor could he let on how much Cindy's premonition bothered him.

In his recliner, he closed his eyes and tried to do what he had told Cindy—trust God and Dan's good sense. "Lord, that's a tall order. I trust You, but I also know what Dan is now up against. Oh, God, protect him, calm his fears, and give him the courage to face whatever lies ahead. Please protect Danny and Timmy from Adolf and his son…please, Lord, Amen."

Dan had identified the leader of the gang as Adolf, a man who looked like Hitler, and his son had AIDS. Years ago, Cap had testified against a man who could have been Hitler's twin. The man was sentenced to fifteen years in prison. Upon being taken away, his teenage son had gone berserk and attacked Cap. It had taken two more officers to pin him down. His mother revealed later that her husband was having sexual relations with her son. Counseling hadn't helped the boy—his lifestyle continued. He became a drug addict and ended up in prison for armed robbery. After he was released, he lived on the streets. Apparently, Adolf took him in and is now blaming me for the problems he created.

Exhausted, Cap nodded off. The front door opening and closing awakened him. Not ready to face the women, he kept his eyes closed while they walked past him.

He heard Cindy say, "I'll put Jonathan to bed and come back down to help you with dinner."

"I cut up most of the vegetables earlier, but you can clean the chicken."

Cap rested his eyes twenty more minutes before he lowered the recliner and strolled to the kitchen. They were putting the prepared items into the refrigerator. "Soup or stew?" he asked.

Mandy grinned. "One of your favorite dishes…chicken and dumplings. Have a seat. I have a sandwich for you."

Cap filled a mug with coffee and carried it to the table. Mandy set a plate down and gave him a hug. "Were you able to sleep?"

"A little," he said, kissing her before he sat down.

Mandy took the seat across from him, and Cindy hurried over to join them. Both looked at him with expectant faces. Mandy blurted, "What can you tell us?"

"Whoa, slow down…let me get awake first."

"I'm sorry, but we've been on pins and needles all day."

Cap nodded and took a sip of coffee as he mulled over how much to tell them.

Mandy said, "The news reported explosions early this morning. Five people were hurt. Why did the gang stop?"

"We don't know why they stopped yesterday, but we do know why they quit today. I already told Cindy that Dan managed to give us information. I'm positive he pretended to pass out before he entered the next market to give us time to work on the information. If what I suspect is true, I now know why Dan and the boys were kidnapped. The man responsible is not only using this scheme to get money but also his revenge against me."

"Why?" both asked.

"Because after my testimony sent him to prison for fifteen years, his son got into lots of trouble and hooked on drugs."

"Honey, your suspicions are too farfetched. You were only doing your job."

155

"I agree," Cindy said.

Cap shrugged. "Maybe you're right, but that's the only logical reason I can come up with." *And may you never know the whole truth until Dan and the boys are home safe and sound.* "Since things seem to be at a standstill, I won't have to go back to the station, but I'll keep in touch."

When the phone rang, Cap answered, recognized the voice, and pushed the speaker button. "Yes, Pastor Richards, what can I do for you?"

"Would it be okay if some of the young people came over tonight around seven to hold a prayer meeting? They're very concerned about Dan and the boys. They said, 'No refreshments...we just want to pray with your family.'"

"Pastor, tell them yes...we welcome them and feel honored to have them."

Mandy said, "They want to pray with us...what a wonderful way to show how much they love Dan. Did the pastor say how many are coming?"

"No, but I'll bring the dining room chairs into the living room and start a fire in the fireplace. It's chilly tonight."

*****

Cindy stared in amazement when Cap ushered in over twenty teenagers and a few parents. The adults took seats, but all the young people sat on the rug. She found it hard to believe so many teenagers would come on an evening that didn't include food and frivolity. A few had come from other churches. Pastor Richards offered encouraging words before he prayed. As soon as he finished, the teenagers began praying.

Cindy's eyes misted as she listened. Young men and women shared their testimonies of how Dan had led them to the Lord or back to the Lord. Many said Dan's counseling had helped and encouraged them. Cindy's heart went out to these young people who loved Dan. Surely God wouldn't allow his ministry to cease. But hadn't there been missionaries killed whose work was equally important? God had allowed them to be slain before He turned the situation around…more people had accepted Christ after their death than before.

Tears streamed down Cindy's cheeks. "But, Lord, I need Dan and the boys." She took courage and added, "not my way, Lord, but Yours."

*****

Cap said after everyone left, "I feel so blessed to know that there are so many young people who love Dan…to know how many kids he's helped." He gazed at Mandy. "We have a wonderful son and, Cindy, I'm positive God will bring him and the boys home soon."

"Oh, Cap, the vision I had of Dan covered with blood still scares me, but after hearing those teenagers, I have to believe God will answer our prayers as well as theirs. I just pray that Dan isn't suffering."

When the phone rang, Cap rose to answer, but he didn't put it on speaker. He listened and said, "I agree. If I don't need to come down to the station, I'll stay here." He returned to his recliner and said, "We need to listen to the ten o'clock news. Ware Mart had an explosion in the store where the money was delayed, and Dan had go back to retrieve it. From now on, all the couriers will have a police escort."

The breaking news was the explosion. A nearby reporter had rushed to the scene for exclusive pictures of the destruction and the injured. She recorded the manager's words before he passed out. "I know who did this. I gave him the money, but he destroyed the store anyway."

When Cap saw their horrified faces, he said, "Calm down. Don't go into panic mode."

Cindy blurted, "Calm down? Dan's been recognized. They'll kill him. They don't dare chance his being spotted and causing a panic in a store before he can get the money."

Mandy said, "The news media has his picture and will blast it everywhere."

"But it's not a good picture, and the manager didn't say Dan's name. Officers were rushed to the hospital to speak to him before he does...let him know how crucial it is for him to say nothing to reporters...that we need time to rescue Dan and the boys. He doesn't know other stores have been targeted, nor does the news media know, and we want to keep it that way."

Tears streaming, Cindy said, "Won't they kill Dan and use someone else?"

Cap shook his head. "As a precaution, Adolf will probably have Dan dressed differently so he won't be noticed, but he will still use him. He knows how much Dan being forced to do this hurts me. He wants Dan to retrieve every penny of that money."

13

Supported between Lefty and Muscles, Dan stood in the hideout living area, pretending not to be aware of his surroundings.

"All right, Baker," Adolf said, "listen and listen well. Either you're a good actor or you're ill. I intend to know the truth. Open your eyes and look at me. Now!"

Dan blinked a few times before he looked up and saw Doc enter with Danny and Timmy. The boys pulled their hands free of his grasp, only to be caught by Adolf. "Not so fast, boys...can't you see your father's not feeling well? Doc, take them outside to play." The savageness in his voice made Dan stiffen.

"Daddy, we don't have our snowsuits on," Danny said. "It's cold out."

Dan remembered the icy wind that had blasted him, but he remained silent. *There has to be a way out of this. Think! Don't panic!*

"I'm waiting, Baker. What's it to be...snowsuits or no snowsuits? It's your decision. How long they stay out depends on how long it takes you to answer."

Sagging in defeat, Dan said, "Doc, would you please put their snowsuits on them."

Adolf nodded to Doc who took the boys by the hand and led them from the room. Dan watched until they entered the hallway before he turned to ask, "What now?" His heart did a double-take. Needles stood gleaming with anticipation, fingering a sharp hunting knife. His smashed jaw kept him quiet, but Dan needed no words to relay the junkie's intention.

"Not yet, Needles," Adolf said. "After Baker finishes his errands, then we'll get our revenge."

"Revenge? You kidnapped my sons and me for revenge? Why?"

"If I could have turned your head with money, your death wouldn't be necessary. Seducing you into becoming my son would have been much more to my liking." He turned to Needles. "You always wanted a brother. Let's see if we can buy you one. Giving a man options is always fair. Bring me the last batch of money." Needles's scowl showed he didn't want Dan for a brother. He stomped out of the room, returned with a suitcase, and laid it on the table.

Doc entered with the boys dressed in their snowsuits, and he in his heavy parka and boots.

"Before you take them out to play," Adolf said, "show them the money."

"Why?" Doc asked.

"I want them to feel it…smell it…crave it. The money will be theirs if their father chooses not to have it."

Doc led them to the table and opened the suitcase. Adolf put an arm around each boy and smiled like a benevolent grandfather. "Think about all the things you'd like to have. I can buy you everything you want."

Dan seethed at this ploy to win his sons. Danny lifted a bundle and fingered it. Timmy picked up another.

Danny's eyes glowed. "We can both have bikes," he said.

"Even a small motorized car," Adolf said, "anything your heart's desire."

Danny put his money down. "Let Daddy have it. He and Mommy need money. That's what they fight about. They'll buy us what we need."

Dan stood shocked, but proud—shocked to learn Danny had overheard him and Cindy quarreling—proud, because of the unselfishness in his son's heart.

"Even small motorized cars," Adolf said, "anything your hearts desire." When the sliding glass door closed, he smiled in amusement. "They can still have all they want. With a cool million, you can send money to your wife and youngest son while you show Danny and

Timmy the world. I'll treat you well. I'll play grandfather to your sons, which I'll do anyway, with or without you." Dan said nothing, refusing to be baited. "You could even visit the Holy Land. Isn't that what preachers dream about?" He laughed his cruel vicious laugh. "Too overcome to speak? What's it to be...son or not to be my son?"

Dan shook his head in disgust. "I pity Needles having you for a father. No wonder he turned to drugs and acquired AIDS."

Adolf's nostrils flared, his black eyes shot darts of hatred. "My son has AIDS because of your father. His testimony sent me to prison when my son needed me most."

"That's a cop-out, and you know it. How long has he used you, Needles...from puberty? A loving father would never treat his son like yours treats you." Dan's agitation made his heart thud against the bomb.

Needles raised the knife. Sunlight flashed across the gleaming steel. Adolf caught his arm. "Not now, tonight." His commanding tone made Needles lower the blade. Adolf's last word suddenly registered on Dan's brain. "Yes, tonight," Adolf said. "Did you think your ploy canceled our plans for today? You've merely changed them. We're waiting for Einstein to plant a few more bombs after he and Snow White eat breakfast. Yes, there is a Snow White. She didn't have an alias until you provided one."

The door banged open and slammed shut. Einstein rushed into the room breathless and angry. Adolf's eyes went wide. "What are you doing here?" he demanded. "Why aren't you planting bombs?"

"They're planted, and I have an even bigger explosion ready to deter the cops." He gave Dan a furious glance. "Your preacher here passed information."

"He what? How?"

Dan's heart froze as Einstein continued. "At breakfast, my girl said she heard he'd written on gum wrappers. She didn't know what...only that the cops will be watching the main roads into the San Bernardino Mountains."

"What did he write with?" Adolf asked, turning his attention to Dan.

"A crayon." Einstein spat the word.

Black eyes bored into Dan's as Adolf's lips grew so tightly compressed, he looked ready to explode.

Dan swallowed hard. His courage waned. He could take the man's ramblings, but the silence grated his nerves. What retaliation was he plotting?

Lefty, Muscles, and Cookie shifted glances between Adolf and Dan as if waiting for fireworks to begin.

"What are we going to do?" Einstein asked. "He guessed right where the hideout is."

Adolf shifted his gaze to his men who looked worried. "It may cost us extra time, but we can skirt around them."

"They'll have the stores staked out," Lefty blurted.

Adolf rolled his eyes. "They've always been covered. That's why Einstein's planting bombs. Nothing's changed. And once we start our errands, I'm banking on the cops being concerned about people getting hurt to the point they'll just watch us until we're finished, then concentrate on catching us. We've got our bases covered. Relax."

They nodded as if satisfied.

When Adolf pivoted, Dan found it hard to breathe. "Now, for you...you've annoyed me for the last time. I'm going to have Doc bring your kids back in. You have a choice...either you take their snowsuits off and shove them back outdoors to play, or I'll let Needles undress them in their room. If you say one word to your boys, Needles wins."

Dan watched Needles's eyes grow unusually bright, and he licked his lips as Adolf took quick strides to the glass door, slid it back, and yelled, "Doc, bring the boys here." Danny and Timmy ran to Dan as he knelt to receive his sons, hugging them in anguish.

"We had fun," Danny said. "We're helping Doc build a snow fort."

Dan contemplated their next stay outdoors as he unzipped Timmy's snowsuit and helped him out. He prayed his sons could sense his torment.

Danny sat on the floor to pull his off. He looked up. "Daddy, what's wrong?"

Dan bit down on his lip and helped Danny to his feet. He glared at Adolf as he took his sons by the hand and led them back to the door. As he gazed into their troubled faces, he mouthed "I love you," opened the sliding door, and turned them toward the icy air.

"No, Daddy," Danny cried. "It's too cold."

They fought to keep from being pushed outside, but Dan's strength prevailed. He gave one last shove and closed the door. The bitter wind blasted him, sending icy jabs through his heart. His tears matched theirs as he watched them pound on the glass, begging to be let inside.

"Come here," Adolf ordered.

"God protect them," Dan prayed to regain his composure before he turned to face their tormentor. He took his time walking toward Adolf, wishing he were holding a gun. Vow or no vow, this man deserved to die, and Dan wanted to pull the trigger. He saw Needles's eyes no longer glowing with anticipation. Robbed of two boys to play with, he'd gone back to fingering the knife. Lefty and Muscles gazed at Adolf as if awaiting orders. The fate of Dan's sons didn't appear to concern them. Dan saw Doc and Cookie in the kitchen. Maybe they couldn't bear the sight of two miserable boys.

"Stand next to me," Adolf said. "Watch your sons suffer. Do you think they'll love you for being so cruel? Instead they'll love me. I will let them in and give comforting words while I rub their cold little backs before I send them to Cookie for warm soup and hot chocolate. Look at your sons one last time. Remember them well and carry this picture to your grave. You've managed to gain a one-day reprieve, but you'll not enjoy it with your sons."

Danny and Timmy no longer pounded on the glass. They pressed their noses against it and cried.

Black slits of steel narrowed in on Dan. "What information did you pass? Did you write San Bernadine Mountains on that paper?" When Dan hesitated, he yelled, "Answer me."

Dan knew he'd lost. For his sons' sake, he had to reveal something. "I only gave the information the Feds wanted. They couldn't decipher the first wrapper, so I wrote…Leader-Hitler look-alike. I did put S B Mts with a question mark on one."

"On the others?"

"H's son—AIDS on another and your descriptive names on the rest."

"You said nothing about the rendezvous area?"

Dan wanted to kick himself for not thinking about that. He shook his head.

Adolf glanced at the boys then back to Dan. "I'm inclined to believe you, but your sons' lives are in jeopardy. Are you positive?"

"Yes. For what it's worth, I didn't think about it. Please let my sons in." Dan watched in torment until he could stand no more. "I yield. Isn't that what you want? I'll cry uncle or whatever you say. I'll do anything you want."

"Anything?" Adolf smiled with smug satisfaction. "You and Needles? Now that's an interesting prospect."

With hatred spewing from his eyes, Needles shook his head and made slashing motions with his knife.

Adolf laughed. "I think he has other plans. Anything you said. You and me?"

Dread and revulsion raced through Dan, robbing him of breath.

"Anything?" Adolf's tone demanded an answer.

Dan bowed his head and closed his eyes as he nodded.

"Look at me when I'm speaking. Are you willing to become my son?"

Dan knew what being held Adolf's prisoner entailed. This had to be one of Adolf's empty threats, another mind game. The vileness made him want to vomit. To protect his sons, he'd promise anything and trust God to deliver them from Adolf's ruthless plans.

Adolf tapped his foot. "Well?"

Dan's eyes flashed, but he said calmly, "If you and Needles leave my sons untouched and return them to their mother, I'll come away with you."

"Good. To tame Daniel, the lionhearted would be quite a challenge. I'll consider that after I let my grandsons in. Poor little tykes must be cold. They'll love me for saving them." After he slid the door open, his arms encircled the boys. "You poor dear boys, that was mean of your daddy to shove you outside." He pulled them closer and kissed Timmy on the forehead.

When he started to kiss Danny, his son kicked Adolf in the shins. "You're the mean one."

Adolf yelped and swore as they ran to Dan.

Dan embraced his sons. He might never see them again but at least he knew they harbored no ill feelings against him. Adolf had fooled himself, not two small boys. He prayed Adolf would take his anger out on him, not Danny. He rubbed their backs in an effort to warm them as their teeth chattered.

Doc and Cookie rushed out of the kitchen. "We'll get the kids warm," Doc said, lifting Danny.

Cookie picked up Timmy. "I have hot soup ready."

They carried the boys to the kitchen and closed the door. Dan stared at the kitchen door, grateful his sons were being cared for but depressed at seeing them whisked away. Would he ever see Danny and Timmy again?

Needles tapped his father on the shoulder and pointed to the knife.

"I did promise you some fun, didn't I? Show Baker what you intend to do to him tomorrow night."

Dan's hair stood on the nape of his neck as he watched Needles pantomime. The act would have been comical if a clown had been performing. Needles wasn't clowning. His hacking, chopping, and slicing motions left nothing to Dan's imagination. He understood all too well that Needles wanted to dismember him alive—bit by bit.

Needles suddenly stopped. He nodded at Lefty, then Muscles. His malicious expression made Dan want to bolt. The muscle-men seized Dan's arms. Needles approached with slow, deliberate steps until Dan could gaze directly into the addict's eyes—ice blue pools of hatred as Needles fingered the knife blade. He reached for the zipper tab of Dan's jacket and inched it down. Holding the knife in his left hand aimed like a gun, he used his right to unbutton Dan's shirt from the bottom up, pausing between buttons to glare. When he came to the bomb, he lifted one corner of the shirt.

Dan knew Adolf wouldn't allow his son to kill him, but how far would he let him go? The torture of waiting raised beads of perspiration across Dan's brow. He swallowed hard and moistened his dry lips.

Adolf laughed. "I think you're getting to him."

Needles grinned with satisfaction. He placed the tip of the knife under Dan's right rib cage. A prick made Dan stiffen as the blade broke the skin. He willed himself to stand still. "Lord, give me courage," he prayed as the blade penetrated. His and Needles's eyes locked in mutual hatred. Dan's never wavered as the knife slid deeper. He fought to control his breathing and hide his terror.

"Enough, Needles!" Adolf ordered. "I'm sure Baker gets the point. Now back off!"

Needles's sadistic smile said, *Must I? I am so enjoying this.* He withdrew the knife and raked it across Dan's midsection, leaving a six-inch gash.

Dan clamped his mouth tight to keep from crying out.

Needles's lip curled, giving him a vicious, mad-dog look. Before he sheathed his knife, he wiped the bloody blade on Dan's shirt.

Dan couldn't explain the calmness that came over him, the sudden pity he felt for this man held in Satan's grip. Humanly speaking, it made no sense. Earlier in his hatred, Dan had wished for a gun. Now he didn't. "Needles, vengeance for what you've done is in God's hand," he said without a trace of venom. He could say no more. Lightheaded, he didn't dare glance down at the warm blood spilling over his skin. Seeing the bloody knife was enough.

A black veil obliterated his vision. Still standing, he could hear every sound but couldn't see.

"Help him to his room," Adolf said.

On the way back, Dan blinked over and over—nothing.

Lefty and Muscles stretched him out on the bed in his semiconscious state.

"Baker," Doc said after they left, "I'll give you a shot of Novocain before I stitch up your wound. I don't know why Adolf keeps his son around. He's demented, a menace to himself and this whole setup. Baker, look at me."

"Doc, I can hear, but I can't see."

"You're fighting against passing out. I have something that will help."

"I don't want anything. Just stitch me up and leave."

Doc began cleansing the wound. "How did you come up with the stupid gum-wrapper stunt? Where's the crayon now?"

The firm pressure Doc applied to stem the blood revealed his anger. Dan winced, but the pressure didn't stop, nor did Doc apologize. *Is he angrier with me than he is with Needles?*

"Do you expect a SWAT team to come rushing in to save you? Forget it. I bet it never occurred to you that Adolf holds the winning hand…that he has his ace planted. Now Einstein's planting more bombs to keep the cops at bay. He'll detonate them too. Don't act like you're not hearing me. Your expression shows you're grasping every word."

The black veil lifted, but Doc's image was blurred. Dan blinked to clear his vision, but he could do nothing to dispel his shakiness or queasiness. Miserable, he could only stare. In a gentler tone, Doc said, "Novocain's next. Man, your nerves have taken a beating. You're trembling. Looks like I'll be adding tranquilizers to your medication," he said, injecting Novocain close to the wound.

The throbbing in Dan's midsection eased, but his queasiness increased. He tried to relax, but he couldn't ignore Doc's tugs and pulls. He gazed at him in misery, fighting to hold out until Doc finished.

Their eyes locked, and Doc stopped stitching. "Can you make it across the hall?"

Dan nodded, not knowing whether he could or not, but barfing on the floor was better than doing it on the bed.

Doc helped him rise. "Go slow. Breathe deeply."

Dan made it to the bathroom and grabbed the rim of the wash basin. With one hand, Doc put pressure on the half-stitched wound. The other held the bomb firmly against Dan's chest to keep it from hitting the wash basin rim every time Dan leaned forward. Dan didn't know if he felt better or worse after the spasms produced nothing of consequence. Relieved when the spasms stopped, he sank to the closed toilet lid and pressed his back against the tank.

"You know," Doc said, "you've eaten next to nothing the past two days. Your shakes may be due partly to that. I'll have Cookie bring you some of the soup we gave Danny and Timmy."

"Are they all right?"

Doc smiled. "They're fine now. For a while, Danny kept yelling, 'Make those mean men leave my daddy alone. We want to go home.' They did some crying, but Cookie finally consoled them."

"Thanks to both of you. When I testify, I'll bring out your good points."

"You really do expect to be rescued, don't you?"

Dan nodded. "I don't know how God intends to do it, but His hand is better than Adolf's."

"Your naive faith amuses me. By the way, where's the crayon?"

"I flushed it."

"You're lying. It would float."

"Wrong. Try it."

Back in Dan's room, Doc finished stitching the gash in Dan's midsection and covered it with layers of gauze. "You'd better try and sleep after you eat, get all the rest you can. We're leaving extra-early, and you're going to need your strength."

"We're leaving? That sounds like you're coming?"

"I've been around each day. You never spotted me, did you?"

Dan shook his head.

"Tomorrow I'll take Einstein's place. He's staying in town with Snow White tonight and will keep in contact with her tomorrow."

"I have to sleep with this bomb?"

"You got it...your penance for dropping gum wrappers."

"What if I decide I've had enough and try to yank the bomb off?"

Doc stiffened. "Don't! You want to kill your kids too?"

"Then the bomb's for real?"

"You had doubts?"

"I was hoping this was one of Adolf's mess-with-my-mind-games."

"Well, it's not. None of us likes having explosives in the lodge."

Alarmed, Dan said, "Does Einstein keep the bombs here?"

Doc shook his head. "Adolf won't even allow him to have stuff in the car. What isn't destined to explode at the touch of his finger is stored within easy reach in Orange County." He pointed to Dan's chest. "That's the only bomb here, and we don't like knowing that any more than you like wearing it. At least Adolf makes Einstein keep the detonator in the car. Are you desperate enough to try blowing yourself up?"

Dan shrugged. Doc frowned but said nothing before he shackled him and left. That should give him something to think about, Dan thought, but knowing now that the bomb wasn't a hoax gave him more cause to worry too. Exhausted mentally and physically, he closed his eyes and tried to relax. His mind whirled in turmoil. He glanced at his watch—a little past eleven. How could so much have happened in such a short time-span, not just the events of the past hours but the last five days? How was Cindy coping? He wished they'd parted on better terms. He'd wanted Sunday night to be special, wanted to make up for not being there all week. What if he'd let her come with him? He was glad she hadn't, glad she was safe.

"You look tired," Cookie said, carrying a tray. "Want to eat in bed?"

Dan sat up. "No." The chain thudded to the floor as he eased off the mattress. Still lightheaded, he stood a few moments before walking to the table. He gazed at the chain in disgust as it slithered behind him like a loathsome snake.

Cookie set the tray on the card table and pulled out the opposite chair. "Doc told me to stay, make sure you eat."

Dan stared at the soup. The aroma aroused his taste buds, but he didn't feel like eating. He closed his eyes but couldn't give thanks for his food. "Lord, this is crazy. A condemned man being watched by a crooked cook who's been ordered by a crooked doctor to make sure the condemned man eats so he can have strength to finish running crooked errands before he's killed. But I think Doc and Cookie have open hearts. Help them see the error of their ways and come to You before it's too late. And give me strength for what's ahead...my trust is in You, Amen."

He gazed at Cookie and stirred the soup—chicken noodle. *Just what the doctor ordered.* The thought struck him funny. He started to laugh but clamped his left hand over his midsection. His laughter died to a moan.

"You okay?" The look Cookie gave him suggested he worried more about Dan's mind than his health.

"I haven't flipped, Cookie. It just struck me funny that you're babysitting me, and Doc orders me a kid's meal."

"Not quite. Taste it. I spiced yours."

Dan took a spoonful, grabbed the glass of milk, and gulped mouthfuls. "Wow, did you!" It perked Dan up and sparked his appetite. "I like it."

Cookie beamed. Dan finished the soup and started on the ham sandwich Cookie had brought. While he ate, Cookie talked about his childhood, how Doc always watched out for him, especially after their folks died.

"You're brothers?"

Cookie nodded. "We weren't lucky like you. We didn't end up with nice folks. We'll make sure Danny and Timmy get home. Needles wants them bad. He hates your guts."

Did Cookie know the room was bugged? Dan hoped no one was listening. Talk like that could get Cookie and Doc in trouble, maybe killed.

Cookie stood and stacked the dishes on the tray. "I told Adolf I'd still cook turkey for tonight and give them sandwiches tomorrow."

Dan had never heard the man talk so much. In the beginning, he hadn't talked at all. Now he seemed at ease. "I'll look forward to dinner tonight."

"I'll come eat with you. Not fair you eat alone."

Dan smiled and nodded. "I'd like that." After Cookie left, Dan stretched out on the bed. The soft spot in his heart asked, "How will I ever be able to testify against you?" He felt calmer. He didn't know if it was due to the food or to Cookie, but he knew he could now do as Doc suggested—sleep.

The scraping of a chair across the floor awakened him. He turned over and winced. The Novocain had worn off.

"You're hurting?"

The sound of Adolf's voice made Dan fume. He opened his eyes and saw Adolf sitting next to the bed. "What do you think?"

"The pain had better not keep you from working."

"Don't worry, you'll get your precious money, but you'll never spend a penny of it."

"Are you Daniel, the prophet now?" Adolf asked, raising one eyebrow.

Dan cocked his head. "Maybe I am."

"Then tell me, Prophet Daniel, am I taking you or your sons with me?"

"Neither. If Needles had his way, it would be my sons, but he'll never get the chance."

"Just as Doc said, you expect the cavalry to come charging in here. You are so naive. Like Doc told you, I have all the aces."

A picture flashed in Dan's mind—four aces, all black. "They're spades," he said more to himself than to Adolf. Amazed at the vision, he stared at Adolf and laughed. "All your aces are spades. You're not going to live to spend that money."

Adolf scooted the chair back and stood. "You've flipped. Doc said your nerves were playing havoc with you. They're playing havoc with your mind."

Dan held out his hand, praying it didn't tremble. It didn't. "Spades, Adolf. Four…black …aces of spades."

14

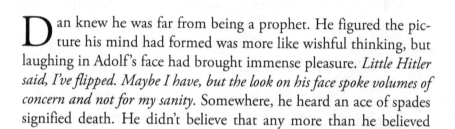

Dan knew he was far from being a prophet. He figured the picture his mind had formed was more like wishful thinking, but laughing in Adolf's face had brought immense pleasure. *Little Hitler said, I've flipped. Maybe I have, but the look on his face spoke volumes of concern and not for my sanity.* Somewhere, he heard an ace of spades signified death. He didn't believe that any more than he believed finding a penny would bring good luck. God had control over his life, not a card or a penny.

Is Adolf superstitious? If he is, maybe fear of death will make him slip up, bring about his own destruction.

Dan listened to the sounds coming from the living area—the clatter of dishes, muffled voices. He had no desire to eat with crooks, but he longed to share the warmth of their fire. He wished they would build one in the hearth facing this side of the lodge. The chain would prevent him from standing in front of the blazing logs, but at least some heat would reach him. He shivered and wondered if the weather had turned colder, or was he getting the shakes again. Were they due to loss of blood, or was his constant fear that Adolf might harm Danny and Timmy playing havoc with his nerves? Maybe Doc's right—they're due to not eating much. At least the codeine Doc gave him had made his headache go away, and his stitched midsection no longer hurt. Maybe he'd be able to enjoy his condemned man's last meal.

Cookie entered with a tray carrying two heaped plates, mugs, and a carafe of coffee. He set it on the table. "Be right back." He returned with a heater in one hand and pie in the other—two extralarge slices of pumpkin pie topped with whipped cream.

Despite the heartache of no longer being able to see his sons, Dan enjoyed eating an early Thanksgiving meal with Cookie. The chef had set the heater three feet away, directing it toward Dan, but he started shaking so much he had to hold his coffee mug with both hands.

"Still cold?"

Dan nodded.

"You need my cooking…more fat to keep you warm."

"If you held an honest job in a restaurant, my family and I would be regular customers."

"I want my own place, want to be my own boss. Soon I'll have enough money."

"Dishonest money."

"You're preaching again."

"That's my job. I love God. You love cooking. We each have our special calling." When Cookie stood and started stacking the dishes, Dan said, "God loves you, Cookie."

The chef stopped and glared at him. "He doesn't love me! He took my good parents…gave me bad ones." He turned his back and finished loading the tray.

Dan knew his words, falling now on deaf ears, would be useless. He tapped Cookie on the arm, and when the man turned, Dan held out his hand. "I love you as a friend."

Cookie's frown changed to a smile. He grasped Dan's hand. "Friend." He gathered everything but the heater and hurried out of the room.

Dan thought about these brothers who lost good parents. Life was rotten for plenty of kids, but not all turned to crime. Doc, obviously, for a short time at least, rose above his circumstances. Was he driven to succeed in order to get Cookie out of a bad situation? Doc had mentioned that Cookie poisoned some men he didn't like and served time. Did his brother get into trouble because Doc was in prison and not around to look out for him? How long had Doc sheltered Cookie—since childhood? *What a responsibility he's shouldered. Like Doc, so many youngsters are pushed into adulthood before they're ready. Some never experience childhood. Will the world ever come back to the place where kids can stay kids through childhood?*

Dan realized nothing remained sure in life—something could happen to him and Cindy, but he knew beyond doubt God would take care of their sons. He mulled over their arguments over the past year. *When I get out of this nightmare of a mess, I'm going to spend more time with my family.* Dan propped his elbows on the table and laid his head against his folded hands. "Lord, raise up others to take over some of the responsibilities that have fallen on me. Cindy has been patient, so unselfish, but it's not fair she has to bear the brunt of raising our children. She seems tired all the time. I know money's short, and we can't do much, but at least we could enjoy being together, enjoy simple pleasures. Lord, I'm trusting You to bring us back together, Amen."

Dan sighed and glanced at his watch—six-thirty. Today seemed endless. They were leaving extra early tomorrow. *Will Doc be here soon with the sedative?*

Awhile later, he heard footsteps, but not Doc's. Adolf entered with the handcuffs and blindfold. "On your feet…I have a message for you to deliver to your father. Call him at home and tell him we won't stand for the police watching the roads. We're setting off six bombs before morning, and we have others to detonate if we spot one more tail…car, plane, or interference of any kind."

Dan scrambled to his feet. "You kill anyone, and I'll find some way to explode this bomb. Before I set one foot in a store, I insist on listening to the news."

"Yes. Yes. I remember your threats. You just deliver this message."

"How do you know my father will be home? Did Snow White tell you? Is she working in law enforcement?"

"You have an overactive imagination." The words said with nonchalance didn't fool Dan—Adolf's lips quivered.

Little Hitler studied Dan through squinted eyes filled with distrust. "No, I think I'll deliver the message."

Dan laughed. "Afraid I'll tip him off about Snow White?"

"Hardly. Your conjectures are of no consequence."

"You lofty, lying son of the devil, you're scared stiff."

"I fear neither God nor man!"

"Only death."

Adolf's face colored. With eyes blazing, he whacked Dan's face with the back of his hand and stomped out of the room before Dan could recover from the staggering blow. Dan stood blinking as he waited for the footsteps to fade.

In the bathroom, he applied a cold washcloth to his reddened cheek and stared at his reflection. "Was it worth it?" he asked himself and answered, "Yes."

*****

Adolf stormed toward his bedroom, grabbed his jacket, and headed for the door where he met Doc on his way to Dan's room. "Don't give Baker any codeine or sedative tonight and remove the heater." He drew in a quick breath. "And that bomb stays harnessed to him until he finishes his errands…even if Einstein returns."

"You look ready to explode. What'd Baker do now?"

"Nothing a phone call to Einstein won't take care of." He slid into his jacket and zipped it. "I'm going into town to call Captain Baker and deliver our ultimatum." He stomped to the door, flinging it open and slamming it behind him.

During the ride into San Bernardino, he plotted revenge against the whole Baker family. Before entering the town, he pulled off the highway, dialed Captain Baker's house, and drummed his fingers on the dashboard. Three rings later, the captain answered, and Adolf said, "Don't talk, just listen. Back off or else. Six bombs will be detonated tomorrow morning. More will explode if we spot one tail, whether it's someone on foot or in a car. If we so much as hear a helicopter, yours or otherwise, we'll detonate another bomb."

Back on the road, Adolf headed for the nearest saloon and parked in front. Before going inside, he contacted Einstein. Eyes bright with anticipation, he said, "I have another job for you. I want you to rig every car at Captain Baker's house. Let's say, have them explode when they reach sixty-five so we have a nice freeway pileup."

"You want all their vehicles rigged?"

"Yes. I don't know which one they'll use. I envision them on their way to church Sunday morning. If their god chooses to have them die before that, so be it, but I want that whole family eliminated!"

*****

Doc rushed into the bathroom and glared at Dan. "Why'd you have to go and rile Adolf?"

Dan shrugged.

"Well, he ordered me not to give you the codeine or anything to help you sleep tonight. And I'm to remove the heater Cookie so graciously left."

"Good thing I've already eaten, or I'd be sent to bed without my supper."

"You're pleased with yourself, aren't you?"

"It was kind of nice to intimidate him for a change."

Doc touched Dan's cheek and shook his head. "You're going to have some bruise."

"If I'd turned the other cheek, I'd have a matched pair."

"What did you say to set him off?"

"Nothing much. He's just getting edgy. Did you come in here just to see my face, or did you have another reason? Your closing the door suggests a private conversation. What gives?"

"I wanted to thank you for being nice to Cookie. Offering your hand in friendship meant a lot to him"

"I like him, and I like you. If you'd forsake this insane scheme, I'd try to help you both. What if something happens to you? Who's going to watch out for Cookie?"

"Would you?"

Not expecting the problem thrown back at him, Dan's eyes widened, but he said, "I don't know how I could help him, but I'd try. I'd like to see him open his own restaurant."

"Thanks, I think you mean that." Doc reached into his shirt pocket and handed Dan two tablets. "The codeine will help you get through the night."

"Isn't crossing Adolf dangerous?"

Doc smiled. "Without me, Needles is doomed to die. I hold the formula to the elixir that has managed to put his AIDS in remission."

"Proven formula? Or is Needles your guinea pig?"

"With a million dollars, I can set up the facilities to prove it."

"I know a Christian doctor who would help you do this honestly."

"Forget it! You just get me that money. If you do, I'll make sure you get to see your kids when we return."

"How, tell Adolf you'll withhold Needles's medication?"

Doc shook his head. "Adolf is vain. He wants your sons to love him and knows they're unhappy with him now. Not letting the boys see you tomorrow might make them hate him. Adolf plans to tell them you're going to let him take them on a trip. He's promising Santa's Village and a plane trip to Florida to see all the attractions there."

"Adolf will never allow me to see my sons. He knows I'd turn them against him."

"Not if I tell him I told you to go along with the scheme that Cookie and I vowed to deliver your sons to your wife."

"You're going to convince Adolf you've convinced me you're going to cross him? And you're asking me to convince my sons they should go with Adolf despite his past actions?"

"Yes, if you want to see your sons and hold them one last time. I'm not a miracle worker. I can't promise your life, but I can give you a few hours with Danny and Timmy, if you can trust me long enough to do your part."

Trust? Is Doc trustworthy? Couldn't this be a ploy to get me to help Adolf? "You're asking a lot."

"Didn't Cookie and I keep our promise to keep Needles away from your sons?"

Dan nodded and held out his hand.

Grasping it, Doc said, "Good. You keep your part of the bargain, and I'll keep mine, so down that medication and go to bed. You have a busy day tomorrow." While Dan swallowed the pills, he added, "I hope you'll be able to sleep with that bomb."

After he left, Dan retrieved what he'd seen in the wastebasket—an old fashioned, double-edged razor blade. Would it be sharp enough to cut through the bomb harness? He'd threatened to explode the bomb if someone died in one of Einstein's explosions, but he had to be sure Danny and Timmy would be safe. Dan shook his head and dropped the blade back in the wastebasket. *What am I thinking? Vengeance belongs in God's hands, not mine.*

He opened the bathroom door and gaped in surprise.

Doc held out his hand. "If you took the razor blade, give it to me."

Awestruck, Dan couldn't speak. *Did Doc plant the blade?*

Doc motioned him to fork it over.

"I don't have it."

"Then you were bluffing."

Dan shook his head. "I did retrieve the blade, even planned when to use it, but killing any of you would be sinful. I'd be sealing your fate. I can't do that. I can't condemn any of you to hell. That's God's job. As long as you have breath, there's still time for you to change from your wicked ways."

"Save your breath." Doc hiked his thumb toward the bedroom. "Go."

Stretched out on the bed, Dan listened to the howling wind. He wished a storm would develop, one so fierce it would keep the gang holed up for days. Maybe they'd abandon their plans. He dreaded tomorrow.

He had only agreed to Adolf's nauseous proposition so he could rescue Danny and Timmy from the cold and keep them out of Adolf's clutches. Now, after talking with Doc, he realized the boys remained in imminent danger with Adolf laying the groundwork, enticing them to come with him. They loved Santa's Village and wanted to see Disney World. *I'd stand a chance with Adolf, but Timmy and Danny would be helpless pawns.* "God, why don't you strike Adolf down? Doesn't he deserve hell? I know I should hold out hope for every man no matter how rotten, but he's gone too far. If I'm wrong, change his heart." Putting the matter in God's hands helped Dan relax and fall asleep. Toward morning, he began to dream:

Standing in the archway with the chain around his ankle, Dan stared at four coffins near the sliding glass door. Needles stood on one leering at him while fingering his knife. He threw his head back, gave a soundless laugh, and pointed the knife toward the closed kitchen door where the boys stood. Jumping to the floor, his knife slicing the air like a swordsman beheading a foe, he gave Dan a deadly glance before charging Danny and Timmy. The boys bolted and tried to run to Dan. Needles blocked their path with his swinging knife. His sons turned about-face and ran to the kitchen door. It wouldn't open. They ran to the sliding glass door. Needles scrambled over the coffins and cornered them. His knife lashed out.

"No," Dan screamed and awakened. Gasping for breath, he trembled in the tomb-cold room and drew the blankets tighter. Over and over, his mind replayed the nightmare—his sons' frantic faces as they ran. Their eyes widened with horror when Needles cornered them. Tortured by the scenes, Dan began to shake uncontrollably. *Stop. It was only a dream brought on by your fears.* "Lord, please let that be the case. Please let Danny and Timmy come out of this ordeal unscathed." After he drew in deep breaths to calm down, a strange peace came over him—God's assurance his sons would soon be safe.

With calmness came reason, and he began to review the first part of the dream—four coffins. Was there a connection between them and the four aces of spades? Could God possibly be showing him four men would die? How? Who? Would he be one of them? "Lord, if I am to die by Needles's hand, give me the courage of Daniel when he faced the lions."

Footsteps in the hallway disrupted his thoughts. Someone opened the door and flipped on the light. Dan shielded his eyes from the brightness. "Good, you're awake," Adolf said, entering. "That was some nightmare you had. I was in the kitchen pouring a cup of coffee when I heard you scream. I almost scalded myself."

Dan trembled when he sat up.

Adolf laughed. "Nerves getting raw?"

"It's cold in here." Dan swung his legs to the floor and leaned against the bed until a wave of lightheadedness passed. "I want to listen to the news. I meant what I said last night."

"Ah, yes, the brave pastor willing to give his life to save others… even offered yourself in place of your sons. You know, I thought that over but decided you have too much bravo for my taste. Your sons, however, are moldable."

"You'll never touch them."

"Are you back to the ace of spades? If you think that bothers me, think again."

"I'd be plenty worried if I were you. I had a dream. I saw four coffins lined up in the other room. You were in one of them."

Adolf laughed. "Is that why you screamed? Were you pained to see me dead?"

"Hardly." *So much for rattling Adolf.*

"Then why did you scream? Let me guess. Was Needles after you? No, no, that wouldn't make you cry out. He must have been after your sons. Am I correct?"

Dan said nothing.

Adolf raised an eyebrow. "Your face says he was. Did he get them?"

"No," Dan said, angry with himself for trying to fake out the master of deceit.

"Too bad. You notice I'm not quivering or shaking in my boots over your insane prophetic dream." His lips twisted in a mocking smile.

Prophetic? If Adolf refers to it as that, maybe he is taking it seriously. "I want to listen to the news."

"On the way down, Doc can turn on the radio, but this early in the morning he may only find music." He surveyed Dan head to foot. "Get out of those blood-awful trousers and that horrible jacket." He wrinkled his nose with disgust. "You'll find clean trousers in the closet and an Angels baseball jacket. I couldn't get your cap back, but there's a red stocking cap that should set the jacket off nicely. After we get back and Einstein removes that bomb, you can change your shirt. We can't have your sons seeing that blood when they eat with you tonight. You look surprised."

"I thought I couldn't see Danny and Timmy again?"

"Doc insisted on celebrating with the rest of us…said it wasn't fair for him to be stuck with your boys. I benevolently agreed."

Benevolent? You don't have a benevolent cell in your body. "How soon do we leave?"

"As soon as the others eat and get dressed."

Doc came in a few moments later to have breakfast with Dan. He wore glasses and a debonair black wig that hid his graying hair. Make-up made him look twenty years younger. "Don't you look the dandy," Dan said. "All duded-up and ready to go."

"I'd rather stay here," Doc grumbled.

"Whether you stay on the fringe of crime or in the thick of it, you're still as guilty as the others."

Doc glared at him before he leaned down to unlock the padlock and scowled while Dan changed into clean underwear and trousers. When Doc remained sullen while he ate with him, Dan knew he had ruffled Doc's feathers.

They barely finished when Lefty sauntered in with the handcuffs and blindfold. "Adolf said it's time to go." Doc guided Dan down the slippery path.

"Too bad you can't see the stars," Lefty said. "The sky's crystal-clear."

"That's why it's so blasted cold," Doc grumbled. After Dan lay on the van floor and the door slid shut, the doctor said, "Get that heater on. I'm freezing."

"You're softer than Baker," Lefty said. "He never complains."

"If it will do me any good, I'll complain plenty. I already ache. These handcuffs wrench my shoulders. Since Doc didn't give me codeine this morning, my head's splitting. My stitched wound is being rubbed raw against the floor. And we've barely started. Could you at least remove the handcuffs so I can get more comfortable?"

Silence.

Dan hadn't been exaggerating his discomfort. Every twist and turn increased his agony until he couldn't think, only endure. He needed to get his mind elsewhere. To remain positive, he started quoting Bible verses silently. After a few, he decided to recite the Ten Commandments.

Lefty laughed. "He thinks he's Moses."

Doc said, "Shut up, you two. I'm trying to sleep."

Silence fell once more. A while later, Lefty pulled over and stopped. Now what? Dan wondered. Where were they? They should be close to Redlands. "Why did we stop?"

"Shut up," Doc said.

Being kept in the dark when you're blindfolded is worse than being kept in the dark when you can see, Dan thought with disgust.

The phone rang. Dan heard Einstein's voice say, "All clear."

So that was why they were waiting. Had Snow White assured Einstein the police were no longer watching the roads? "Turn on the radio. I want to hear the news."

"Later," Lefty said and started the engine. Sooner than Dan wanted, the van stopped at the rendezvous spot. The door slid back, and Lefty lifted him out and to his feet. As usual, the others left before the blindfold and cuffs were removed. Dan rubbed his wrists. "I still haven't heard the news." When Lefty gripped his arm, Dan said, "I'm not going to bolt." The southpaw's strong grasp didn't lessen. "You can listen as soon as you get in the car."

Doc turned on a flashlight and directed the beam on Dan. "Unzip your jacket and raise your shirt." After Dan did, Doc said, "You weren't kidding." He inspected the stitches on Dan's blood-smeared midsection. "You'll live."

"You're so comforting. Could I at least have some codeine?"

"I'll give you some in the car. We can't have you passing out." The flashlight beam picked up the late-model gray sedan stolen for today's dirty work. After Doc took his place behind Dan, he leaned over the seat and handed him two tablets. Dan swallowed them and turned on the radio. He immediately found the news—national then local. Six bomb explosions had rocked the area within minutes of each other around two-thirty, one in Anaheim near a school, one in Fullerton on Interstate 5, another in Orange obliterated a newly constructed apartment complex, the one in Corona destroyed a gas station. Flames could be seen for miles. Two explosions in Riverside caused extensive damage to the shopping mall, injuring a guard. "Details are sketchy," the newscaster said. "The police are not commenting."

Lefty clicked off the radio.

"Leave it on," Dan said, turning it back on. "Details are still coming in."

Two more reports came as the story developed, but details remained sketchy. "Like the explosion in Ware Mart, it's a miracle no one has been killed," the newscaster said. "If the bombs had been set to go off hours later, who knows what carnage would have resulted?"

Dan blurted, "You bombed Ware Mart? Why? You got your money."

"But not on time," Lefty said. "The other stores needed a warning. At least Einstein must have taken your threats seriously and planted his bombs with care. Guess you can relax."

"Sure," Dan said. "Just pretend none of this is happening."

Minutes later, Lefty parked in front of Quick Stop, the convenience store where Dan had passed out. Dan suddenly felt as if he were reliving a nightmare.

"Time to go to work," Lefty said.

Doc leaned over the seat. "Remember, you're being monitored. That listening device is so sensitive it can all but hear you think."

Dan stared at him, recalling their conversation last night. Had Einstein heard them?

As if reading his mind, Doc added, "He has to be within range to pick you up, but you can be sure right now he's counting your heart beats just for fun."

Intentional or not, Doc had relieved one of Dan's fears, but that didn't help him relax.

Inside the store, the manager remained stone-faced throughout the transaction.

Lefty had already started the car when Dan reached it. "Anxious to leave?" Dan said. "Be my guest." He waved his hand in dismissal.

"Give that money to Doc and get in," Lefty growled.

"Do I detect a touch of nervousness?" Dan said, passing the case through the back window to Doc.

"Shut up!" Lefty said.

Dan took his place in front. At least, he wasn't the only edgy one. He turned and watched Doc thumb through the bills with gloved hands before he placed them in a large suitcase. Unlike Einstein, he took care as he tossed the briefcase out the window.

No one was spotted tailing them, but Dan hoped somehow the police were tracking them.

Before they hit the next store, Lefty asked permission to buy coffee and use the men's room.

Adolf said, "Make it quick, and Baker is not to go in alone. Keep an eye on him every second."

Back in the car, Dan's nerves acted up again. His hand shook, and he almost dropped the coffee Lefty handed him.

Lefty laughed. "Look who has the shakes. You've been thinking about Needles and his knife?"

Dan ignored him.

Doc leaned over the seat. "Here's something for your nerves. I apologize for not giving you some this morning. I knew you had to have the pain pills, but I guess I wanted you to have the shakes. Your remark about staying on the fringe of crime ticked me off. I shouldn't have let it interfere with my judgment, but…" He shrugged. "Anyway, I'll hand you more when I give you the codeine."

"Thanks," Dan said, swallowing the medication with the last gulp of coffee. Depressed and exhausted, he leaned his head back and closed his eyes. Doc had looked concerned and sympathetic, but he was still a crook, not a friend. Dan felt abandoned, helpless—as despondent as he had been after his parents' death. *You're no longer a kid. You didn't rely on God then, now you do. He's your hope and strength.*

"Are you all right?" Doc asked.

Dan nodded. "I could use another cup of coffee."

Lefty returned, grumbling about having to go back for refills. Dan was halfway through his second cup when Adolf phoned and told Lefty to proceed to Ricard, a drug store.

Even at this early hour, the store was busy. Dan had to weave between people to reach the office, and every time he turned, he saw Muscles, but the ex-boxer stood out of sight as he knocked on the door. When Dan showed the manager the card, the man shoved the briefcase across the threshold and slammed the door. Dan walked back to the car, mulling over with disgust how Adolf's plan appeared to be succeeding. Had the bombings and the threat of more caused the police to back off? Maybe it was better that way—let the crooks have the money and catch them later. He hoped the gum wrappers would help identify them.

In the car, Dan decided to put the matter out of his mind. He had enough to worry about. *Don't think about Needles's knife. Act as if today is the first day of your life, not possibly the last.*

While Doc counted the money, Lefty drove through a residential area until Doc said, "Contact Adolf…the money's all here."

Adolf told them to proceed to the JR market in Fullerton.

This market was crowded with Saturday shoppers. He scanned the area as he threaded his way to the office but didn't spot a gang member. The manager opened the door to Dan's knock, glanced at the card but stared at Dan with disgust as he grabbed the briefcase, handed it to him, and slammed the door.

Back in the car, Doc counted the money while Lefty drove around until he was told to go to the next market. Twenty minutes later when Dan entered Shop-Smart, he tried to keep a positive frame of mind, but his spirits plummeted when he saw the manager's face. The man stood in the doorway glaring as if Dan was a scumbait crook.

"Do you have the money?" Dan asked, holding his breath. He didn't want any more bombs detonated.

The manager nodded, retrieved a briefcase, and shoved it across the threshold, looking as if he wanted to spit on him. "I hope they nail you alive in a coffin and burn it."

The words stunned Dan. He tried to convince himself it didn't matter what the man thought, but it did. Dan snatched the briefcase and turned heel—angry with Adolf and his gang for the ordeal he and others were suffering. He scowled at Doc when he tossed him the briefcase and threw the black business card in his face.

"What's eating you?" Doc asked.

Dan slid onto the passenger seat, slammed the car door, and glared at Lefty who whipped out his gun. "You know," Dan said, "the manager has the right idea…nail each of you in a coffin alive and cremate you."

"Cool it," Lefty said, "or you'll get yours now. We don't need you anymore."

Startled, Dan could only ask, "Why?"

"Figure it out for yourself, bright boy."

"Adolf said he contacted twelve corporations. You've only hit eight stores."

Lefty laughed. "Looks like you and the cops fell for it."

15

Still laughing, Lefty pulled out of the parking area and looked toward Dan. "You don't think it's funny that we fooled the police?"

Dan turned his head and stared out the right window. Blue sky had replaced most of the clouds. He wished his fears, like rain, could dissipate as quickly. *If Adolf really did dupe the police, I can't expect them to rescue us.* He believed Doc and Cookie would do their best to save Danny and Timmy but knew they wouldn't risk their necks to help him.

"Lord, I don't know what lies ahead but please give me courage to endure whatever Needles has planned." As morbid as the picture was of dying such a cruel death, Dan also found the air charged with expectancy. Dark as his outlook was now and growing blacker by the minute, faith assured him God was in control.

Doc said, sitting behind him, "You're awfully quiet."

Dan turned. "What's to say?"

"Do you need some codeine?"

"Your concern seems ludicrous when you know I may be dead in a few hours."

"Yeah, Doc," Lefty said, "Why waste it?"

"He needs it." Doc leaned forward and handed Dan the medication.

"Sure seems a waste when he's going to be wasted." Lefty howled over his play on words.

Dan saw the flash of anger in Doc's eyes. The man was a doctor foremost, crook second. What emotional conflict raged within him? "Will you shed a tear for me, Doc?"

"Should I?" His eyes now reflected the steel-hardness of a man determined to do what he had to do.

Dan decided to try one last time to reach Doc's heart. Maybe Lefty's would soften too. "Do you two realize your money will have been purchased by blood? My blood. But Christ shed His to purchase your lives…to free you from the penalty of sin. Only accepting Him and what He did can spare you eternal torment in hell."

Lefty guffawed, "We're goners, Doc. We're gonna be finger-lickin'-good crispy critters."

"Hellfire and brimstone," Doc chuckled. "But I've got to hand it to you, Baker. At least you're persistent."

Dan shook his head and resumed staring out the window. They'd soon be at the rendezvous spot, then the hideout. He thought about his sons. He hadn't taught Danny how to ride his new bike, and he'd always looked forward to playing baseball and basketball with his boys. Dan wanted to grow old with Cindy. He didn't want to die, but he had to be practical in case God had other plans. He turned again.

"What do you want now?" Doc asked.

"I'd like to write a letter to Cindy…give her some advice and information to help make things easier." He sighed as he thought of her struggling alone. "I want to tell her how much I love her." He saw skepticism in Doc's eyes. In disgust, he said, "I won't say anything to endanger any of you. You can all read it and have a good belly-laugh, but please let me write her and make sure she gets the letter."

"I don't know," Doc said.

"Hey, Doc," Lefty said, "let him. A man should get a last will and testament. You can nail it to his chest so the cops can find it." He again gave his irritating horse laugh. "Unless, of course, Needles goes too crazy with his knife and there's not a big enough piece left."

Dan tried to erase the picture Lefty painted, but it came through—blood red. He glared at Doc, then at Lefty. "You're all heart…both of you. Too bad they're frozen." He pressed his head against the seat and watched the cars whiz by like the last moments of his life.

At the rendezvous area, Dan saw Adolf standing by the van. Lefty pulled close and rolled down the window.

"You're late," Adolf said. "The others have already ditched the stolen cars and headed back. Einstein has the cops occupied."

Dan flung the car door open and jumped out. "What did he blow up?"

Adolf whisked out his revolver. "I didn't ask. Lefty, cuff Baker and get him in the van. We'll wipe down the car and leave it here. Doc, ride in back with Baker. I'll drive."

"Turn on the news," Dan demanded before he was forced to the floor.

"Too upsetting," Adolf said. "Nice soothing music is what you need."

Whatever Einstein had done appeared to have worked. No phone calls came saying they were being tailed. To Dan, the whir of the tires repeatedly said "Time is running out." When they reached the hideout, he realized what few precious minutes he had left, unless God intervened. Since he hadn't been blindfolded, he could see the blue interior of the large van. *Never again will I ride up this rutted gravel road,* he thought as they ascended, rounded the curve he knew so well, drove up the driveway, and stopped. Lefty lifted him out to his feet. Dan surveyed the area around him.

Adolf stood beside him. "Do you like your surroundings, Baker? It's a perfect winter setting…the placid blue sky above the snowy evergreens…so picturesque, so peaceful." He laughed. "And soon you'll be in your heavenly rest."

The tormenting words didn't faze Dan as he surveyed the lodge and tried to picture the steep hill behind it.

"You don't look perturbed."

"Why should I be? There's too much beauty around me to waste my time on morbid thoughts. God has given me the assurance that my sons and I will be home soon."

Adolf laughed. You'll be in a coffin."

"No, Adolf, you will, and I will never have to see your black eyes spewing hatred again."

Adolf stomped to the steps and turned, "Lefty, escort Baker into the lodge then park the van by the kitchen door for Cookie and Doc." He stomped up the porch steps but left the door ajar.

Muscles, awaiting Dan, hiked his thumb toward the hallway, followed him to the bedroom, shackled him, and left.

Einstein sauntered in, his face beaming with pride. "Want out of that rig so you can enjoy your last few hours?"

Dan fought to remain calm. "What did you bomb?"

"Marvelous, simply ingenious...railroad tank cars filled with gas. I gave the cops fifteen minutes warning. You should have seen them flood the area and scurry to evacuate. They did a good job."

"You'll never get away with this. They'll hunt you down and lock you away for good."

"By the time they start looking, I'll be long gone. Smile. Congratulate me. This is my finest hour." He let out an insane laugh like the Joker in *Batman*. "And Snow White's waiting for me to pick her up so we can get married."

Dan shook his head. "You may think you've gotten away with this, but you won't escape the wrath of God."

Einstein eyed him with scorn. "And you can't escape the wrath of Needles." He unlocked the harness padlock, removed the bomb and sauntered into the hallway.

Dan blew a sigh of relief. At least that was one load off his chest—literally. Now if he could only be free from the other threats hanging over him.

Doc entered a short while later with paper and pen. "I'll be the only one reading what you write. A man's last wishes shouldn't be held up for ridicule."

"Thanks, Doc, I appreciate that."

"You'd better write fast. I'll be bringing the boys soon. Just before I do, I'll come and remove the chain. That will give you time to shed that bloody shirt. You'll find your jacket in the closet. Adolf said to tell you that you can keep the red cap to wear tonight or the other one, depending on which one you want to be found in. He ordered me to add...of course, if Needles scalps you, it won't matter."

"He really likes painting the blackest picture possible, doesn't he? I'm surprised he wants me to change jackets. The white baseball jacket would show my blood more than my navy one. Why did he make me wear it in the first place?"

"Before the injured Ware Mart' manager passed out, he told a reporter he knew who blew up his store, but he didn't say your name. Adolf figured the cops must have gotten to him before the media did and stopped him from revealing the information to them. As a precaution, Adolf decided to change your image."

Dan shook his head. "So many explosions…so much havoc. Einstein will be caught…so will all of you…even if I'm not around to see it."

Doc thumbed toward the closet. "You have thirty minutes to change and write."

Dan slipped out of the white baseball jacket. Only his respect for the Angels kept him from throwing it on the floor, but he did throw the bloody flannel maroon shirt down before he put on the blue one then donned his navy jacket and stocking cap.

At the card table, he stared at the paper and pen. Mentally, he had written his letter in the van, and words flowed from his mind as he wrote:

Hi, Hon,

I bet you never thought your ole Daniel would wind up in a predicament like this, did you? The lions haven't eaten me yet, but I can sure feel them breathing down my neck. I thought about giving you some advice regarding our affairs but decided against it. That seemed too negative as if I'd lost hope. I haven't. I know the boys will be home soon. God assured me of that. I'm counting on being there and saying this in person. I'm writing just in case God's plans differ from mine.

As soon as we can, you and I are going to take a long vacation and get reacquainted—recapture the love and longing we once had. We're not returning home until we do. I'm going to smother you with love until you beg to come home.

I've neglected you. I'm sorry. I was so caught up ministering to others that I put you and the boys on the shelf like books I could enjoy later. I've been wrong and I pray I live, if only to be able to right this.

You've never complained. I've seen the hurt and disappointment in your eyes when I say I have to go out again. You've always been patient and understanding. I appreciate that, but you made it too easy for me to put aside what should have been my first priority before others, you and the boys. I've noticed how tired you've been from having to bear the brunt of raising the boys. I'm sorry.

Last Sunday night, that seems ages ago, I really had a wild night planned. I was going to try and make things up to you. I pray I still have the chance. I love you, Cindy. Always have. Always will. Although you hate them, I love every freckle on your face and your girlish laughter, which has been silent much too often lately. I plan to bring that back, smother you with love, pamper you, and embrace you until you beg me to let you go.

If I don't get the chance to do this, forgive me for not doing so these past few years. Again, I'm sorry. To end this on a positive note: meet me under the avocado tree tomorrow night after the boys fall asleep. Let's put them to bed early.

I love you, Cindy. I love you.
Dan

Dan stared at what he had written, wishing he could revise it. Not his best piece of work but at least it was from his heart. He hoped Cindy would be able to sense what he hadn't been able to express adequately. He closed his eyes, picturing her in his mind and willed his words to reach her—I love you, Cindy. I love you. "Lord, wherever she is, let her feel my love right now." He glanced at his watch and made a mental note of the time—five after one.

He recognized Doc's footsteps and smiled when he entered.

"Finished?" Doc asked.

Dan nodded and handed him the letter.

Doc read it and raised an eyebrow. "You're going to meet her under an avocado tree?"

"We have five acres of orange and avocado trees. One avocado tree has branches touching the ground, making for complete privacy. October isn't our normal season for romantic interludes, but I bet we won't even feel the cold."

"You're still expecting a miracle?"

Dan remembered reading his watch and realized that was optimistic, and he no longer felt depressed. "Yes, I am." He smiled. "If I get my miracle, will you believe then that God is worth trusting?"

"You never quit, do you?"

"With my last breath, I'll try to convince you Jesus is Lord."

Doc shook his head, his lips drawn in a grim line. "This room is still bugged, and you are expendable, so don't try to escape if you want your sons to live."

Dan nodded.

Doc removed the chain and hurried out of the room, and Dan shoved the links behind the dresser.

Cookie entered with a large tray of sandwiches, milk, and coffee. "Adolf said you get one hour with Danny and Timmy. Doc and I are going to leave early. We don't want to be here. You're a good man. If God loves you, why is He going to let you die?"

"He won't, Cookie. He won't fail me."

"If He lets you live, then I'll know He is good."

Dan watched Cookie leave. Despite all the evil Adolf had devised, Dan knew God would bring good out of it. "Lord, did You allow me to go through this ordeal so Doc and Cookie would have a chance to see Your power and believe in You?" Dan felt confirmation in his heart.

He heard Danny and Timmy running down the hall and knelt to receive them with outstretched arms, hugging and kissing them. "Boy have I missed you." He glanced up and saw Doc. "Sure you don't want to eat with us? Looks like Cookie brought plenty."

Doc shook his head. "Cookie and I have some packing to do."

"Are we going home?" Danny asked.

"Since these men have their money, we don't need to stay here any longer."

"Adolf said we could go with him to Santa's Village then fly to Disney World, but I want to go home. I miss Mommy and Jonathan."

"So do I," Dan said, relieved he didn't have to pretend he'd given permission. After they started eating, he asked, "What's the first thing you want to do when we get home?"

"I want pizza," Timmy blurted.

Danny looked thoughtful. "Can you teach me to ride my new bike? You were going to do that Monday."

"One pizza and one bike lesson coming tomorrow," Dan said. "Will you two do something for me?"

"What?" they chimed.

"Will you go to bed early without protesting? Mommy and I have lots of talking to do."

Danny snickered, cupped his mouth, and leaned close to Timmy. "They're gonna kiss." Both giggled.

Dan pretended not to notice. "Can I count on you boys to be good?"

They nodded with smirks on their faces. Suddenly their eyes went wide when the table started shaking. Milk and coffee sloshed.

"Daddy, we're having an earthquake," Danny said.

"Sure feels like it," Dan said unperturbed as the room rocked gently.

"That was fun," Danny said. "Will we have another one?"

Timmy blurted, "Do it again, Daddy."

"He can't do that," Danny said like a well-informed older brother. "Only God can."

Dan smiled when Timmy looked to him for confirmation. "That's right. The room may rock again, maybe several times...probably small aftershocks from last week's big earthquake. Nothing to worry about."

Danny said, "If we have another one, will you sit under the table like Mommy did and play rowboat?"

Dan chuckled. "You boys can crawl under the card table. I don't think I'd fit."

They were still eating when Doc entered. "Did you feel the earthquake?" Danny asked.

"Sure did." Doc's smile looked feigned. "You boys need to come back to your room now. Adolf wants to talk to your father."

"So soon?" Dan asked. "We haven't finished eating."

Doc's face contorted as if he were trying hard to find the right words. "The natives are getting restless," he blurted. "They started drinking the minute they arrived...Needles even sooner...had a bottle with him in the car. Cookie and I want to take the boys home. Now."

His face puzzled, Danny asked, "Daddy, aren't you coming?"

"Later...go with Doc. Tell Mommy I'll be home soon." He mustered a faint smile. "Doc, I'm counting on you. I'm pretty sure Cindy will be at Captain Baker's."

Doc nodded and held out his hand. When Dan grasped it, he said, "I'll make sure they get home safely." His eyes misted. "Take care," he added as if he didn't know what else to say.

Dan knelt and hugged and kissed each boy. "See you soon. Since you'll see Mommy and Jonathan before I do, kiss them for me. Okay?" They nodded.

Panic hit when Dan saw Adolf in the doorway. Would Doc get the boys away in time? "Off with you now." He gave them an affectionate swat on their bottoms. "Lord, help them escape."

Adolf stepped back to let them by before he came in, his articulate speech somewhat slurred. After Muscles hurried to shackle Dan and left, Adolf said, "We're having a great celebration, but Needles is eager to start the entertainment. I'll let you enjoy the warmth from the fireplace for a few minutes...before he begins." His deep guttural laugh spewed viciously. "You have ten minutes to pray while Needles finishes packing and I pass out the money. I think I'll check on Doc and Cookie."

Had he heard him tell Doc where Cindy would be? Did he realize Doc and Cookie were going to leave right away?

Adolf turned and studied Dan. "You look perturbed. I'm only going to say goodbye. I decided not to keep your sons, at least not Danny. He's too much like you. Timmy, now, he's young enough to be molded." Dan's hands clenched. "Ah, that really gets to you, doesn't it? Why can't you be like some ministers who preach tolerance for all lifestyles? Unfortunately, it's too late for you." Adolf turned to leave. When Dan started to follow, he did an about-face and pointed. "Stay in this room, or I'll make your kids watch Needles have his way with you." His savage tone and sadistic expression made Dan back away. Adolf spat his last words. "Pray while you can."

Dan sank to his knees. "Lord, don't let Adolf make Danny and Timmy watch me die. Protect my sons!" He stood and started pacing. What if Adolf decided to carry out his threat? Would he allow Needles to take revenge on the boys afterward or before? Dan knew the crooks would rejoice seeing him in unbearable torment. Endless possibilities of what they might do assailed him.

*****

When Doc left Dan's room, he automatically stopped at the bathroom to make sure Timmy and Danny urinated before they left the lodge. He realized the task was no longer irksome. He'd come to love these two good-natured kids. In his suitcase, he had one million dollars to fulfill his dreams, but his conscience robbed him of joy. He couldn't wipe out the vision of what Needles planned to do to Baker, nor could he shake the picture of Dan kneeling beside his sons' bed, praying. The man genuinely loved God. He loved Danny and Timmy, and they loved him. He sighed—*all I see that's good in life is going to end.*

Doc helped the boys wash, grasped each slightly damp hand, and headed for the bedroom. From the deep recesses of his mind came another picture. He and Cookie were probably older than Danny and Timmy, but their real father had knelt and prayed at their bedside. Doc mentally heard his mother singing "Jesus Loves Me." Tears brimmed as he realized he would never see his parents again unless—

Danny tugged Doc's hand when they reached the room. "Please, let Daddy come home with us."

"I can't do that, Danny. Adolf wants him here."

"Why?"

"It's too complicated to explain."

Adolf barged into the room. "Not gone yet?"

"Cookie's packing his stuff now."

"Well, hurry up…Needles wants to play." His mouth curved into a satanic smile. "Do you boys want to know what Needles wants to play? He wants to play Daniel in the lions' den with your father. Of course, poor Needles can't bite, so I guess I'll have to give him a knife."

The boys clung to Doc and started crying. "Stop it! Haven't you tormented this family enough? You're getting your revenge. Leave the boys alone."

Adolf laughed. "You're no fun, Doc, no fun at all." Viciousness replaced laughter. "Get these kids out of here before I change my mind and make them watch." Adolf turned heel and stomped from the room.

Tears streaming down his cheeks, Danny gazed at Doc. "He's going to kill Daddy! Don't let him."

"Danny, I'm no Daniel. I can't face all those lions in there, but we can pray for God to save your father. Get in bed under the covers. It's cold in here."

Both continued to cry as Doc prayed. "I'm not sure how to do this, God, but these dear boys and their father have convinced me You're real. I believe in You. Cookie says he won't believe unless You save Baker, and I want Cookie to know You as his Savior too."

Doc finished and tried to console the boys, but they wouldn't stop crying.

Cookie ran into the room. "Danny? Timmy? What's wrong?"

"I'll tell you later," Doc said. "Let's get everything in the van fast before Adolf changes his mind. You boys stay there. I'll put your snowsuits on you when I get back. I won't be long." Not taking time to put on his parka, Doc raced with Cookie down the back hallway to the van outside the kitchen door. Doc told Cookie what Adolf had said while they threw the last items into the van. "Warm this buggy up. I'll get Danny and Timmy."

Doc ran back to the lodge. *God will have to take care of Baker. My job is to save the boys.* He dashed into the room. "Okay, let's get your snowsuits on." When he started to pull back the covers, a thunderous blast rocked the room. Doc threw himself over Danny and Timmy. Shards of wood and plaster crashed around him.

*****

Above the sounds of the gangs' whoops and hollers, Dan heard his sons sobbing. "Lord, what's happening? Why hasn't Doc left?" When he stood to go check, a thunderous sound rocked the room. A rumble sent his mind reeling, his heart pounding as the depths of the earth groaned and shuddered. A loud horrifying thud reverberated. The floor buckled, throwing him into the wall, then to the floor as glass broke and timbers crumbled.

Stunned, he lay motionless, too dazed to think. Dan grabbed the bed, pulled himself up, swayed, and fell to his knees. *What happened? I've got to get to the boys.* Ignoring the jabs of jutting wood, Dan started crawling toward the doorway. The chain caught on the separated floorboards. He freed it and crawled toward the bolt that looked solidly embedded. He cringed when the room shook again but grasped the metal hook and pushed and pulled with all his might. Beam after beam crashed behind him before the swaying stopped, and he managed to stand to get more leverage. The bolt gave way, toppling him backward. Stunned, he lay staring overhead at a one-foot chunk of plaster hanging by a thread. Mesmerized, he watched it sway back and forth before it dropped. Rolling over and covering his head, Dan barely escaped the chunk shattering beside him. Was the whole building ready to collapse? *I've got to make sure Doc and Cookie got away with the boys.*

Dan stood and looped the chain over his arm as he edged his way to the hall. He stared at sunlight streaming through an enormous gaping hole in the roof of the large unused room. He shuddered at the sounds of settling debris. *What if the boys haven't been whisked away?* Dan's heart pounded while he climbed over wood and plaster to reach their room. His breath came in gasps as he shoved the door open enough to reach in and toss aside the mound of debris blocking it. Inside, he scanned the apparent empty room but froze when he saw a man's leg dangling over the edge of a debris-covered bed and heard faint cries coming from the bed. He dropped the chain to fling aside debris and recognized Doc's shirt. Faint whimpers coming from underneath him spurred Dan to move faster. "Danny, Timmy, I'm coming." Two distinct low cries quickened his heartbeat. He uncovered Doc, stunned but moving, and lowered him gently to the floor. Danny and Timmy wailed. He yanked back the covers, and the boys scrambled into his arms. Dan wept. "Thank God. You're safe."

They started shivering. "Slide under the blankets. I've got to help Doc." After tucking the covers around them, he knelt beside Doc. "Can you hear me?" Doc opened his eyes and struggled to sit up. Dan propped him against the chest of drawers. "Are you all right?"

Doc nodded. "The boys?"

"They're frightened but okay. Thank you for protecting them."

"They were staying in bed to keep warm while Cookie and I packed the van. He was going to warm it up so we could leave immediately. I was about to get the boys out of bed and into their snowsuits. What happened? Have you seen anyone?"

"No, I came straight here. I think we had a stronger aftershock."

"Help me to my feet. Let's get that chain off you." Doc took the key from his pocket and removed the chain from Dan's ankle. "Let's get out of here." He reached under his shirt and pulled out a revolver. "Take this in case we meet trouble." When Dan made no move to take it, he said, "You don't know how to shoot?"

"Yes, but..."

"You don't have to kill anyone, just injure them so you can get away. I have another gun."

Dan stared at the lethal weapon with distaste but took it. He raised his jacket and started to stick the revolver under his belt.

"No," Doc said. "Be ready to use it in case we run into trouble. I'll get the boys snowsuits." He reached for them lying on the recliner. "We've got to…" A noise drew their gaze to the doorway. "Watch out," Doc yelled and pushed Dan.

A knife whizzed past Dan and penetrated Doc's chest. The doctor cried out. Recovering his balance, Dan pivoted. Needles, standing in the doorway, fired a gun. A bullet tore through Dan's jacket, searing his arm. Staggering, he fired Doc's gun. Needles's arm flew up, sending his second bullet into the rafters as the junkie crumbled to the floor.

Disoriented, Dan stood transfixed, staring at the red stain spreading across Needles's chest. The revolver slipped from his shaking hand. He heard Danny and Timmy crying but stood powerless to move or think.

"Baker," Doc gasped. "Snap out of it."

Dan sank to the bed.

The boys crawled out from underneath the covers and clutched him. "Daddy," Danny cried, "I want to go home."

Don't think about what you've done. Concentrate on what you need to do.

Danny touched Dan's sleeve. "You're bleeding."

"I'm okay, but Doc's hurt bad. Stay under the blankets while I help him."

The doctor's eyes were closed, his breathing labored.

"Tell me what to do, Doc."

"I'm finished. Leave."

"There has to be something I can do."

"Save your sons…I made peace with God…help Cookie." Dan nodded, too choked to speak.

Doc reached up and touched Dan's sleeve. "Bind that," he said and slumped.

Dan bit down on his lip while he searched for a pulse—none.

"Daddy, please take us home." Danny's voice shook from fright.

"I need to fix my arm first." He removed his jacket and ripped a strip of sheeting from the boys' bed. He recovered his composure while he bound his upper arm, thankful the bullet hadn't penetrated—only grazed him. He slipped back into his jacket. If Needles had survived, someone else could have. He gazed at the gun. With revulsion he picked it up, praying he wouldn't have to use it.

"Okay, boys, let's get going." They crawled from under the covers, dropped to the floor, and ran to him. Dan set the gun on the bed while he retrieved Danny's snowsuit, boots, and mittens from the chair. "Get these on while I help Timmy."

Danny finished before Dan fastened the large diaper pin at the neck of Timmy's snowsuit. "Help your brother with his boots while I put on Doc's parka and boots." Dan grabbed the flashlight on the chest of drawers, shoved it into one of the deep parka pockets and Doc's gloves in the other.

The boys scrambled to their feet, their eyes wide when he grabbed the gun. Danny blurted, "Who are you going to shoot?"

"I hope no one. I'm only taking this to protect us. Now, stay behind me and obey. Stop when I tell you and don't move until I say it's safe. Come only after I call you. Understand?"

They nodded, but when they saw Doc, their lips quivered. Dan yanked a blanket off their bed and covered the body.

Danny frowned. "Won't Doc get cold with just one blanket?"

Gently, Dan said, "Doc is dead."

"Is he with Jesus now? He told God he believed in Him."

"Then he's with Jesus."

Dan kept an eye on the doorway, alert for any sound in the hallway. Where was Cookie? *Surely, if he were alive, he would have come by now.*

When he started toward the doorway, Danny grabbed the parka. "Don't leave!"

"I'm not. I only need to move Needles and some debris."

Danny gazed at the body. "Is he dead?"

Seeing fear in his son's eyes, Dan knelt and pulled him close. "Easy, son, he can't hurt you. He's dead."

"Make sure. Adolf said he was going to let Needles kill you."

Shocked, Dan said, "When was this?"

"Just before the earthquake. Doc said only God could save you. He prayed, Daddy."

Tears of gratitude filled Dan's eyes. "Doc was a good man. We'll miss him, but we'll see him again someday," he said to comfort them as well as himself. He lifted Danny's chin. "I'll make sure Needles is dead. Okay?"

Danny's lips puckered as he nodded.

"Wait here."

Dan kept the gun ready as his quick strides carried him across the room. He checked Needles's pulse—nothing. He stuck the revolver in a pocket. Feeling queasy, he gazed at the ceiling while he dragged the bloody form as far away as he could from the doorway.

He hurried back to the boys. "Needles can't hurt anyone, Danny. He's dead." Dan grabbed the folded stadium blanket from Doc's chair and draped it over his left arm.

"Why are you taking that?" Danny asked.

"We may have to walk, and it's cold out. Let's hurry home to Mommy and Jonathan."

Their faces brightened but only for a short while. When they reached the hallway and Dan retrieved the gun, their faces again reflected fear. "I'll stay in sight," he said, surveying the area to his left. He listened but heard nothing to indicate anyone was in the unused room. "I'm going to check the back corridor. Stay here." A quick peek told Dan no one had been there since the earthquake. Blue sky had replaced the ceiling, and timbers blocked both bedroom doors. While Dan rushed back to the boys, he wondered if everyone had fled or had someone heard them and was lying in wait. "Okay, let's go, but stay behind me. Danny, help Timmy if he needs it." Dan kept the gun poised and his eyes alert for the slightest movement. Listening was pointless. He and the boys were making too much noise. So much debris lay strewn about, Dan had to kick some aside to clear a path. At the end of the hallway, he stopped and stood transfixed.

Danny said, "Wow! How did that rock get there? Look at the snow. What happened?"

Equally dumbfounded, Dan shook his head. The rock, almost three feet in diameter, lay embedded in the floor. He had seen the gaping hole earlier, but the boulder had been out of view. Other than the hole in the roof, he saw little damage to the room, but the archway was packed with earth, rock, and snow.

"What happened?" Danny asked again. "Where is everybody?"

"Looks like maybe the earthquake triggered a landslide. I don't see how, but the force must have lifted that boulder and tossed it right through the roof. If anyone was in the other room, they're either trapped or buried. We'll send help back." Dan's vision of the four coffins flashed through his mind. Had Adolf, Muscles, Lefty and Einstein been gloating over their ability to pull off their scheme? Where had Needles been—in his room?

"Okay, boys, we've stayed long enough," he said but stood mesmerized a few more minutes, viewing God's awesome power. He picked up Timmy and tugged Danny's hand. "Let's go."

Outside, Dan closed the door. *To keep crooks out?* He laughed inwardly over the irony. Suddenly realizing Timmy hadn't said one word, Dan set him down and stroked his forehead. "Are you okay?"

Timmy's face puckered as he wailed, "I want Mommy."

Dan hugged him. "So do I. Let's find a car and drive home fast."

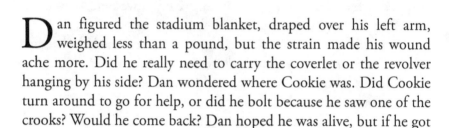

16

Dan figured the stadium blanket, draped over his left arm, weighed less than a pound, but the strain made his wound ache more. Did he really need to carry the coverlet or the revolver hanging by his side? Dan wondered where Cookie was. Did Cookie turn around to go for help, or did he bolt because he saw one of the crooks? Would he come back? Dan hoped he was alive, but if he got buried under hallway debris trying to get to Doc, then the van was still here.

Visions of the four coffins flashed again. Dan tried to convince himself God was reaffirming the deaths of Adolf, Einstein, Lefty, and Muscles. The doubting Thomas in him wanted further confirmation. "Lord, please protect us and convince me no one's around."

Danny tugged on his sleeve. "Can we go now?"

Dan nodded. He set the gun on the porch railing and bent down to tie Timmy's hood securely over his ears before he did Danny's. When he picked up the gun again, Danny's face puckered. "Do you still need that?"

Dan didn't want to frighten them, but until convinced they were safe, he wanted them to be on guard too. "I'm just being cautious. I'll put it in my pocket for now."

While they went down the slippery steps, Danny grasped the porch railing, and Dan held Timmy's hand. He stopped a moment to survey their surroundings. He needed to see if the van was still here, and he also wanted to make sure no one had escaped by way of the back door. "Let's check the kitchen to see if we can find food to take with us, then we'll check the garages to see if we can find a car. The walkway may be slippery, so stay behind me while I check." With his hand on the gun in his pocket, Dan kept alert for danger ahead as well as underfoot. His heart sank when he didn't see the van, but it gave him hope that Cookie had gone for help.

The kitchen door stood ajar—rock, mud, and snow covered the area. The doorway into the living room was packed high with debris. Had the whole hillside crumbled?

"How can we get something to eat" Danny asked. "The refrigerator is buried."

"Guess we'll have to wait until we get down the mountain. Let's hope we can find a car in one of the garages." Dan took his sons' hands while they walked the snowy driveway down to the garages. He tried each door and shook his head. "They're all locked. We'd better start walking."

"How far?" Danny asked.

"More miles than you've ever walked, but it's downhill. You'll have to keep moving until you're tired, then I'll carry you one at a time. When I need a break, you'll both have to walk. Okay?"

Danny nodded. Timmy stared at him as if he didn't have a clue what Dan was saying, like he did when he needed a nap. *He's too tired to understand. How long can he hold out?* Convinced the crooks were dead, he left the gun in the deep parka pocket and retrieved the gloves. Dan glanced at his watch—three-thirty. He figured the snowy winding gravel road to be almost two miles. Even if he were in top-notch condition and could carry the boys, darkness would fall before they reached the paved road. Adrenaline pumping full speed wouldn't help him beat the setting sun. *What if another earthquake causes more hillsides to give way?* That thought brought a glimmer of hope. Emergency crews would be clearing debris.

"Let's ask God to protect us."

The boys bowed their heads.

"Lord, we have a long walk ahead. We trust You to keep us safe, Amen." Silently he added, *I need strength. Please send help.*

He held Timmy's hand while they walked, but it wasn't long before the youngster began to pull back, making Dan go slower. He decided to play Mother-May-I with the boys by going ahead and getting them to catch up. They didn't want to play his way. Dan tried guessing games, racking his brain to make up easy questions. Their interest lasted only a short while. He led them in simple songs to bolster their spirits.

Danny stopped singing. "My throat hurts."

So much for that brilliant idea, Dan thought, disgusted he hadn't taken into account the effects the cold air might have. He judged they'd gone a mile when the boys lagged, and Timmy started crying.

Dan picked up the three-year-old, and they were able to walk a little faster until Danny plopped down on a log. "I'm tired, Daddy. Carry me."

"Okay, Timmy, time to get down." Whimpering, the boy grabbed his neck, and Dan tried carrying both boys. The strain made his left arm throb, and he clenched his teeth whenever they rubbed against his stitched midsection. He endured the pain a few minutes more before setting Danny on the ground. "I'm sorry, but you're going to have to walk."

The temperature dropped as the sun lowered. Danny whined. "I'm tired and cold."

Dan took the blanket, folded it crosswise, and wrapped him. He secured the material with the diaper pin from Timmy's snowsuit. "That should keep you warmer." *And I'm glad to get rid of that blanket.* Timmy reached up to be carried, and Dan picked him up. The air turned icy; the sky dark. The moon highlighting the snow made Dan think of the poem "A Visit from St. Nicholas." He recited the verses while Timmy slept.

"Isn't it a little early for Christmas?" Danny asked.

"Thanksgiving is next month. Christmas won't be far behind, and you're going to get a special gift this year for letting me carry Timmy. I'm proud of you."

After they rounded a curve and passed through an opened gateway, Dan said, "Hey, look, there's the main road, and I see a sign. Let's go see what it says. Maybe it will tell us where we are. Maybe there's a town close by." Dan pulled out the flashlight and brushed off the snow, but he didn't have to use it to read it. The moon high-lighted the black letters—NO TRESPASSING. Dan's heart sank.

Danny burst into tears. "Carry me."

Dan realized his son could endure no more. "I'll carry you too for a little while." How long could he bear the pain? How long would his legs hold out? He saw a large boulder where Danny could stand. When Dan shifted Timmy, he snuggled closer and buried his face against the fur on Doc's parka. "Danny, take my hand and stand on the rock. I'll bend down so you can grab my neck before wrapping your legs around my waist." Dan clenched his teeth, prepared for the pain, but he couldn't stifle a moan when Danny's legs brushed his midsection.

"Daddy, what's wrong?"

"Try not to move around."

"Are you sick? Doc said you didn't feel good the other day."

"I'm just very tired. I'll carry you for as long as I can, then you'll have to walk. Okay?"

"But, Daddy, I'm tired," Danny whimpered.

"I know, son. Rest while you can."

Dan relegated pain and weariness to the far recesses of his mind. The moonlight made it possible for him to pick out nearby objects and focus his attention on them. Forcing one foot in front of the other, he managed to reach first one tree, then another, and followed a wooden fence, hoping it would end at a driveway leading to a house. The railing turned and headed up the hill. Dan went back to striving to reach trees. A strand of glittering wire caught his eye. He strove to keep his gaze fastened on it, but from time to time, the strand disappeared. Maybe the wire was only visible from a certain angle, or maybe his eyes were getting too tired to see anything clearly. He blinked several times. In the distance, he saw the outline of a sign. Dan's mind said, *Hurry, go see what it says.* His feet refused. Twice his eyes closed as he dragged to reach it, making him realize he was reaching the end of his endurance. He concentrated harder, putting one foot in front of the other, left-right-left-right. Dead on his feet, his head swimming, unable to think, unable to pray, Dan plodded like a zombie driven by an unseen force.

Danny screamed, "Daddy, you almost fell."

Jarred out of his trance, Dan stared into space unable to comprehend where he was then realized he was walking down the middle of the road. He looked for the sign he'd been striving to reach. Either he had staggered past, or it had been another figment of his imagination. "I can't carry you anymore," he mumbled. Danny didn't balk when Dan leaned over and set him down. Timmy clung tighter to his neck and started crying. Dan pried his fingers loose and put him on the ground. "I'm sorry, Timmy, you're going to have to walk, but first I need to rest on that log." Immediately, Timmy climbed on his lap. Dan fought the urge to close his eyes. "We can't sit very long."

"Can't we wait here for someone to find us?" Danny asked.

"It's too cold. We've got to keep moving as long as we can."

Danny pointed down the road. "What's that?"

The light of the moon revealed a van that had plowed into a tree about two hundred feet away. "Looks like a car. Let's go see." He took their hands while they walked down the road to look at the wreck. Dan shook his head as he surveyed the crumpled front end and the shattered windshield. The flashlight revealed an empty van with blood on the front seat before the beam died. Was the driver in the hospital or the morgue? From a practical standpoint, one person's misfortune was his small miracle. "I hope it's not locked. We can climb inside and stay warmer until someone finds us." He pulled and tugged on all the doors, but none would open.

Tired and discouraged, Dan brushed snow off the back bumper and sat. "We're not going to walk any longer. After I pin that blanket around you and Timmy, I'll sit here and hold you. Someone will come for this car." Both fell asleep after they settled on Dan's lap. He braced his feet on a rock and his back against the van. Clasping his hands around his precious sons, Dan closed his eyes.

*****

"Let go of the boys. I'll take them."

Dan vaguely heard a man's voice. He moved his head side-to-side to escape a light flashing across his face.

"Let go of the boys," the voice repeated softly but more insistent.

Gentle slaps on his face made Dan open his eyes. Groggy, as if he were coming out of one of Doc's drug-induced sleeps, he stared, seeing but not comprehending. Dan tightened his fingers when someone tried to pry them apart.

"I want to help you," a man said. "My car's warm."

Warm? The word penetrated Dan's fogged brain. He opened his eyes and shivered.

"How long have you been sitting here?"

Dan shrugged.

"Do you remember hitting the tree? Why didn't you stay in the van to keep warm?"

"Not our van…doors jammed…been walking for hours."

"Let me put the boys in my car, then I'll give you a hand."

With relief, Dan relinquished each sleeping son and watched the man place them in the car.

The stranger returned and helped Dan to his feet, gripping his right arm when Dan's legs buckled. "Can you make it with my support?"

"I think so. Just give me a few minutes to get some feeling in my legs." He squeezed his numb toes.

The man scanned the back of the van with his flashlight. "This stuff looks pretty expensive. The person must have been planning on setting up housekeeping…a gourmet cook from the looks of these fancy pots and pans."

When the light shone on a heater and a package of pull-up diapers, Dan sank on the bumper. "Lord, no." He laid his head against his palms.

"You know the driver?"

Dan gazed into his concerned face. "It's Cookie's. He's a chef. I think he was driving."

The man put a hand on Dan's shoulder. "Maybe he's okay. We'll hurry down to the ranger station. They can find out where he was taken and his condition." He helped Dan to his car.

The warmth overwhelmed Dan as he laid his head back.

"My name's Bob Jensen. What happened tonight?"

"I'm Daniel Baker…tremor caused an avalanche or landslide… long story." Exhausted, he closed his eyes. Explanations would have to wait.

At the ranger station, Mr. Jensen ran to the building and returned with two rangers who carried the boys inside. Dan leaned on Mr. Jensen while they followed the men into a lounge where a fire blazed and a portrait of Smokey Bear smiled down from the mantle.

Danny awakened. "Timmy, look."

Startled, Timmy jerked upright in the ranger's arms and glanced around the room.

"I'm here," Dan said. "Everything's okay."

Danny pointed to the picture. "It's Smokey."

When Timmy beamed, the dark-haired ranger said, "Would you like a toy bear?" He set Timmy on the couch.

Dan watched his son nod shyly.

The man winked. "Be right back." He returned with stuffed Smokey Bears and gave one to each boy. "Little man, let's get your mittens off so you can hold that bear better."

"Check his hands for frostbite," Bob Jensen said. "His father mentioned they'd been walking for hours."

The ranger examined Timmy's hands. "They're cold but otherwise fine." He tugged off Timmy's boots and unzipped the snowsuit. Timmy clutched the bear in one arm then the other as the man pulled down on the sleeves.

Too tired to move, Dan could only stand and watch others take care of his sons.

The tall ranger came over to Dan. "Wouldn't you like to shed that parka?"

Dan blinked a few times. "What?"

"Aren't you getting hot in that parka?"

Dan nodded, slipped off his gloves and pulled down the zipper tab.

"I'm Chad Cooper. Let me give you a hand with that. You look tired enough to drop. You'd better sit in that recliner. How far did you walk tonight?"

The minute the parka was off, Dan dropped into the chair. He slid back his jacket cuff to look at his watch. *Almost seven?* "We left around three-thirty, but I have no idea how long we sat on the bumper."

The dark-haired ranger joined them. "I'm Chuck Nelson. The boys seem none the worse for wear. Who are you and what happened tonight?"

Before Dan could speak, Bob Jensen said, "This is Mr. Baker. He told me that the tremor caused an avalanche."

Ranger Nelson lifted Dan's arm and fingered the bullet hole on his bloody sleeve. "Since when do avalanches shoot bullets? Chad, fetch me the first aid kit. Mr. Jensen, would you take the boys to the kitchen and fix them something to eat?"

"Sure thing."

Danny forsook his bear immediately and ran to Mr. Jensen. Timmy made no move to join them. "Come on, Timmy. I'm hungry. Aren't you?"

Clutching his bear tighter, Timmy turned fear-glazed eyes toward Dan.

"It's okay, Timmy. I'll be right here. I'm going to call Grandpa to come get us."

Danny ran and grabbed his brother's hand. When he tugged, Timmy balked before he finally went along.

After Mr. Jensen and the boys were in the kitchen, Ranger Cooper left the room and returned with a first aid kit. He set it on the end table and picked up Doc's parka and searched the pockets, pulling out the flashlight and revolver. He eyed Dan with suspicion. "I thought this jacket seemed weighted." He held out the gun. "You've been shot and you're carrying a gun. Explain."

Dan stared at the revolver, reliving the shooting and seeing Needles's lifeless bleeding form. Shuddering, he managed to say, "I killed a man in self-defense so we could escape. I took the gun for protection." Dan shivered again.

Ranger Nelson placed his hand on Dan's forehead. "He's not feverish."

"I got chilled," Dan said. When the ranger opened the first aid kit, Dan heaved a sigh. "This really isn't necessary. It's only a gash, and I bound it to stop the bleeding."

"Give me a hand, Chad. Help me get his jacket off. At least you were dressed warm."

Dan unzipped it, started to take out his arm, winced and yielded to the rangers. Not wanting them to see his stitched wound, he said, "There's no need to take my shirt off, just tear the sleeve. It's shot anyway." He laughed dryly. "No pun intended."

Neither man cracked a smile. They seemed intent on studying the wound after Ranger Nelson unbound it. "Chad, bring me a wet washcloth. I need to clean off this dried blood before I use the alcohol swabs."

When Chad returned, he gave him the wet cloth and said, "I need to call the police."

"I need to phone Fullerton Headquarters," Dan interjected. "My father, Captain Baker, needs to know we're here. My sons and I were kidnapped six days ago. He knows the whole situation. I'm sure he and the FBI would like to handle this."

Both rangers seemed to be pondering this while Ranger Nelson took care of Dan's arm. "I see," he said, wrapping gauze around the newly cleansed wound. When Dan shivered again, the ranger helped him into his jacket.

Dan bit down on his lip, trying to stop his trembling. "I must've gotten colder than I thought."

Mr. Jensen came out of the kitchen with a tray containing sandwiches and three mugs. "You, boys, sit here at the dining room table. I need to talk to your father." He carried a mug over and handed it to Dan. "I thought you could use some cocoa too."

"Thanks." Dan held the mug with both hands. Unable to control his shaking, cocoa sloshed. He set it down on the end table, pressed his head into the recliner, and clenched his hands in frustration.

The two rangers exchanged a few hushed words before Ranger Nelson said, "We'd better have Doc, who lives nearby, come check you over."

"Doc?" The word unleashed Dan's emotions. He fought for control, but tears streamed down his cheeks.

Danny rushed over, climbed onto Dan's lap and threw his arms around him. "Don't cry, Daddy. Doc's with Jesus now."

Dan embraced him and gradually grew calmer. "Thank you, Danny. Daddy's okay now. You can go back to your cocoa." He gazed into the concerned faces of the three men. "Guess I just needed a hug." His hand barely trembled when he lifted the mug to his lips, took a sip, and set it down. "Doc died saving me. Earlier, he threw himself over my sons to protect them from falling debris." He drew in a breath and slowly let it out. "When you said the word *Doc*, it hit me square between the eyeballs. It's been a rough night, but I don't need a doctor. I'm tired, and my nerves have taken a beating, but all I really need is to call my father and have him come get us. It's been six days since I've seen my wife. Believe me, sleeping in my own bed snuggled next to her will do more for me than any doctor can. Please, may I use the phone?"

Ranger Cooper retrieved the portable phone and said, "I'll call." He looked at Dan as if he suspected he was trying to pull a fast one. "What's the number?" After Dan gave it to him, the ranger dialed, asked for Captain Baker, waited a moment and said, "Sir, we have a young man here with two small boys who says he's your son."

Dan heard Cap shout, "Praise the Lord."

Suspicion vanished from the ranger's face. "He wants to talk to you."

Dan took the phone and managed to relate in a calm voice how they had escaped. "A man picked us up and drove us to the ranger station. We're okay. Please bring Cindy."

When Danny ran to Dan, Timmy followed and climbed on Dan's lap. Danny tugged on Dan's sleeve. "I want to talk to Grandpa."

"Not very long."

"Grandpa, Needles killed Doc with a knife then he shot Daddy, but Daddy shot him and made sure he was dead. Needles was…"

Dan rolled his eyes and grabbed the phone. "Enough, Danny," he said sharply. "I'm fine, Cap. The bullet only grazed me, but we're all tired. The sooner you get here, the better." He handed the phone to Ranger Cooper. "He wants directions."

The ranger gave him the information, pushed the off button, and called the San Bernardino police.

Danny's face puckered. "Why are you mad at me?"

Dan hugged him with tenderness. "I'm not angry, just tired. But this is police business, and we should only talk to them."

"Oh." With guilt written on his face, Danny cast a furtive glance at Mr. Jensen.

Dan said, "I take it he talked a lot in the kitchen."

Mr. Jensen nodded. "Normally, I would have chalked up his conversation to an overactive imagination, but that bullet wound lend credence to it."

"What did he say?"

"He didn't like Mr. Adolf, Needles, Lefty, Muscles, and Einstein…said they took them from their mommy and put some smelly stuff over their faces. It made them sick. Timmy threw up."

"What else?"

"He said Doc and Cookie were nice, and that all seven men were going to get one million dollars. For ransom? That doesn't jibe, nor does Mr. Adolf's offering Danny his share if Danny would come to live with him and the guy named Needles."

"Ransom never figured into it, only money and revenge." He smiled at Danny and ruffled his hair. "And I've never been more proud of you." He looked up at the three men. "He told Adolf, 'Give the money to Daddy. He knows what I need.'"

Chad Cooper again eyed Dan with suspicion. "Did he give you the money?"

"No. His offer was repugnant. Adolf and his son were…" How could he explain yet keep Danny in the dark? "Intimate partners… Needles was dying from…AIDS. I could have the money if my sons and I would go live with them."

Danny tugged on his sleeve. "Without Mommy?"

"Yes, but I knew we'd never be happy without her, not for all the money in the world." He hugged his son but gazed at the men.

"Please, no more questions. I've got to call the nearest hospital and check on Cookie."

Danny's eyes widened. "What's wrong with Cookie?"

"He was driving that wrecked van and was probably taken to the nearest hospital. Do any of you know the number?"

"It's 555-6000," Ranger Cooper said. "I'll dial and put it in speaker."

A man answered the phone and said, "Sorry, the receptionist had to leave for a moment. Can I help you?"

"I'm trying to find my friend whose van hit a tree near the Ranger Station. Has anyone been brought in there tonight?" Dan gave him a description.

"Yeah, I happen to be the orderly who wheeled in a man like that who kept muttering, 'Got to save them.'"

"That must be Cookie. Any idea what his condition is?"

"I heard the fly boys talking about rushing him to St. Jude in Fullerton for brain surgery. Hate to tell you, man, but he may not live."

Dan's heart sank. "Thanks." He punched the off button and set the phone on the end table.

Danny climbed on Dan's lap. "Daddy, Cookie has to live. He doesn't know Jesus. Pray for him." Tears poured down Danny's cheeks. "Please!"

Dan bowed his head. "Lord, we know You hold Cookie's life in Your hands. He told me he would only believe in You if You saved my life. Please let him live and learn how wonderful You are, Amen."

"Please, Jesus," Danny cried. "Don't let him die. I love him."

Dan kissed one sobbing boy then the other until they stopped crying. By then, he'd recovered his composure. "Why don't you and Timmy try to sleep? God will take care of Cookie."

"When will Grandpa get here with Mommy?"

"Pretty soon. The time will go faster if you sleep."

Both snuggled closer and closed their eyes.

"They're good kids," Mr. Jensen said. "And you sound like a preacher."

"Youth pastor," Dan said with weariness.

"How can Danny love a crook?" Mr. Jensen asked.

"Cookie only fixed meals and took care of my sons." A wave of sadness hit him, and he closed his eyes a moment before he continued, "Doc was his brother, but Doc's dead now. His last words were, 'Help Cookie.' The guy's a decent fellow who's deaf and has had nothing but bad breaks. His dream is to own a restaurant. What he can do with food is fantastic, but he'll probably end up in prison and never realize his dream. I wish I could prevent that. I wish I had money to hire the best lawyer. I wish I could buy him a restaurant." Dan laid his head back. "I wish. I wish."

"You're beat," Mr. Jensen said.

"Beat? Yes." He looked at Mr. Jensen. "Beaten? No. God can do what I can't."

Mr. Jensen smiled. "Yes, He can. He works in strange and marvelous ways." He extended his hand. "I have to leave, but I'm sure God will see to it that our paths cross again."

Dan couldn't explain the peace filling him as he grasped the man's hand. "I'll look forward to it. Thank you for rescuing us. You surely were our guardian angel tonight."

Mr. Jensen laughed. "I'm hardly an angel. I just happened to be in the right place at the right time."

After he left, Ranger Nelson said, "Would you like a sandwich, more cocoa or coffee?"

"Nothing, thanks. Mr. Jensen seems like a nice gentleman. He acts at home here," Dan said, trying to push his ordeal aside, but his throbbing head and arm made that impossible.

"The three of us went to college together," Ranger Cooper said. "His wife died last year. He lives in Orange County, but whenever he comes up to his cabin, he pops in here for a visit."

Dan saw concern register on the rangers' faces.

"Why don't we stretch the boys out on the couch so you can be more comfortable?" Ranger Cooper said.

Dan nodded and allowed them to carry his sleeping sons to the couch. Neither awakened. The men exchanged a few words before Chad Cooper approached. "We really feel we should have the doctor come check you over. You're in a lot of pain."

"Nothing I can't handle, but I wouldn't refuse whatever you have that's extra strength. As to a doctor, I have a family physician and dear friend who I'm sure has been contacted and is waiting to examine me as soon as I get home. I'm surprised the San Bernardino Police aren't here by now."

"Since we relayed what you said about your father and the FBI, they're probably coordinating. Chuck would you get Mr. Baker something for his pain?"

Chuck nodded and returned shortly with a glass of water.

Dan tried not to appear eager when he accepted the tablets, but after gulping them down, he prayed they were fast acting. "Think I'll follow my sons' example and get some sleep." He leaned his head back and closed his eyes.

17

Reveling in a valley of peacefulness, Dan clung to his dream—the sensation of warm moist lips caressing his. As he had for six days, he concentrated harder to visualize Cindy nestled against his chest. He inhaled the spicy fragrance of her perfume and the sweet scent of clean hair. Dan moaned with longing.

"Open your eyes."

The soft-spoken command penetrated Dan's dream-like trance. *Cindy?* He stared, too overwhelmed to speak. When she kissed him, pressing his head against the chair, his ordeal vanished. He pulled Cindy onto his lap and kissed her with six days' worth of longing. They continued to cling to each other. "Let's go home," he whispered.

Cap cleared his throat. "Sorry to break this up, but we need to talk."

Dan stiffened as if he'd been jabbed with a needle.

"It's okay," Cindy said, her eyes showing sympathy and understanding as she slid off his lap.

"Where do you want to go?" Dan muttered in disgust.

"I was told we could go to the kitchen for privacy and fresh coffee."

After they set steaming mugs on the table and took seats across from each other, Cap's brow furrowed with concern. "One of the rangers told me about your having the shakes and breaking down. I hate asking you questions so soon."

"But you're a cop, and I'm a witness."

"You sound resentful."

"Couldn't you have given me five minutes with Cindy? You shattered the first peace I've felt in six days."

"Sorry. I know it was rotten timing, but now that you've gotten that off your chest, can we talk? A SWAT team will be here shortly. You need to show us where the hideout is."

Dan shoved his chair back, stood, and walked to the window. Bracing his hands against the sink, he stared at the night sky before he turned and glared at Cap. "The gang's not going anywhere. Four are buried under an avalanche of snow, rock, and mud. Doc has a knife sticking in his chest...I triggered the gun that killed Needles...Cookie may die before the night ends, and the money's all there. God wrapped the whole package and dropped it on your doorstep. What more do you want?" Dan blurted, shaking and breathing hard.

Rushing to him, Cap placed his hands on Dan's shoulders. "Son, I'm sorry. Forgive me. I thought the sooner I put you through this, the quicker you'd be able to put it behind you."

"Sorry, I lost my cool. It's been a long six days. Returning to the hideout is the last thing I want to do. I'm exhausted. But you're right about getting it over with so I can get my life back together."

"You accounted for seven of the gang, but eight stores were hit. Was there an eighth person?"

Dan gave a half-hearted laugh. "I guess God did leave one package for you...Snow White, Einstein's girlfriend. She shouldn't be hard to track down. I think she worked in law enforcement since she kept Einstein informed of every police move."

"You're right, she shouldn't be hard to trace."

The station's phone rang, and Ranger Cooper came into the kitchen. "That was Police Chief Captain Marshall. He's been waiting outside for the SWAT team and said it just arrived. I told him you'd be right out."

Cap said, "Dan, it's time to leave. Cindy can stay here with the boys."

"If the SWAT team just arrived from Orange County, you must have sped one hundred miles an hour to get here...sirens blaring all the way."

"The team's from San Bernardino. Cindy and I came by heli-copter. Captain Marshall met us at the chopper pad and drove us, and we'll return the same way. He's provoked because the San Bernardino police weren't called immediately. Why weren't they?"

"The rangers were busy tending to the boys, and my wound. They called right after I talked to you. What difference does ten to twenty minutes make? Except for Cookie and Snow White, the crooks are dead."

"Did you see all the bodies?"

"No."

"Then you can't be sure."

After they left the kitchen, Dan saw a police officer talking to Cindy and the rangers. The man took long strides toward them.

"Daniel Baker, I'm Captain Marshall. You'll ride in the front seat with me. Can you pinpoint on this map where the hideout is?" He spread a detailed map of the area on the dining table. "Here's the ranger station."

"A van got wrecked tonight. Can you locate the area for me?"

The captain tapped the paper. "About right here."

Dan saw a side road a few miles farther. He mentally walked it to the wide curve. In his mind, he saw the lodge. "Take this nameless gravel road on the left. It leads to the lodge…roughly two miles. There's a wide curve before you reach the driveway."

"You're sure?"

"Pretty sure. When we reached the main road, there was no signpost at the end of the one we came down. But there was a NO TRESSPASSING sign nailed to a tree"

Cap's eyebrows shot up. "You hiked that far carrying the boys after having been shot? No wonder you're tired."

"The bullet only grazed me, and Danny walked most of the time."

Captain Marshall opened a notebook. "Draw me a layout of the hideout. You're sure it was a lodge?"

"Yes." Dan sketched quickly while he talked. "Two side by side massive rock fireplaces separated the two large living rooms." He pointed to the room he had drawn. "The landslide filled this area with mud, snow, and rock, burying the four men in there who were getting their money. I think the leader's son must have been packing. You'll find him in this room with Doc."

"The bomb guy?"

"Einstein."

"Do you happen to know if he kept explosives at the lodge?"

"I asked Doc that last night. He told me Adolf wouldn't even allow him to have them in the car. They're stored somewhere in Orange County. The only bomb up there should be the one I wore. Einstein probably took it to his room." Dan tapped the sketch. "This one, but that section of the lodge is pretty well destroyed. Doc said the detonator was kept in the car...Adolf was too paranoid to have it close."

"Where would the car be?"

"In one of the garages, but I found them all locked."

Captain Marshall glanced at Cap and back to Dan. "How sensitive would you say that bomb is?"

"As far as being accidentally detonated...the earthquake didn't trigger it, nor did the jarring ride each day. They had me lying face down behind the front seat of a van. We bounced so hard over the rutted road, I feared it would explode. And I don't think Adolf would have made me sleep with the thing if he'd thought there was the remotest chance it might explode."

Cap's eyes widened. "You had to sleep with the bomb?"

"My penance for passing information. Why all the questions?"

Captain Marshall pursed his lips. "I'm weighing my decision whether or not to take you and your father up there now or after the bomb squad goes over the area."

Dan drew in a breath and exhaled. "Look, I don't want to wait around here, nor do I want to come back tomorrow. I want this to end now."

Captain Marshall glanced at Cap who said, "It's your call. Since Dan had to sleep with that bomb, I'd say without someone to trigger it, we're safe."

The door banged open. The SWAT commander barged in and took quick strides toward Captain Marshall. "We've been waiting ten minutes. Are we going or not?"

"Mr. Baker sketched a layout." He tore out the sheet and gave it to the garbed man before showing him the map. "This is the probable turnoff to the hideout. I'll fill you in when we get there." He grabbed the notebook and map. "Let's get going."

When Dan glanced at Cindy, she smiled wanly and blew him a kiss. Outside, Dan slid onto the passenger seat, and Cap took the backseat of the patrol car while they waited for Captain Marshall to speak to the SWAT team commander. After the policeman returned, he said, "We'll follow them. Mr. Baker, if the side road they turn on isn't the correct one, tell me immediately."

They passed the wrecked van, and Dan uttered a silent prayer for Cookie before saying, "I think Doc and Cookie's money is in the van. You may want to have a wrecker haul it someplace secure." He kept his eyes focused on the road but found nothing to change his mind. When the SWAT team vehicle turned and started up the side road, Dan's heart pounded harder the closer they came to the curve. He watched the vehicle stop short of it. Men peeled out before Captain Marshall pulled in behind. Dan, Cap, and the captain joined the heavily garbed armed men.

"Are you positive this is the area?" the team commander asked Dan.

Dan nodded. "A steep driveway leads to the lodge which is just around the bend."

"How much tree coverage?"

"Plenty, but I really don't think you'll run into trouble."

He eyed Dan with disdain. "Men have died believing that. These men are under my command, and I don't intend to lose one." He turned heel and stomped to the head of the group. Captain Marshall, who had just suited up, hurried to join him. Thoroughly rebuked, Dan climbed in the front seat of the squad car with Cap and watched the team hike the hill.

When the men disappeared around the curve, Cap said, "While we wait, why don't you give me a rundown of the past six days."

After Dan gave his father an overall account, Cap's brow furrowed. "You said Danny and Timmy were shoved outside in the cold to make you reveal what information you passed to us. That's all Adolf did in retaliation?"

The knife and Needles's sadistic smile flashed before Dan. Remembering the slow penetration of the steel blade, he held his breath.

Cap touched his arm. "What did Adolf do?"

Dan drew a quick gulp of air, and shuddered.

"Son?"

"Give me a minute." Dan took a deep breath before telling Cap about Needles's viciousness. "Adolf stopped him but made it clear his son could do whatever he wanted after they divided the money. That's why Cookie and Doc were so anxious to get the boys away."

"Do you think Adolf would have let them leave?"

Dan laid his head back. "I don't want to think about it."

"Unzip your jacket and pull up your shirt so I can see your wound."

"There's nothing to see. Doc stitched the gash and wrapped gauze around me."

"When we get home, I want it checked."

"Fine." Dan rested his head and closed his eyes.

"I haven't heard any gunfire. I hope that means no one's alive and all are present and accounted for."

"They'll only find Doc and Needles."

"So you keep saying. How?"

The mobile phone rang, and Cap answered. Dan heard Captain Marshall say "You can come up now. Our thermal imaging viewer has scanned the lodge for heat areas and found nothing to indicate anyone's alive."

Walking up the driveway to the lodge, Dan and Cap met the SWAT team commander who said, "We only found two bodies."

"The rest are buried in the debris-filled room," Dan said.

"Guess we'll have to dig to make sure, won't we?" the man's tone implying Dan couldn't possibly know.

"Of course...or you can want for the snow to melt." Dan didn't care how the officer took his sarcastic remark. For six days, he'd been through the mill. Suddenly he wanted to slug someone.

Cap moved in front of Dan. "May we go in now? Dan needs to identify the bodies."

"Be my guest." He spat the words as he gazed at Dan with contempt. "Captain Marshall's waiting for you in the room with the dead guys."

Cap and Dan stood at the foot of the stairs while the rest of the team filed out of the lodge, joined their commander, and headed down the hill. "Your tiredness is making you surly," Cap said while they climbed the steps.

Dan stopped when he reached the porch and turned to face his father. "Maybe I've just come out of shock and I'm beginning to get angry."

"I'll buy that. But how about directing your anger toward the right side? Think about the pressure that commander's under."

"And I've been through hell!"

Cap sighed. "Then vent steam my way."

"Why?"

"When I talked with you on the phone, you sounded good, so I suggested to Captain Marshall we come up here tonight instead of tomorrow. I didn't realize what Adolf had put you through until you told me in the squad car."

"What about the boys? Didn't you take into consideration what they've been through?"

"Dan, I'm sorry. I blew it. I apologize. For what it's worth, I did run this by Cindy. She didn't like the idea but agreed it was better for you to get this over with tonight so you could relax tomorrow. I don't want to argue about this any longer. Captain Marshall is waiting." He opened the door and gestured Dan to enter.

Dan scowled at his father before he walked across the threshold.

Inside, Cap said, "Show me where Doc and Needles are."

Dread replaced Dan's anger. "Down the hall...last door on the right." He made no move to follow Cap.

"Aren't you coming?"

"I can't go in there."

"Dan, you're the only one who can identify them."

"I killed Needles."

"In self-defense. Your teenage nightmares still haunt you. Are you going to add this to them? Son, you're no longer a kid."

Dan lagged behind while his father stepped over debris and waited for him in front of the opened door. Reaching it, he stiffened, his mind refusing to let his feet enter the room. "Needles's body is the one just inside…to the right. Doc is near the window, propped against the chest of drawers." Dan saw the police officer, waiting.

Cap's hand gestured him forward. "Identify them for us."

Dan took a deep fortifying breath and walked into the room. He forced himself to look at Needles. "God, forgive me," he blurted.

"Forgive yourself, Dan. God doesn't hold you responsible." Less forcefully, he said, "Show us Doc's body."

"I told you where it is."

Cap waved his hand again. "Show us," he ordered.

Captain Marshall, who could have easily walked over and looked, stood still as if waiting to see whose will was stronger.

Dan scowled as he passed in front of both men and pointed. "There!" he said, stepping aside to allow Captain Marshall to approach.

Cap placed an arm around Dan while the captain pulled back the blanket and said, "Is this Doc?"

Dan nodded, his eyes misting. "He pushed me, Cap. That knife was meant for me." He shook his head sadly. "Doc only joined the gang to get money to open a clinic for AIDS patients. He formulated a drug to help them. It was keeping Needles alive. That's why he could stand up to Adolf and protect the boys. Now he's dead, and so are the others, except Cookie. Somehow, Cap, I've got to help him."

"Why are you so positive Adolf and the others didn't get away?" Cap asked.

"Would you believe God told me?"

"How?"

Captain Marshall cocked his head with interest, but his face reflected skepticism while Dan related his vision and dream.

"Aces and coffins," Cap said. "Visions and dreams like Daniel of old. Your mother sure named you right."

"Ahem," Captain Marshall coughed, taking a small tape recorder from his breast pocket. "I need to make out a report. Do you mind being taped?"

"No," Dan said. Too tired to stand much longer, he went around the bed to sit where he couldn't see Doc. After the two men followed and stood in front of him, Dan said, "What do you want to know?"

"I'd like you to start at the beginning and tell me everything."

Dan rolled his eyes. "You've got to be kidding. Maybe you've got all night, but I don't! I have two small boys who need to be home in bed getting their lives back to normal."

Cap laid a hand on his shoulder. "Easy, Dan, I'm sure Captain Marshall can see you're exhausted. The only pertinent information he needs right now is where you think the money is. Fair enough, Captain?"

"That, and at least a recap of what happened tonight and descriptions of the supposedly buried men."

"They're dead!"

"Then show me their bodies, otherwise I need to put out an APB on them."

"Dan, he's not being unreasonable."

Heaving a sigh of defeat, Dan gave the officer a quick rundown and descriptions. "Logic tells me most of the money is buried under the rock and snow—five to six million, depending on whether or not Needles took his to his room. And, as I said before, Doc and Cookies' money should be in the van."

Captain Marshall cocked his head in puzzlement. "You've accounted for seven crooks, but eight stores were hit. Did Adolf take two million?"

"No, they each received one million. I told Cap about Adolf's mole in the police department, but I guess I forgot to mention her to you."

"Leave her to us," Cap said.

"Then I think we're done here," the officer said. "I imagine you'd like to get back to your family."

Dan nodded and fell in behind the captain who walked briskly down the hallway but stopped in the large empty room that now housed a boulder and asked, "Do you think aftershocks from last week's earthquakes triggered the landslide?"

Dan gazed from the gaping hole to the gigantic rock. Again awe-struck, he said, "Whether God caused it by divine means or natural ones doesn't matter, but He sure answered Doc's prayer and mine."

"As well as ours," Cap said. "Do you believe in prayer, Captain?"

"Well…yes," he stammered, "but I've never seen one answered like this."

"Nor have I, but last night, we had a roomful of teenagers in our home praying for Dan and the boys. I have never felt more proud, yet humbled at the same time. I listened in wonder as these young people poured out their hearts to the Lord. The power of their prayers filled the room like a gigantic wave of love engulfing evil." He placed his hands on Dan's shoulders. "I knew, no matter what happened to you, your ministry would never end." His eyes misted, and while hugging Dan, he said, "They love you, son, and so do I."

The door slammed behind the SWAT commander who barged into the room. "Are you finished in here, Captain Marshall? I'm going to ride back to the ranger station with you. I already dismissed my men, told them I'd go back with you and have my son pick me up later. I have a few more questions to ask Mr. Baker before I make out my report."

"What do you want to know?" Dan asked, wondering how many times he was going to have to repeat his story.

"I've been waiting out in the cold. I'd like to question you where it's warm."

Dan held back retorting, "Stupid, why didn't you come inside where the wind wouldn't whip your butt." He shrugged and headed for the door.

Outside, Cap said, "Dan, you take the front seat. I'll sit in back with the SWAT commander."

Afraid I'll spout off again?

At the ranger station, Dan saw Cindy cradling Timmy and cast her a faint smile. Danny lay peacefully asleep on the couch. *The sooner we get this over with, the sooner I can go home.* The SWAT commander pulled out a chair at the dining table. Before he could sit,

Dan took quick strides to the kitchen and grabbed a seat at the table. The commander stomped in and pulled back a chair. His scowl told Dan the man didn't like losing control of the situation—didn't like Dan deciding where they would talk. *You may not like it,* but *I'm not about to be interrogated within earshot of my sons and chance awakening them. They deserve to sleep and doggone it, I'd like to go home and get some shut-eye.* "Shoot," he said, knowing he sounded as disgusted as the commander looked. He ignored Cap's stern gaze as he and the policeman took the two remaining seats.

Captain Marshall interjected, "I really don't think we need to take up anymore of Mr. Baker's time. I have on tape his statement concerning tonight."

"All well and good, but I want to know why he's so hell-fire-sure four men perished in that room."

That's really been bugging you, hasn't it? Knowing the man would disregard visions and dreams, he simply said, "Adolf, Lefty, Muscles, and Einstein were in there celebrating…Needles was in his room packing. Cookie had taken the suitcases to the van, and Doc was with the boys. That accounts for all seven."

Before he could go on, the commander snorted, "No Snow White?"

"Yeah, there is a Snow White."

The man shoved his chair back, stood, and glared at Dan. "You're quite the comedian, aren't you? Captain Baker, maybe you can get your son to give me straight answers."

Cap motioned him to sit. "I know you two didn't get off on the right foot tonight, but he is telling you the truth. The seven men went by descriptive aliases. Snow White happens to be the alias of their mole in law enforcement."

"Do you have anything more to add?" the commander asked Dan.

"No, the proof lies under the debris. I'll identify the bodies after you find them."

"Mr. Baker gave me descriptions of the four men," Captain Marshall said. "Since it's possible they could have escaped, I'll put out an APB on them."

"Good. I'll get together with you tomorrow and listen to that tape." The commander stood, nodded, and walked out.

Captain Marshall pursed his lips as he shook his head. "He's normally not this inconsiderate. I think he needs a good night's sleep too. Mr. Baker, I hope you're right about the bodies. Having those men dead would be a godsend." He stood and offered Dan his hand. "I'll give all of you a ride to the chopper pad."

The wheels touching the pad at Fullerton Headquarters awakened Dan. Sluggish, he sat upright and pushed the remnants of sleep aside. "I'll carry Timmy," he said and reached for his son cradled in Cindy's arms.

"Hon, you've done enough for one night. Besides, I haven't been able to hold him for days."

Dan conceded and allowed Cap and Cindy to carry the boys to a squad car.

Cap withdrew his keys and unlocked it. Dan opened the back door for Cindy, and as soon as she was seated with Timmy on her lap, Cap placed Danny next to her and asked Dan, "Do you want to sit in front or back?"

"Where's your car?" A strange expression crossed his father's face as if he were hiding something. "You had an accident?"

Cap sighed before he said, "No."

"What's going on?" Dan asked. Cap had never been one to hesitate answering a straightforward question.

Resting his arm on top of the squad car, Cap said, "Adolf's bomb expert was extra busy. He rigged all our vehicles. If it weren't for Cindy's premonitions, we might be dead."

Cindy said, "In my mind, I saw the car explode just before Cap reached for the door handle."

"She screamed so loudly, it's a wonder that didn't trigger all the bombs."

Dan stiffened. "What do you mean by all?"

"All of our cars were rigged to explode when the speedometer reached sixty-five, but the bombs are being diffused."

Dan's mind went into overdrive. "What about your house… our house…the orchard? Why didn't you mention this earlier?" He'd thought his roller-coaster ordeal was over, but once more he plummeted from high to low as despair, anger, and fear again raised their ugly heads to torment him. He started shaking.

"That's why," Cap said. "Now calm down. Our houses and property have been gone over with a fine-tooth comb. No explosives were found. If I wasn't convinced we're safe, I wouldn't have left Amanda home with Jonathan, and we'd all be staying at a motel." Cap put his hands on Dan's shoulders. "It's over, son. Let's go home."

Dan bit down on his lip. "Will it ever be over?"

"If you're right about Einstein being dead, then he can't raise havoc again."

"It's my fault, Cap. I intimidated Adolf and felt smug about it. That's why he plotted revenge against all of you."

"With a mind as evil as his, who's to say he didn't have this planned all along?" Cap looked him square in the eyes. "Think about it. That man was a skunk of the worst kind. Now put this behind you."

"Sure. Just like that?"

"Yes. Now get in the car. Amanda, Jonathan, and Dr. Kincaid are waiting."

"Why Dr. Kincaid?"

"Because I asked him to come over and check you and the boys."

"I'm fine!"

"Like fun you are. It's either him or the emergency room."

Dan shrugged. "Let's go home."

"Good, I thought you'd see things my way. Now, back to my original question, do you want to sit in front or back?"

Dan saw Danny stretched out with his head on Cindy's knee. He closed the door. "I lost back seat privileges." He took the front seat. "Home, James."

When Cap rounded the corner of their street, Dan saw Dr. Kincaid's sedan parked in front of the house. The man was a trusted friend and godfather to the boys as well as the doctor for the rest of the family, but Dan had never let the man examine him. Call it foolishness, stubbornness or whatever, but he had a hang-up about allowing the doctor, from whom he'd fled as a teenager, to give him a physical. Dan had refused then to let Dr. Kincaid see the marks left on his back from his father's beatings. *And now? It's better than the emergency room.*

As soon as Cap pulled into the driveway and stopped, he jumped out and soon had Danny gathered into his arms, and Cindy carried Timmy into the house.

The minute Dan came inside, Amanda threw her arms around him and hugged him so tightly he winced. "You're hurt!"

"Mom, I'm okay. Maybe a little worse for wear, but basically I'm fine."

"I think I should be the judge of that," Dr. Kincaid said. "Amanda, where can we go?"

"Dan's old room. He can show you."

The doctor ushered Dan forward. "You lead. I'll follow."

Dan caught the scent of Cindy's perfume and saw her clothes hanging in the closet. He hoped Dr. Kincaid would give him a quick once-over and leave. He longed to snuggle in bed with his wife. Maybe getting his life back to normal would make it easier to put the last six days behind him.

The doctor closed the door. "Okay, let me help you out of your jacket and shirt. Your father told me about your stitched midsection and your arm."

"When was that?" Dan unzipped his jacket and allowed the man to ease his arm out of the sleeve."

"He called from the helicopter."

"Man, I must have conked out fast."

"Now, let's get that shirt off." When Dan made no move to unbutton it, he said, "You look ready to bolt again." He shook his head. "Daniel, Daniel, after all these years, are you still afraid to let me see the scars left from your beatings? I know they're there. Cap told me years ago."

Dan shrugged. "Memories are hard to reason with."

"I'm more than godfather to your sons...I'm your friend. Please don't shut me out of this area of your life."

Dan hung his head a moment before smiling at the man he admired and trusted. "I apologize." He unbuttoned his shirt. "Do you have any codeine? I have a terrible headache."

18

Dan glanced around the room as he gradually awakened Sunday morning. No longer surrounded by rustic hewn walls, peace rolled over him like a warm gentle breeze. He was safe. Growing more alert, his mind grasped the full meaning of this. His heart overflowed with gratefulness. *Praise God, I'm free! Danny, Timmy, and I are free!* "Lord, thank You for answering my prayers. I don't think I could have endured another day." A flash picture of the gaping hole and the gigantic boulder made him add, "You truly are an awesome God. My trust is in You alone, Lord. You have never failed me. Thank you again, Lord, Amen." *Never again will Adolf torment me with threats of harming Danny and Timmy. No longer will a chain or bomb mentally weigh me down.* He pressed his head into the pillow and gazed heavenward. *It's over. It really is over.*

Dan reveled in the sensation of lying warm on a soft mattress. Having Cindy snuggled next to him would have made waking up perfect. He ran his hand over the sheet where she had lain—cold. *Some husband I am. I conked out last night before she could climb into bed. Some friend Dr. Kincaid is. Why didn't he tell me that sleeping pill was so fast-acting?* He glanced at the clock—almost seven. If he asked, would Cindy come back to bed? He heard Jonathan crying and shook his head. *I think I've lost out for the moment.*

He stared out the window at the big apple tree he'd climbed countless times. It seemed strange to lie in his old room and see nothing to suggest it had ever been his. The bookcase no longer housed his bowling trophies. He saw no evidence his bug collection had ever cluttered the walls.

Dan enjoyed the creature comforts of the bed a few minutes longer before rising to shower and dress. He didn't like what he saw in the mirror, but there was no way to disguise the haggard face staring back. He glanced at Cindy's array of cosmetics. *I don't think I want to look like a clown.* Would that be better or worse?

Leaving the image of the older man in the bathroom, he put on his best smile and hurried downstairs to the kitchen.

Cap and Amanda sat at their table sipping coffee while Cindy fed cereal to Jonathan. "Good morning," Dan said to everyone but walked straight to Cindy. He kissed her hard, longing to lift her from the chair and carry her to the bedroom. Her barely perceptible moan told him it had been a long six days for her too. For a few seconds, they gazed at each other with love and understanding. He leaned down and kissed Jonathan on the forehead. "Hi, big guy, remember me?"

Jonathan squealed and raised his arms above the highchair tray.

Dan reached for his son, but Cindy said, "Wait until after he eats."

"Then let me feed him."

As they changed places, Jonathan started pounding his highchair tray with his spill-proof cup.

"Okay, I'll hurry," Dan said, filling the spoon. He took the cup from Jonathan and offered the cereal.

The baby batted the spoon, sending globs flying onto Dan's face and spattering his arms. Cap, Amanda, and Cindy started laughing. Dan glared and grabbed a napkin to wipe off the mess.

Amanda pushed back her chair and hurried to the sink. "I'll get you something better." She snatched one of the baby washcloths lying on the counter, moistened it, and rushed back to Dan. She lifted his chin and proceeded to wash his face.

"Mom, stop that. I'm not a baby. I can do it." When Dan reached for the cloth, she pulled her hand back.

Her eyes twinkled. "And deprive me of a privilege I never had? Besides, consider this your penance."

"For what?"

"For not giving me a kiss this morning."

Her grin told him she wasn't upset, but he realized he had virtually ignored his parents. "Mom, I'm sorry. Let me get this mess off so I can make amends."

Amanda tossed him the wet cloth, and while he cleaned off the splatters, Cindy wiped down the tray.

Dan rose to hug and kiss his mother. "Am I forgiven?"

She brushed a lock of his hair back in place. "Of course, and since I know you must be hungry, I'll serve breakfast." Amanda studied him a moment. "You certainly look better than you did last night. I really expected Dr. Kincaid to take you to the hospital."

"Mom, all I needed was a good night's sleep." *What in the world did I look like last night?* Dan couldn't picture himself appearing worse than the haggard guy he'd seen in the bathroom. He gazed down at Cindy who had taken over feeding Jonathan. The baby accepted each spoonful with eagerness. "He used to eat like that for me too. What got into him today?"

"Sorry, I forgot to warn you. For the past six days, I've had to hold his hands the first few bites. He may only be six months, but this ordeal has upset him too. Why don't you go talk to your father while I finish here?"

Dan poured a cup of coffee and set it down at the other end of the table before going to his father. He put his arm around him and grinned. "Do you need a good-morning kiss before I sit?"

His father chuckled and held out his cup. "A refill will suffice."

"Good." He took coffee to his father and sat across from him. "Thanks for holding down the fort."

"My pleasure, but I'm glad you're back to take over."

After a leisurely time around the table, Cap and Amanda rose to dress for church.

"I'll get Jonathan ready to go with you," Cindy told his parents.

"We're not going?" Dan asked in surprise.

"Dr. Kincaid told you he wouldn't put you in the hospital as long as you stayed here and rested. No phone calls, no visitors."

Cap said, "I already took our phone off the hook."

"I have no say in this?"

Cap grinned. "Nope. Consider yourself under house arrest. You're safe for now."

"From what?"

"The press. Last week we wouldn't let them interview Cindy... told them she was in seclusion. We told them they can't interview you because of the ongoing investigation of the explosions. Your escape and rescue made the eleven o'clock news, but not soon enough for the papers. Today's paper has a two-page spread on yesterday's chaos, and you're still a prime suspect."

"I heard about the six bombings on the way down yesterday morning, and Einstein bragged about the tank cars. Knowing how much misery he's caused makes me sick. How many has he killed, Cap? How many has he injured?"

"No one has died, but quite a few have been injured, including the Ware Mart manager. He told a reporter at the scene that the man destroyed his store because he had to come back for the extortion money demanded from the corporation. As soon as the media reported this, other managers started talking. One identified you." Cap shook his head. "You actually told one of the managers who you were and that you were being forced to do it?"

"What I was doing horrified me. I had to set the record straight."

"And Adolf enjoyed every minute of your torment, but he did take precautions by changing your appearance. The press was told you and the boys were kidnapped...that you were being forced to do this, but it didn't help...you were still at large, there were more explosions and the media linked them with the heists. You're still a prime suspect and guilty in many eyes. As soon as people know that you and the boys escaped and the bombings stop, things will quiet down, but then the media will be clamoring to interview you. Protecting you from reporters will give you some privacy and some normalcy. You will have police protection at home and a discreet escort wherever you go. So enjoy your next few days."

"I don't suppose Cindy and I could escape to Hawaii?"

"You're going to need that trip more after the news media gets their fill...not before."

Dan drew in a deep breath and sighed. "You're probably right."

After his parents left the room, Dan shoved his chair back and went to Jonathan, "Well, little man, since we don't have much time to play, let's go have some fun while I dress you." He glanced at Cindy. "Okay by you?"

"His clothes are laid out."

"I hear Danny and Timmy. Do you want me to help them get ready for Sunday school?"

"No, they're staying home too."

"Could I change your mind?" Dan ignored Jonathan's out-stretched arms and put his around her, drawing her close and kissing her with the fervor denied him for six days. "We could play catch-up all morning," he whispered, realizing their closeness was affecting her too.

Cindy leaned back against his arms, her eyes glazed with desire. "Dan, please don't make this so hard. We can't think about us right now. We have kids."

Her words hit him like a cold shower.

With her finger, she traced his lips and lifted one corner of his mouth into a lopsided smile.

Dan hated it when she tried to make him smile when he felt grumpy.

"We'll go home after lunch, and tonight I'll be all yours. Our avocado tree is waiting, the one we like with the branches reaching the ground. I raked up a mattress of leaves where we can lay our double sleeping bag."

"Then why not let Mom and Dad take Danny and Timmy with them so we can rush home now for a couple of hours?"

"Honey, the boys need to spend time with us. At church, they'd be made over and get undue attention before we have the chance to help them deal with what they've been through. They had night-mares, especially Danny. I was up and down all night."

"And I slept only because Dr. Kincaid made me take that fast-acting sleeping pill."

"You needed sleep." Her warm brown eyes revealed the depth of her love. "Think you can wait 'til tonight?"

"Yeah, but can we at least put the boys to bed early?"

She nodded. "But this morning, let's concentrate on helping them. I thought family devotions and a time for sharing by the fireplace would be more beneficial than church."

"You're probably right." *Probably?* Dan knew she was right. He, as well as Danny and Timmy, needed to deal today with what they had been through. Nightmares might not go away quickly. Last night in despair he'd voiced, "Will it ever be over?" In bed this morning, he'd told himself it was over, but he knew there would be lingering effects. If he had to seek professional help, he would do so for himself and the boys. Right now, he'd let Cindy handle the situation. She knew how little kids thought and how to reach them—get them to share their feelings.

After Danny and Timmy ate breakfast, Cindy said, "The boys need a bath, and I need to get a shower. While we get ready for the day, why don't you read our mail in the basket on the desk?"

Dan rekindled the fire before he took the basket and settled in Cap's recliner. He sat in awe as he read the encouraging cards and letters people had sent Cindy—so many praying and expressing love for his family. He saw the newspapers on the end table and picked up the Saturday paper. The front page shattered the warmth of being loved and respected—so much speculation, so many accusations. He hated seeing his picture with the caption—Prime Suspect, Daniel Baker. Pictures of the Ware Mart explosion and the injured surrounded his. He read the article and shook his head in disgust. Did he dare read the Sunday paper?

He picked it up and looked at the front page and saw his picture with the same caption. Yesterday's heists were mentioned but hardly noteworthy compared to the pictures of the six early-morning explosions. Einstein had really been busy. At least he gave the police time to evacuate the areas near the train. Dan shuddered. Twenty-five people had been injured; many hospitalized during the crime spree. Dan laid his head in his hands and prayed for all the victims.

When Cindy put her arm around him, he looked up and shook his head as he put the paper aside. "So much speculation…they jump to the conclusion that since the old stone house was bombed, then a new mafia gang must be behind the crime spree. Since I have been identified as the man who retrieved the money, then despite the FBI saying I was forced to do it, I'm still a prime suspect, and they surmise I'm working for the mafia, and that's how I can afford to own this house on prime acreage."

"Honey, you know the papers...anything to sell papers. Soon you're escape will be headline news."

"Can't be soon enough for me." A thought crossed his mind. "You know, maybe all this publicity will help the church grow. Maybe people will come to check it out."

"That reminds me. The produce crates will be here next week, and the young people are ready to pick and pack our bumper avocado crop. We should get enough money to pay our taxes."

"Praise God for good news."

When the boys came running into the room, he lowered the recliner and told them, "We're going to have devotions in front of the fire." They immediately ran and sat on the hearth rug. He and Cindy joined them. It reminded Dan of legends being related around a campfire as Cindy dramatically recited the boys' favorite Bible stories.

She asked questions after each, trying to get them to open up and express the emotions the characters must have felt—fear, anger, despair, hatred. Timmy mainly mimicked his brother, nodding or saying yes whenever he did. Dan listened and watched his sons' reactions.

They agreed that Shadrach, Meshach, and Abednego must have been frightened when they were taken from their homes and terrified when they were thrown into the fiery furnace. Danny's countenance darkened when she started talking about Joseph. His mouth drew into a grim line as she related how mean his brothers were to toss him into a pit. When she mentioned his being dragged away to Egypt, Danny blurted, "They dragged me across the floor, but I kicked one of them before they put that smelly stuff on my face. Timmy threw up all over the bed. And my shoulder hurt."

When Cindy cast Dan a worried glance, he mouthed, "We'll talk later."

She hugged the boys. "But you're both okay?" They nodded, and Danny seemed to relax, but the minute she started talking about Daniel in the lions' den, he started shaking. Wild-eyed, he screamed, "Adolf wanted Needles to play Daniel in the lions' den with Daddy and kill Daddy with a knife. I hate Needles. I'm glad Daddy killed him!"

When Dan saw hatred spewing from his son's eyes, he bowed his head. Hate had made him place his hands around Needles's neck. Would he have killed Needles if Muscles hadn't knocked him out? He'd told Doc that murder or attempted murder was never justified in the eyes of God. Hate equated murder. Dan laid his head against his palms and wept.

Danny wriggled onto his lap, pushing Dan's arms apart until Dan wrapped them around him. He gazed into Dan's face with eyes no longer glazed with hatred but ones filled with concern. "Daddy, why are you crying?"

Dan pulled him closer, fighting for control and the right words. He took a few deep breaths and glanced at Cindy. Tears streamed down her cheeks as she nodded for him to handle it. *Pray for me, Honey, I need all the help I can get.*

"Daddy! Why are you crying?"

He kissed his son on the forehead. "Because I see so much hatred in your heart. Danny, I had to ask God to forgive me for hating Adolf, Needles, and the others."

"You hated Cookie and Doc?"

"Cookie? No. Doc? Yes, at one time I hated him too."

"Why? Doc was nice."

Lord, don't let me get sidetracked. "We'll talk about that later. The point is, Danny, hate is wrong. To God, hate is a sin as bad as murder. When I fired that gun, I never meant to kill Needles. I only wanted to disable him so we could escape." Shock, puzzlement, and disbelief registered on his son's face. Dan glanced at Cindy, desperately wanting her to take over. When she said nothing, he knew it was up to him. "Danny, I may still have hate in my heart that I need to confess. Will you kneel with me?"

Timmy scrambled over Cindy to join them. With an arm around each boy, Dan's heart burst with an overwhelming sense of love. "Dear Jesus, I am so grateful for Your bringing us all back together. I am overwhelmed by Your willingness to forgive us when we sin. I ask forgiveness now for any hatred left in my heart. I know I asked before, but I feel the need to confess again the sin that displeases You so much. Erase this last trace of bitterness and make me pleasing to You, Amen."

While he listened to his son, Dan squeezed his eyes to stem his tears, but they slipped through the lashes when Danny sobbed, "I don't want to be a murderer, Jesus. Please forgive me for hating all those bad men."

How Timmy could possibly understand what was happening, Dan didn't know, but his three-year-old started crying, and after Danny finished praying, Timmy said, "I sorry, Jesus."

Dan sat back on his haunches and hugged both boys, feeling more love for his sons than he thought possible. "Feels good, doesn't it, to ask God for forgiveness and feel his love pour over us?"

Danny nodded.

Timmy cocked his head. "What's forgiveness?"

"Remember when you spilled milk the other day and said you were sorry?"

Timmy nodded.

"What did Mommy say?"

He thought a moment. "That's okay."

"Forgiveness is God saying, 'That's okay. I still love you.'" When Timmy beamed, Dan hugged his sons again. "And you will never lose God's love or mine or Mommy's."

After church, Cap and Amanda brought home dinner—fried chicken and all the fixings. Danny finished eating and asked, "Can we go home now, Daddy? You said you'd teach me to ride my new bike."

Before Dan could answer, Cindy said, "We'll leave after I finish helping Grandma in the kitchen, but your father can't teach you today."

"Why?"

"He needs to rest. He can play quiet games instead."

"A little exercise will do me good."

Cindy gave him a don't-argue-with-me-Daniel-Baker stare. "Dr. Kincaid told you to rest a couple of days, and you said you would."

Danny blurted, "But he promised to teach me to ride."

"And he will, Danny, but not until later this week."

"No, not later this week," Dan asserted. "I promise you, Danny, you'll get your lesson tomorrow and, Timmy, you will get your promised pizza for lunch. End of discussion."

While Cap packed the car and Cindy helped Amanda, Dan took the boys for a walk. "Do you remember what I asked you to do?"

Timmy looked at his brother as if he hadn't a clue.

Danny's mouth drew into a pout. "Do we have to go to bed early tonight?"

"Yes."

Danny pondered this and shrugged. "Okay."

*****

Frustrated over his inability to make love to Cindy, Dan rolled off the bed Monday morning and walked to the window. He clenched his hands and stared out at their special avocado tree. Did he dare take a chance tonight?

Cindy came up behind and wrapped her arms around him. "It's okay. Tonight will be better. You have too much on your mind right now."

He turned. "When did that ever prove a problem?"

"Don't be so hard on yourself. Your nerves are frayed, and you're still worried about Cookie."

"I wanted last night and this morning to be perfect. I wanted to make up not only for the past six days but all the nights you've spent waiting up for me. For all…"

She pressed her finger against his lips. "You can do that after we've shared a peaceful day, and again, when we go to Hawaii. Now call the hospital to settle your mind about Cookie. I'm sure he came through the operation fine."

While Cindy showered, Dan dialed the hospital. To his relief, Cookie was alive. He remained unconscious and in serious condition but showed signs of improvement. Dan was told, "It may be days before he can have visitors, and you'll have to get police clearance to see him. The man is a criminal suspect and under police guard."

He hung up and bowed his head. "Lord, Cookie needs You. Help him see his need. Give me wisdom and the right words when I break the news that Doc is dead. Lord, I love Cookie. I don't want him to go to prison. Lord, I trust You to save him, comfort him, and fulfill his dreams, Amen."

Just before breakfast, Dan listened to the news and was glad to hear he and the boys were home safe and sound. "No arrests have been made, but it appears the bombings have stopped. Until Pastor Baker can be interviewed, or the police assure us the chaos is over, we'll just have to pray that it is."

After breakfast, Cindy insisted Dan should rest again today.

Dan put his arm around Danny. "I promised I'd teach him to ride his new bike. A promise is a promise. Right, Danny?"

Danny's head bobbed like a puppet's.

"Can I come?" Timmy asked, running to Dan.

"Sure. You can ride beside us on your tricycle."

The long asphalt driveway leading from the house to the street made a perfect place for Danny to learn balance and pedaling. Danny stopped pedaling when they reached the end of the driveway. "Why is that police car parked out front?"

"To make sure no news reporters come to the house. We can't talk to them until the crime investigation is complete. The police need to find out who all those men were." Dan was glad that satisfied Danny.

Within half an hour, Danny had the hang of it well enough for Dan to feel comfortable releasing his hand from the back of the seat. By then, his running alongside Danny told him why Dr. Kincaid had insisted he rest a few days. The strenuous exercise made every wounded part throb, but he refused to go inside where Cindy would notice and chew him out for overdoing. Dan opted for sitting on an overturned trashcan to rest while he watched Danny.

242

When the pizza delivery truck pulled into the driveway around noon, Timmy squealed, "Pizza."

While they ate lunch, Dan gazed at Jonathan's high chair. "I miss him."

"I know," Cindy said, "but you must admit, having Cap and Amanda keep him today has helped us relax."

"True, but I'll be glad when he's home...doesn't seem normal around here without him."

Dan heard the doorbell ring and looked at Cindy in surprise. "Are you expecting someone?" She nodded and rose to answer the door. When Dan saw Cap and Amanda with Jonathan, he said, "I thought you were coming over later." He rose and gave his mother a hug. When Jonathan squealed and raised his arms, Dan took him. The baby laughed with glee and threw his arms around Dan's neck.

"He really missed you," Cindy said.

Dan sniffed. "I think I'll play with him later. He needs changing."

Amanda took him. "I'll do it."

Seated in the living room, Dan asked Cap, "How come you decided to come early?"

Cindy answered, "You and I are spending the afternoon at the park before we go to dinner. I made reservations at the Starlight Inn for four o'clock so we can get a table by the window."

Dan raised an eyebrow. "We get to spend all afternoon and evening alone?"

Cindy looked at Cap who said, "Afraid not. Actually, you'll be going to the park with another couple who will pick you up. After walking awhile, you will apparently go your separate ways for a few hours then come home. Another couple will pick you up to take you to the restaurant, but they'll eat at a different table."

"Okay, out with it. This is overkill if you're protecting me from reporters. What's the real reason?"

"Despite the headlines reporting your escape, a few angry people say you are responsible for all the explosions and want to see you dead. We're taking precautions until the bodies are recovered and everyone involved is identified. Cookie will soon be able to give his statement. As soon as all the facts are in, your name will be cleared completely. Are you worried?"

"Not really."

"Good. Don't let any of this spoil your day…have fun. Earl and Julie will be here soon."

Dan didn't mind being with Earl and Julie. He and Cindy knew them, and they were fun to be around, but he was glad when they parted ways for a few hours, even though they were being watched.

Hand in hand, he and Cindy strolled along the winding path around the park lake. He stopped to stare at the snow-capped mountains no longer shrouded by smog, but memories shrouded him. He saw himself in the lodge, facing his tormentor.

Cindy tugged his fingers. "Are you worried about people wanting you dead?"

He shook his head. "No. I have a heavenly bodyguard, I have two officers watching my back side and the one holding my hand has ESP."

"I'm not an officer."

"You've worked hard to get back in shape and ready to return to duty as soon as Jonathan is weaned. And Mom and I are ready to take care of the boys."

Cindy gazed deeply into his eyes. "You still have that faraway look. If what Cap said isn't bothering you, what is?"

Dan glanced at the mountains and sighed. "I see ugliness in those mountains…a nightmare that won't go away."

"Then change their image, Dan. Think about all the great times we've had in those mountains…the fun and laughter we've shared. Then shift your mind to our avocado tree."

"And you?" He took her hand and kissed it. "You're amazing. With a few words, you've painted a whole new picture." He lifted strands of her long hair and let them slip through his fingers. "You are my here and now. No longer do I have to imagine our special moments." He pulled her into his arms. "I can embrace you and inhale the heady scent of your perfume before I kiss you."

"Dan, people are…"

His lips silenced her.

When he drew back a moment, she blurted, "Earl and Julie are watching."

"So let them stare. I love you." Overwhelmed, he shouted, "I love you" and kissed her harder.

When a young voice said, "Way to go, man," she pulled away, blushing and giggling like a new bride as a teenage boy on his bike raised his hand in a high-five. "Right on," he said and rode off.

Dan chuckled. "I think I just got a teenager's sign of approval."

"And you have mine. I love you, Daniel Baker." She entwined her arms around him and kissed him.

Dan lifted her chin and gazed into her eyes shimmering with love. "God has given me the best wife a man could ever wish. You brought me here to this park and made reservations at the restaurant to help me recapture all that is wonderful and right with my world. Thank you."

At the restaurant, waiting for their prime rib, they gazed out the window at the mountains. A few clouds had developed to lend more beauty to the sunset. Dan knew why she'd chosen this restaurant—he had proposed here.

She flashed him a loving smile. "Was the view this gorgeous the night you proposed?"

"All I saw was you in that royal blue sundress with white flowers adorning your hair."

"Cap gave me an envelope this morning. Inside was the letter you wrote me." Her eyes misted. "I wish I could express what your words mean to me."

Dan reached across the table to hold her hand. "I wanted you to know I've been aware of your unhappiness. We've got a good marriage, but we've allowed it to become frayed around the edges. I took your hand almost eleven years ago and slipped a ring on your finger. I don't have a ring, but I give you my pledge to be a better husband."

During dinner, they discussed ways to improve their marriage. By the time they returned home, Dan felt revitalized.

Amanda sat rocking Jonathan who again squealed when he saw Dan. Lifting him from her arms, Dan kissed his son's tummy, caught a whiff, and laughed. "Who wants him this time?"

Cindy took Jonathan. "After I change him, I'll put him in his play pen in the boys' room and let them entertain him so we can visit. Be right back."

Dan kissed his mother. "Thanks again for your help with Jonathan and for the support you gave Cindy."

"We supported each other."

He glanced at Cap and saw his we-need-to-talk look. Dan gave a slight nod. "And here I thought this was strictly a welcome-home party tonight."

Cap raised his hands in defense. "Hey, I don't like this any more than you do."

An awkward silence descended. "Let's at least sit in here," Dan said. "Or is this a private discussion?"

"The living room is fine."

Cindy returned when Cap said, "You need to be brought up-to-date."

Dan sighed. "I know. I just wish I could escape all the aftermath. I don't want to see Cookie go on trial. I won't testify against him, Cap."

His father raised an eyebrow. "You'll refuse?"

"No, but I will say nothing incriminating. I will do everything in my power to help him. As far as I'm concerned, he was only a cook and babysitter. I don't want to see him imprisoned!"

Cap smiled unexpectedly. "Bob Jensen called me. He asked a lot of questions about Cookie."

"Why would he do that?"

"He's the best legal mind in the state. He's offered to defend Cookie."

Dan's mouth dropped open. "He's that Bob Jensen…the lawyer who represents the rich and the famous?"

Cap nodded. "Has a hideaway cabin tucked in the hills where he escapes to unwind. That he should pick you up and be touched by your concern for Cookie is indeed providential. And he's providing his services for free." Cap grinned. "See, not all my news is unpleasant."

Too overwhelmed to speak, Dan pondered God's goodness before he laughed. "I'm ready now."

"For what?"

"You and Mary Poppins always give sugar along with the foul medicine. So what's the bitter pill?"

"Tomorrow's morgue day."

Dan gasped as if someone had belted him in the stomach.

Cindy jumped up, put her arm around him, and glared at Cap. "Did you have to be so blunt?"

Dan laid his hand over hers. "I'm okay. I just wasn't expecting a horse pill." No one smiled.

Amanda broke the silence. "All our nerves are shot."

"I apologize," Cap said, "for being insensitive last night and now."

"Apology accepted. Let's get this business over with. Tell me the latest developments."

His father related that four men had perished under the avalanche of snow.

"What about the money?" Dan asked.

"All accounted for, which made each victimized corporation happy."

"Snow White?"

"Only one woman didn't show up for work today…Leslie Adams."

Dan stared in disbelief. "Leslie? That's why she was at St. Jude Hospital the day I was kidnapped. I fell for her sob story about her dying aunt, even offered to talk over a cup of coffee. She said she had to rush home. We walked out together, but Leslie wouldn't let me escort her to her car. She set me up. Did you arrest her?"

"We almost nailed Leslie at her apartment this morning but missed by five minutes. Remember Sergeant Bentley, the racing buff who spends his spare moments at the track?"

Dan nodded.

"He spotted her car on the freeway and flashed Leslie to pull over. She gunned it, and he gave chase…clocked her at ninety. Then she must have decided to give up because she slowed and stopped.

The car blew. Bentley told me it was the biggest car explosion he'd ever witnessed. If he'd been closer, he'd be dead instead of in the hospital. The lab boys are checking what's left of the vehicle."

"I don't understand. Why would the car suddenly explode?"

"I think Einstein rigged it to explode the minute she'd come to a full stop. He must have decided two million made a better partner than a wife."

"Are you sure she was Snow White?"

"There were enough explosives in her apartment to flatten a square mile. And we found a marked detailed map of the intended bomb locations. All have been accounted for."

Dan's mind replayed his last conversation with Einstein. The man had seemed exuberant, almost slap-happy—like the Joker in Batman enjoying his evil deeds. *What a cruel joke to play on Leslie.*

Cap waved his hand in front of Dan's face. "You okay?"

"Just frustrated. I wish I could have counseled her, helped her turn her life around…what a waste. All the crooks are dead except Cookie, and only Doc repented. I wish this could have ended better."

"You've always been an idealist. Life is far from idealistic."

"I should have tried harder," Dan said, feeling sick at heart.

"Dan, I know you. You did your level best under trying circumstances. Face the facts. Garbage stinks no matter how much you wish otherwise or try to find good in it."

Cindy rose and put a hand on Dan's shoulder. "He's right. Forget what you can't change. Concentrate on Cookie. The boys say nothing but wonderful things about him. They speak well of Doc, but I sense they adored Cookie. Danny begged me all day to let him go with you to see him. I told him not until Cookie feels better."

"Thanks. The doctor told me he'd call as soon as Cookie regains consciousness so I can be the one to break the news of Doc's death. That's going to be hard." He glanced at his father. "I will have police clearance to see him, won't I?"

Cap nodded. "You and Bob Jensen will be allowed to visit but not the boys."

"Why not?"

"Isn't that obvious? I don't care how much you like him or claim he's a decent man…he's a criminal. In desperation, he could grab Timmy or Danny in order to escape."

"He wouldn't do that, Cap. I'd swear to that."

"Sorry. They'll have to visit him in jail."

"Jail? That's no place to take children!"

"Wrong! That's the best place for them to see a man who's committed a crime."

Amanda stood with her hands on her hips. "Enough wrangling…we came to celebrate. For the rest of the evening, no more talk of crime, punishment, the law, or anything related to police business. Is that clear?"

Dan had never seen his mother scowl so ferociously at his father.

Cap had never looked meeker. He raised his hands in defense. "Okay…small talk it is." He turned to Dan. "How did your day go? Did Danny learn to ride his bike?"

"That's better," Amanda said. "Now maybe it will be safe to leave you two alone a few minutes while I dish up the cheesecake and Cindy gets the boys."

For some reason, the interchange between his mother and father struck Dan funny. He clamped his hand over his mouth to stifle his laughter, but the floodgates of his emotions burst. He laughed until tears rolled down the spillway. and he had to clamp his hands over his stitched midsection. The release lifted a ton of debris off his shoulders and washed it away. His relief amazed him. He laid his head against the recliner and smiled at his father.

Cap grinned. "Welcome back, son."

19

That night under the avocado tree, Dan and Cindy found release in love. Then laughter—the sky opened and drenched them as soon as they crawled out of their double sleeping bag.

In the bedroom, Dan walked up behind Cindy as she sat at the vanity. Her mirror reflection smiled when he picked up the brush and drew it through her long silky-brown hair.

"You know I become putty in your hands when you do that, don't you?"

"I seem to recall something like that."

"Do you have ulterior motives?"

He winked at her reflection. "Could be."

"We should get some sleep."

"But the night is young and…"

Cindy laughed. "And it was a long six days, right?"

"Right."

About the Author

B orn, raised, and married in Colorado, Donna moved with her husband, Ernest, in 1957 to Southern California where they raised two boys and two girls. Their oldest girl was married before they moved north to Redding, California. Their sons met their perspective brides and married in 1982. That same year, God pushed her into writing fiction. She resisted. Two bad school experiences convinced her that wasn't her field. She tried to ignore the story running through her mind and told no one about it. But God knew, and in His own unique way, He compelled her to write it down. Once He hooked her on the fun of creating, He led her every step of the way in learning to write well. God is awesome. What he initiates, He completes.

CPSIA information can be obtained
at www.ICGtesting.com
Printed in the USA
FSHW011349161220
76762FS